# THE
# SAMSON EFFECT

# THE SAMSON EFFECT

A Novel

Tony Eldridge

iUniverse, Inc.

New York  Lincoln  Shanghai

# The Samson Effect

iUniverse books may be ordered through booksellers or by contacting:

iUniverse
2021 Pine Lake Road, Suite 100
Lincoln, NE 68512
www.iuniverse.com
1-800-Authors (1-800-288-4677)

Because of the dynamic nature of the Internet, any Web addresses or links contained in this book may have changed since publication and may no longer be valid.

This is a work of fiction. All of the characters, names, incidents, organizations, and dialogue in this novel are either the products of the author's imagination or are used fictitiously.

ISBN: 978-0-595-45172-2 (pbk)
ISBN: 978-0-595-69366-5 (cloth)
ISBN: 978-0-595-89482-6 (ebk)

Printed in the United States of America

FOR EMILY

No one could ask for a stronger supporter while writing his first book. Thanks for all the late nights you read and then helped to make this story better, in addition to everything else that you had to do, especially with one-year-old twin boys always needing their mother.

# Preface

When I decided to write *The Samson Effect*, I chose to center my story on something I had intimate knowledge of: biblical history. I was a minister for many years and still take the opportunity to fill the pulpit on occasions.

I wanted this story to be a sheer work of fiction, one that anyone could sit back and enjoy. It is not meant to be Christian literature, and I am not trying to "prove" how things really happened in the Old Testament. I am content to believe the Scriptures, and my personal beliefs on how the things I write about actually occurred are vastly different from the fiction that I crafted.

I did, however, craft my story in a way that looked at the biblical record and asked one guiding question: As far-fetched as my fictional storyline may get, could it still be in harmony with the way it could have happened, based on the biblical text? In other words, I did not want to overtly contradict the biblical text to make my storyline fit.

So, what is left is what I hope you see as a fun, fictional story that you can enjoy.

Tony Eldridge

# CHAPTER 1

**Hebron, Israel**

THE FAT MAN'S skin glistened in the noonday sun. Dirty children ran around him, some kicking a ball, others darting up to the merchants' stands, fingering through trinkets until the bearded owners shooed them away. All around the fat man came the sounds of honking cars, children's playful screams, and men calling out for buyers to purchase their wares. The fat man was burning up in his long-sleeved shirt and khaki pants, but better to suffer the burning temperature than have his pinkish white skin fry under the oppressive rays of the sun.

He removed his hat and mopped his brow with his sleeve, then continued his shopping expedition. As he passed by the street vendors, his eyes caught one particular object being peddled by a thin, wrinkled man. He walked to the booth and picked up a piece of parchment, worn in the weather of time. The ancient Hebrew text was remarkably well preserved. As he glanced over the parchment, he interpreted some of the words he knew from his limited vocabulary. *King David, Mighty Strength*, and *Lord's Protector*. The symbol he saw at the bottom sent chills through his overheated body.

The fat man forgot his discomfort as well as his shopping errand as he fumbled with his cell phone. The old man behind the merchandise asked, "You like? Fifty dollars." The fat man held up one pudgy finger, prompting the old man to wait.

When the call connected, the fat man could hardly control his excitement. "Doctor, I may have found it ... Yes! Yes! Please come quickly; there may be more here." The fat man gave directions and then disconnected the call. His eyes darted from left to right as he found a seat in the shade of the thatch-covered booth. His hands clung to the parchment.

"Fifty dollars. Very old, very valuable. Fifty dollars."

The fat man smiled, nodded, and held up one finger. His hands trembled as he scanned the parchment. Behind him, the old merchant shouted and a twelve-year-old boy came running. The old man leaned down and whispered into his ear. The boy nodded and ran off into the crowd of shoppers.

The fat man looked at the old merchant, who returned his gaze with a smile. He turned to see the boy run up to an armed Palestinian soldier and gesture wildly with animated hands. The soldier looked at the fat man and then took out a radio and spoke into it.

The fat man began to perspire more. He glanced at his watch and then down to his cell phone. "C'mon doctor, hurry up."

Two more soldiers joined the other and the three stood there staring at him. Behind, he saw a cloud of dust rising in the air and made out the doctor's black sedan racing toward him. He slumped in his chair and exhaled a pent-up sigh.

A few minutes later, the sedan pulled to a screeching halt. Dr. Michael Sieff flew from the driver's door. He was the complete opposite of the fat man: slender, tall, and he had a rich, deep color that betrayed the hours he spent working in the sun. The only physical trait the two men shared was their thick, black, curly hair. Michael left the car door open in his haste and ran up to the fat man. "Caleb, what did you find?"

Caleb extended his hand and gave Michael the parchment. The doctor read it with lightning-quick expertise and smiled. "This is it, my friend. Yahweh must have led you to it." He reached over and patted Caleb on the shoulders.

"Fifty dollars. Very rare."

Michael looked to the old merchant and smiled. "I'll give you twenty." After haggling back and forth a few times, they agreed on thirty-five American dollars. As Michael reached into his pocket for his wallet, he heard a hissing crack and felt something flick onto his face. He turned to the wooden post next to him and rubbed his fingers over the hole.

He spun around to Caleb. "Quickly, get in the car—" His words lodged in his throat. Caleb was slumped in the chair, staring at him with wide eyes and blood from the bullet hole in his forehead running down his face. Michael froze. "No," he whispered. Another bullet whistled past him, waking him from his trance.

He thrust the parchment into his pocket and ran toward his car. A spray of bullets from a machine gun cut off his path, forcing him to dart into the throng of people doing their daily shopping. The machine gun sent panicked people screaming and running in all directions. Michael turned to see his assailants, but the chaotic crowd made it impossible. He heard another stuttering crack of gunfire and ran deeper into the crowd.

At the far end of the row of merchants, he saw two men dressed in Western suits point in his direction and begin wading their way through the crowd. He turned, only to find two more men brandishing guns and moving toward him. He removed his hat and wiped the sweat from his eyes, looking for any hope of escape. By now, the crowd around him began to thin as men, women, and children ran for safety from the flying bullets, clearing a path for his assailants. Beyond the market, the soldiers stood rigid, watching the unfolding action but not attempting to intervene or join in the action.

Michael knew he was out of options. There was nowhere to run, no place to hide from these murderers. He bowed his head and raised his hands in defeat. The armed men encircled him, training their sights on him. Michael slowly looked up and turned in a circle to see the open barrels of eight machine guns staring back at him. He almost laughed aloud, knowing one wrong move from him would mean his death, but these idiots would also take out at least half of each other in the process.

As he finished his circle, a smiling, pepper-gray-haired Palestinian led a small, well-dressed band of men into the circle of guns. He walked up to Michael with a smile etched on his face. "Dr. Sieff, my apologies if any of my men may have gotten a little excited. I meant for them to know I only wanted to talk with you, not kill you."

The smug look on the Palestinian's face infuriated Michael. He looked off into the distance to see the soldiers watching, content to keep their distance. He twisted out his own smile. "No offense taken, Azim." He nodded at the eight machine guns trained on him. "Mind calling off your dogs?" The gunmen grunted and shoved their weapons closer to him.

Azim ordered his men to ease back and he stepped up to Michael. As if it was an afterthought, he smiled and said, "Oh, I'm sorry about Caleb."

Michael couldn't control the muscles in his face from tightening. He felt the blood and heat rush to his face. Tempted to wrap his fingers around Azim's neck in spite of the men who would love any opportunity to riddle his body with bullets, he instead hacked up the vilest substance he could and spit it on Azim's leather shoes. For the first time since their encounter, the smile faded from Azim's face. With lightning-quick reflexes, Azim grabbed him by the shoulders and forced him down as a knee sunk into his stomach, knocking the wind out of him. Michael collapsed to the ground, struggling to suck in air. A leather shoe appeared next to his face and wiped itself clean on his cheek. A few moments later, he felt himself being jerked to his feet, supported on each arm by two of the machine-gun-toting dogs.

Azim grabbed Michael by the chin. "Dr. Sieff, I was hoping we could be civil toward each other, but now I can see that'll be impossible." He squeezed his fingers around Michael's chin, and then let go. "Now, the parchment, please."

Michael rolled his eyes, still struggling to take breaths. "I … I don't know what you're talking about."

Azim never broke his gaze, but a slight nod of his head sent one of his men rifling through Michael's pockets. The man pulled out a parchment and handed it to Azim.

Azim finally broke his gaze from Michael and read over the parchment. His expression remained chiseled with angry disappointment. "What is this?"

Michael silently stared at him.

"This is nothing more than a fragment of a recipe."

Michael's breath had started to return to him. "I didn't have a chance to look at it before being shot at." Icy contempt shot daggers from his eyes. "I hope the life of a good man was worth it."

Michael saw the blood vessels building on Azim's forehead and neck. In an even, graveled voice, Azim said, "The Samson Effect is mine. I warn you, stay away from it or you'll be reunited with that good man."

Azim gave the order and everyone retreated, leaving Michael alone. Shoppers cautiously returned to their activities, and children once again began playing in the streets. The soldiers resumed their watch, and Michael heard merchants crying out for buyers.

He dusted himself off and made his way back to the car. Knowing it was futile to ask for help, he opened the rear door and walked over to Caleb. He struggled to carry his friend, but managed to place him in the back seat. Once done, he slipped behind the wheel and started the engine. Michael looked in the back seat and removed his hat, pulling the parchment from it. He shook his head as he looked at Caleb. "Forgive me, my friend."

*     *     *     *

## New Hampshire

Dr. Thomas Hamilton choked the tennis racket with both hands and swung. The ball met the racquet's sweet spot, and Thomas knew he had just won match point. The ball rocketed from his back swing, flew across the court, and fell just out of reach of his opponent's diving attempt. He jogged to the net and shook hands with his opponent.

"Good game, Justin."

"Yeah. Congrats. Sure you don't want my job?"

"Me, coach the boys' tennis team? No way. I'm very content with my graduate students."

Justin wiped his brow on his shoulders. "You do have a plush setup, don't you?"

Thomas smiled and nodded. "Works for me." They began walking down the net to the sideline. "Next Friday?"

"I'll be here."

Thomas reached the sideline and headed to the bench where he had left his towel and duffel bag. A woman in sunglasses wearing white capris and a powder-blue top waited for him with a towel in her hand. Either she's having another crisis or she wants something from me, Thomas thought. He reached for the towel. "Thanks."

"Nice game. In fact, you seem to be a little more intense than usual."

"I'm always intense." Thomas wiped his face and neck with the towel. "I know what you're thinking, and you're wrong."

She smiled at him. Thomas reached over and removed her sunglasses. "You're wrong."

"I am, huh?"

Thomas slid the sunglasses back on her face and put his racket away. He smiled, knowing she was probably right. "Okay, I admit I want to be in practice when Michael and I meet this summer. I've never beaten him in tennis, not once. Came close many times, but he always found a way to pull out a victory."

"I'm sure you're exaggerating just a little."

Thomas zipped up his duffel bag and started walking with her toward the coffeehouse where his last class for the day was meeting. "No, I'm not. From college on, he's always been able to beat me in every sport: tennis, running, cycling, you name it. I've never beaten him!"

They walked in silence for a few moments. Thomas could feel her amusement bubbling up. How many times had he sworn to himself he wouldn't discuss this with her again? With every silent step, he felt her enjoyment increasing.

He sighed. "Ellen, do you know what it's like being the bookish friend of a guy who can do anything?"

She abruptly stopped and removed her sunglasses, unmasking her lovely, wide, round eyes. "Bookish? Thomas, you always place in the top five in the marathon every year, you play pickup games with the basketball team ..." She put her hands on his shoulders and looked reassuringly into his eyes. "You just beat the men's tennis coach."

Thomas had to admit he felt confident his first victory over Michael was looking pretty good. Ellen took a step back from him and put the end of her sunglasses between her teeth. As she looked him up and down, he felt a blush tingle across his cheeks. "Trust me, there ain't nothing bookish about you, Dr. Hamilton." She squeezed his solid biceps playfully and smiled. "And bookish definitely doesn't describe the tall, blond professor who makes every freshman girl's heart race, as well as most of their female teachers'."

Thomas smiled and started for the coffeehouse again. "I knew there was a reason why we're still friends."

"At the sake of ruining that friendship," she said in a mock tone of concern, "I believe I've identified your problem."

"Problem?"

"My professional opinion is that you're suffering from an intense case of sibling rivalry."

"What? I don't have a brother."

"True, but would you say Michael is as close to you as any brother could be?"

"Has been since college."

"You wouldn't believe how many patients I have who suffer from the very same thing."

Thomas held out his hands. "Okay, okay, you win. Thanks for the shrink job." They reached the sidewalk leading to the front door of the coffeehouse. Thomas hugged Ellen and started down the sidewalk.

"But I haven't told you how you can cope with it."

Thomas pointed to his watch. "Later, I promise."

"Oh, wait. I forgot why I came to see you. I need a favor."

"Yeah? What favor?"

"Please, please sit in on my 105 class on Monday. Jeff is taking me away for a long weekend—"

"Ellen, I don't—"

"I've canceled my other classes, but I *have* to give my 105 class their test. We're behind schedule as it is."

"Can't you get a graduate student to sit in?"

"Not all of us have that luxury."

Thomas hated psychology. He searched his mind for a legitimate excuse to use to turn her down, but he ran into a brick wall. "Just sit in and administer the test?"

She ran up and threw her arms around him. "Thanks. I owe you!" She let go of him and, without waiting for a response, floated away.

Thomas sighed and stepped into the coffeehouse. The student server behind the counter had his coffee waiting for him. He stirred in the cream and joined his six graduate students who were stretched out on oversized chairs and a sofa in the corner of the room. He sat down in the armchair across from the couch, kicked off his shoes, and propped his sock feet on the table. The waitress passed by with a scowl and bumped his leg with her knee.

"I've told you a thousand times, Doctor, people put their food on that table."

He smiled. "And for the thousandth time, I'm sorry." He took a sip of his coffee and turned his attention to the students. "Where did we leave off on Wednesday?"

A wiry man with kinky red hair leaned forward. "You were telling us the characters in the Old Testament were all completely loco."

"Not all, and not simply loco. I was saying many of the characters, if living in our time, would be diagnosed with some sort of mental illness. For example, Moses showed signs of clinical depression and anxiety. On numerous occasions, he went to the Lord, overwhelmed with his responsibilities and asked God to take his life.

"And then there was King Saul, who *was* loco." He turned to the redhead and nodded. "Here was a man eaten up by paranoia, killing his own priests and driven mad by the thought that his most loyal subject, David, was trying to usurp his throne."

He paused to let the students comment on his theories, but each one stared back silently. He guessed they were either engrossed in his narrative or afraid a comment would bring them too close to the brink of blasphemy.

"Then there was Samson. He exhibited the classic signs of antisocial behavior: the classic bully, always picking a fight and alienating himself from both his enemies and his own friends. When things didn't go his way, he'd go out and kill someone, often innocent strangers. He also displayed cruelty to animals, on one occasion setting foxes on fire."

He looked around the group and his eyes rested on Angela, the most contemplative and well-spoken of the group. "What do you think about my assessment of these characters?"

Angela thought for a moment. "Well, I suppose our culture may have marked them with some sort of mental illness, but I don't think we have enough information for an accurate diagnosis." She wrinkled her eyebrows as if she were about to ask a question but then relaxed.

"You had a question, Angela?"

"Well, I was just wondering what all this has to do with the dig we'll be on in a few weeks."

Thomas grinned and sipped his coffee. He leaned back in the armchair and started to put his feet on the table, until he remembered the waitress. "Fair question. In my opinion, the best way to find out about ancient civilizations is by letting them tell their story and learning as much as we can about them. Otherwise, we're often tempted to tell their story for them and interpret even the most insignificant find within our own paradigm."

He looked around the group and smiled when he saw nods of understanding from them. His cell phone interrupted their conversation. He answered, spoke for a few moments, and placed his hand over the mouthpiece. "This is our host for the dig next month. Let's wrap up class for the day. I'll see you Monday in our regular classroom."

The students picked up their drinks and books and left to enjoy the weekend. Only Ricky Lettle remained at the counter to finish the sandwich he had started. Thomas returned to the phone. "Michael, calm down. What's wrong?"

*        *        *        *

A few minutes later, Thomas stood across his boss's desk. Dr. Clifton Winfred pulled his glasses from his face and chewed on one end of them. Thomas waited, wondering what was going on behind his boss's squinted eyes. He placed his hands on the desk and leaned toward Winfred. "Well?"

Winfred leaned back in his chair and slipped his glasses back on. "Let me make sure I understand this correctly, Dr. Hamilton. You want me to approve an open-ended sabbatical starting immediately, find someone to take over your classes for the rest of the semester, and cancel the first Israeli dig the university has been able to schedule in over twenty-five years?"

Thomas pushed himself away from the desk, pursed his lips, and nodded. "That's about it."

Winfred looked away and shook his head. "Thomas, you're putting me in a very difficult position. You know I have the utmost professional respect for you, and as a friend, I'd do anything for you—"

"Then approve my request."

"Give me something—anything—to help me say yes."

Thomas rubbed his eyes with the palm of his hands. "I told you, Clifton, I'm not in a position to tell you what I need to do. I was hoping you'd just trust me."

"It's not a matter of trust. The department, the university, for that matter, is under an extremely tight budget this year. I don't have the leeway I normally have; you know that."

Thomas paced back and forth in front of the desk, rapping its surface with his knuckles. "I know, Clifton, but ..." He stopped and looked over Winfred's shoulders at the open office door. He walked over, closed it, and on the way back, grabbed a folding chair and set it at the side of the desk. He sat and leaned toward his boss. "It's about the Samson Effect."

This was the only subject about which Thomas knew Clifton had no patience. Thomas held his breath, already wishing he could suck the words back into his mouth. He braced himself to go yet another round with his boss. Every second of Clifton's silence drained Thomas's hope at an agonizingly sluggish pace. Clifton pinched the bridge of his nose and shook his head. "Please, Thomas, not this again. You're too good of an archaeologist to waste your time on this Holy Grail crusade."

Thomas leaned back in his seat. "Michael just called. He found an ancient text he believes will lead him to it. With his expertise in biblical languages and mine in biblical archaeology, he's confident we'll be able to find it soon. That's why I need to get to Hebron as soon as I can."

"Didn't you hear a word I said? So far, your fetish with this Samson Effect has been innocuous, but I'm not about to let you soil the reputation of this department, not to mention the respect you've earned as an accomplished archaeologist."

"Oh, come on, Clifton. You've seen the evidence Michael and I have found already. If you're honestly concerned about the university's reputation, what do you think will happen to it when someone else makes the discovery?"

"I'm sorry Thomas, but the answer is no."

A sound at the door grabbed their attention. Thomas held out a hand, gesturing for silence, and stalked to the door. He reached out and took hold of the shade covering the window. He looked to Winfred, then back to the door. With one quick yank, he rolled up the shade. A student with curly black hair leaned forward on the other side with his ear pressed against the window. When the shade rolled up, he turned and locked eyes with Thomas.

The student shook off his shocked state and bolted down the hall. Thomas flung open the door and raced into the hallway just in time to see the student fly through the outside doors and into a waiting car. When he heard the tires squeal, Thomas turned and saw the department secretary poking her head through her door.

"Everything all right, Dr. Hamilton? Sounds like you and Dr. Winfred are going at it again."

Thomas looked down the hall and then back to the secretary. "Everything's just peachy."

The secretary raised an eyebrow. "Well, whatever's going on, good luck." She hefted her purse to her shoulder and locked her office door. "See you Monday."

Thomas slipped back into Winfred's office and closed the door behind him. "Who in heaven's name was that?" Winfred asked.

"Ricky Lettle, one of my graduate students."

"What was he doing listening outside my door?" Winfred asked with a harsh edge to his tone.

"I don't know. Who all did you mention the Samson Effect to?"

Winfred furrowed his eyebrows. "Absolutely no one. I'm not about to have my name tarnished because of your foolishness."

"Well I sure haven't mentioned it to anyone. Michael and I have kept this low key to protect our own search for it."

"I seriously don't think you have anything to worry about. You two are the only ones I know foolhardy enough to commit yourselves to this."

Thomas sucked in a breath. "I'm going, Clifton. Michael's arranged to have a private jet take me to Israel tonight."

"You better think long and hard before you leave your students, Thomas. Tenure or not, you won't have a job when you return."

Thomas threw up his hands and chuckled. "Fine, Clifton. The Samson Effect exists. I really don't care which university I'm with when I make the discovery." He walked out of the room without waiting for Clifton's reply.

Thomas left the building and walked to his car. It was Friday evening, and the campus was dead. He pulled out of his parking spot and turned onto the deserted, tree-lined campus drive. As he turned around the first bend in the road, an explosion rattled the car. He looked into his rearview mirror to see a billowing fireball rise from the archaeology building.

Thomas stomped on the brakes and skidded to a stop. He flung open his car door and gawked at the fire, feeling its heat from where he was standing. Confused and in a daze, he thought about Dr. Winfred, then about the student he found outside the chairman's door. He picked up his cell phone and punched the numbers 9–1–1. His thumb paused over the send button. After a few moments of hesitation, his thumb glided to the cancel button and pressed down. He tossed the phone in the passenger seat, sat behind the wheel, and took off. The fire began to fade from the rearview mirror as he made his way to the airport.

# CHAPTER 2

THOMAS LOOKED DOWN at the speedometer. Sixty. He caught himself weaving around cars, but he had no memory of driving from the archaeology building to where he was on Fifty-sixth Street. His mind was reeling from the explosion. He thought of turning around at every light, but he knew the bomb was meant for him. His survival instincts kept his foot on the gas pedal and his car aimed toward the airport.

He picked up his cell and dialed Michael's number. For the third time, Michael's voice mail answered that no one could take his call and prompted him to leave a message. Thomas squeezed the phone and slammed it down on the armrest. He gripped the steering wheel with both hands and took in three deep breaths. "Calm down, calm down." He eased off the accelerator and exhaled through his mouth. The clock on his radio display read 6:45. The campus radio station would be playing uninterrupted classical music until midnight. He turned on the radio and pressed the first preset. Instead of Mozart, Thomas heard the excited voice of a student reporter. He reached over and turned up the volume.

"The explosion at Abbey Hall happened about thirty minutes ago. Details are still sketchy, but here's what we do have. According to Chief of Campus Police Bill Redgrove, police have not been able to determine the cause of the explosion or if there were any casualties. One witness told me a few minutes ago that she left the building about ten minutes before the explosion and that the cleaning crew was there along with Dr. Clifton Winfred, chair of the archaeology department, and Dr. Thomas Hamilton, professor of biblical archaeology. I must impress, however, there have been no positive identifications—"

Thomas reached over and turned off the radio. He picked up the cell phone and hit redial. After a few seconds, he slammed the phone down again.

He reached the airport exit and turned onto the lane leading to long-term parking. He maneuvered into the valet parking lane and asked the attendant to put the car in the garage. He took the ticket and waited for the bus to the international terminal.

\*          \*          \*          \*

Thomas picked up his boarding pass for the chartered flight to Tel Aviv that Michael had arranged. He stood in the security line, anxious to pass through the checkpoint and board his plane. He fought to push the evening's events out of his mind so as not to appear in any way like someone security would be suspicious of. The line moved at a snail's pace, but he was comforted with the thought his charter wouldn't leave without him.

In front of him, a young woman struggled to maintain control of two young children, issuing threat after threat, but having little impact on the rambunctious children. He glanced up at one of the television screens hanging in the terminal. A CNN correspondent was reporting from the scene of a smoldering fire. When Thomas recognized the building as Abbey Hall, he tuned out the unruly children and focused on the closed-caption text scrolling across the bottom of the muted television. Then the image changed to a picture of him taken from the yearbook. Below, the text read that police were looking for Dr. Thomas Hamilton for questioning related to the explosion.

Thomas tore his eyes from the screen, scanning the crowd to see if anyone was pointing a finger at him; but everyone seemed oblivious to him, caught up in their own little world. He casually turned to see a row of monitors extending down the terminal with his picture plastered on them. He felt immediate relief when a live shot of the reporter in front of the smoldering Abbey Hall replaced his image.

When he felt someone tap his shoulder, he involuntarily flinched. He turned to see a man in a suit point over his shoulder. "Sir, they're calling for you."

Thomas turned to see a security screener walking toward him, speaking in an agitated voice. "Sir, please step over here!"

Thomas's heart raced, and his body went into flight mode. He fought his instinct and stepped out of line, following the screener to a table. "Sir, please remove your shoes."

Thomas smiled. "My shoes? Sure." He leaned down, slipped off both tennis shoes, and handed them to the screener for inspection. A second screener asked him to empty his pockets while using a wand on him. Apparently convinced he posed no threat, the screener gave Thomas back his shoes and led him through the security checkpoint.

Thomas retrieved his items, stuffed them into his pockets, and found a chair to sit in while he slipped his shoes on. With his trembling hands, it took him three attempts to tie the first shoe. As soon as he finished, he grabbed his keys and wallet and set off at a fast pace to the chartered flights gate.

As he approached the gate, he once again saw his image on CNN. He dropped his head and walked past the television. When he looked up, his gaze locked onto an armed security guard who smiled and nodded to him as he passed. Once again, he let out a sigh when he passed by the guard. His confidence strengthened as he realized his gate was just around the corner.

His body stiffened when he heard someone call out, "Sir, stop!" He turned to see the security guard power-walking toward him with his hand on his gun. His fight-or-flight instinct kicked in again, but this time he ran. His intellect told him he had no chance to escape and running would make matters worse, but he ran anyway.

Thomas prepared for a Good Samaritan to jump to the guard's aid, but, surprisingly, people simply stepped aside to let them pass. He skidded around the corner, right into the burly arms of two waiting men. After one slapped a giant paw over his mouth, the men manhandled Thomas past his gate. Before his mind could register what was happening, the men burst through a nearby door and dragged Thomas down a flight of dimly lit stairs. At the landing, they passed through another door before coming to a stop.

One of the men turned to look at Thomas. "If you want to make it out of here and see Michael tonight, you'll do as we say. Understand?"

Thomas's wide eyes moved from one man to the next. When he nodded, the guard removed his hand from Thomas's mouth. Thomas recognized the Israeli accent. "Michael sent you?"

"We were sent to make sure you arrive in Israel safely."

"But how are you going to get me on the plane? After 9/11, this airport will be locked down until they find me."

"In less than fifteen minutes the search will be called off, and you'll walk to the plane unmolested."

Thomas looked at each man. Part of him believed them, but the other part knew he'd be tackled and shackled the moment he stepped into the open.

No one spoke for the next ten minutes until one of the men placed his hand to his ear and then turned to the other. "All clear."

The other man opened the door. "Dr. Hamilton, if you'll please come with us."

Thomas paused and then stepped through the door, bracing himself for a gang tackle. The stairway, however, was empty. He followed the men to a door marked "Boarding" and walked through to the outside. A small private jet with stairs leading into the cabin sat a few yards away. As he walked toward the plane, Thomas felt a chill run through him. Workers were busy driving luggage to the airliners parked at the gates and refueling planes. It was as if nothing had happened, as if there was no breach in security at all.

When they arrived at the steps, the two men stopped. The man with the earpiece looked at Thomas. "This is as far as we go."

Thomas stared at him and cocked his head to one side. "But how—"

The man held out his hand to stop him. "Don't worry about it. Just enjoy your flight."

Thomas turned and climbed the steps. As he ducked into the cabin, the first things his eyes saw were the firm legs of the woman who greeted him. As his eyes slowly rose, he saw that they were connected to a slim, beautiful woman wearing a white blouse and a dark navy jacket. Her chestnut-brown hair was pulled into a bun, revealing a creamy neck with just a hint of bronze.

"Would you like something to drink?"

Thomas looked around the flying office before nodding. "Vodka, straight."

The woman smiled and walked to the bar. In a few moments, she was back with a shot on the rocks. Thomas took the drink and sipped it, waiting for the plane to take off. Behind him, he heard a commode flush, water run, and then a man in blue khakis and a polo shirt stepped through the door and took the seat across the table from him.

He extended his hand. "I'm Ambassador Benjamin Ben Hur. I pray that you're comfortable."

Thomas shook the man's hand. "Yes, thank you."

The ambassador pushed the button and spoke into a speaker. "We're ready to take off."

Almost immediately, Thomas heard the whine of the jet engines and felt the plane starting to roll. The woman took her seat next to the ambassador, and the three buckled their seat belts. Within minutes, the plane was climbing and soon leveled out.

The ambassador was reading over papers from his briefcase. Thomas finished off his vodka and set the glass on the table. "Excuse me, Ambassador, but what just happened back there?"

The ambassador peered over his glasses at Thomas. "What do you mean?"

"Without trying to sound flippant, you know very well what I mean. How did you get the police to forget about me?"

The ambassador put down his papers and smiled. "I assure you, Dr. Hamilton, they haven't forgotten about you. As for arranging your way through airport security, let's just say my position carries with it certain privileges."

"And why would an ambassador choose to exercise those privileges for me?"

The ambassador turned to the woman and nodded. "Of course, Ambassador." She unbuckled her seat belt, walked to the front of the plane, and disappeared behind the cockpit door.

"Michael is my nephew. I know of his pursuit of the Samson Effect. In fact, my money is funding his search for it. I understand you and he are very close to its discovery."

"Your nephew hasn't told me what he's found yet, only that he's convinced it'll lead to the discovery." Thomas picked up his glass and swirled the ice around. "If the Israeli government is involved, he must've found something conclusive."

"The Israeli government is *not* involved. This is something between him and me, and now you."

Thomas leaned back in his seat. "May I ask you what you intend to do with the Samson Effect if we discover it?"

The ambassador responded without pause. "My only concern is to keep it out of a certain Palestinian man's hand." His eyes bore deep into Thomas. "Can you imagine what would happen if a band of terrorists found, then used, the Samson Effect?"

Thomas didn't respond; he didn't need to. Both men knew what would happen if the discovery fell into the wrong hands.

✳      ✳      ✳      ✳

When he stepped off the plane, Thomas turned to see the hatch close behind him. He reached into his pocket for the only thing he had brought with him aside from the clothes on his back: his cell phone. As he walked away from the plane toward the terminal, his pulse quickened when he spotted the Israeli soldiers patrolling their post. The two soldiers closest to him had not taken their eyes from him since he had landed. He patted his pockets for his passport, which he knew sat in his bank's safety deposit box.

He pulled out his cell and hit redial just as a black sedan pulled up to him. The backseat door flew open and a familiar voice ordered him inside. The moment he closed the car door, the sedan took off.

"I trust you had a good flight, my friend."

A surge of relief washed over Thomas. "You have no idea."

"Let me guess; in the last twelve hours, you managed to sneak out of your country as a wanted man." Michael grew serious. "I'm sorry about Clifton. I never would have believed he, or you, would be in danger in the U.S."

Thomas rubbed his jet-lagged eyes. "I think I'm still in shock at all that's happened. I didn't even get a chance to go home and pack. No passport, no clothes, no money … nothing."

"It's a good thing you didn't go home. At last report, the police have been to your apartment and apparently found evidence you've been planning the bombing for some time."

Thomas strained against his seat belt as he turned and leaned toward Michael. "What? How could that be? It wasn't me who did that."

"I know, and so does my uncle; but as it stands now, if you go back home, you'll be arrested for murder."

Thomas slumped into his seat, wondering how in the world this could be happening to him. Michael put his hand on Thomas's shoulder. "Don't worry, my friend. Arrangements have been made. You will be relatively safe with me."

Thomas's head whiplashed to his friend. "Relatively? You don't inspire much confidence."

"Well, you'll be safe from U.S. and Israeli authorities. The Palestinians, now, that's another issue."

Thomas looked out of his window as an armed Israeli waved the car through a gate. Once on the road to Hebron, Michael caught him up on the parchment he'd found and told him about Caleb's murder. He promised to show Thomas the parchment as soon as they arrived at his home.

After a few moments of conversation, Michael nodded at the window. "This is Hebron."

Thomas looked out at the ancient desert buildings and dusty footpaths that ran throughout the city as a throng of people milled about the various shops. All around, he saw soldiers walking among the people and armored vehicles patrolling the streets. Puzzled, he turned to Michael. "The soldiers look Israeli to me. I thought you said it was Palestinian soldiers who stood by when you and Caleb were attacked."

"I did. Even though the Palestinians control most of the city, Israel maintains a strong police presence to keep the peace. What happened to Caleb and me demonstrates just how powerful our enemies are."

"What do you mean?"

"I mean the attack was well-planned. A diversion was set up to draw the soldiers away while Azim and his men tried to get the parchment. The Palestinian guards were lookouts to let him know when the Israelis were on their way back."

Thomas shook his head. "But how did he know you'd found the parchment? Sounds like he was waiting for you."

"There are a lot of things I don't know about Azim, but this I do know: he's both intelligent and dangerous. If we let our guard down at all, it will mean our lives."

# CHAPTER 3

"ALLAH HAS BEEN good to us."

Azim sat behind the large, handcrafted mahogany desk he had commissioned from his favorite London artisan. His sister and three associates sat in chairs across from him, nodding and uttering their agreement. He looked at his sister, concerned about her countenance. "My dear sister, what's wrong? You look sad."

Delia's eyes snapped open as she looked into her brother's eyes. "Oh, no, Azim. I'm not sad. It's just …"

As she cast her eyes down, Azim felt a surge of power rush through him. Here, his own sister, who had killed many times at his instructions, still revered, even feared, him. He reached out a benevolent hand to her. In a tender voice he instructed, "Come here, Delia. You've nothing to fear."

Delia slowly rose from her seat and stepped toward her brother. She reached out and took Azim's hand, gently kissing it and waiting for him to speak.

"Now, sister, please tell me why you're upset."

Delia drew in a breath. "It's Ricky. I don't understand why you had to have him killed."

A smile cracked the corner of Azim's mouth. "Because, Delia, we couldn't afford to have him linked to the bombing. I was assured he was strangled quickly and was quite dead before his body was placed in the building. Now there's one more murder blamed on Dr. Hamilton." He reached out and lifted his sister's chin so she was staring into his eyes. "Right now he's enjoying Allah's abundant blessings." He leaned in and lightly kissed her on the lips.

When he broke the kiss, Delia cast her eyes back to the floor. "Of course."

Delia returned to her seat, and Azim instructed one of the three men to approach him. "Rajah, you have my thanks and my praise on a job well done. Your plan to leave Michael unguarded in the city worked perfectly."

Rajah took Azim's hand and kissed it. "Allah was with me. All glory to Allah."

"Yes, Allah was with you then as he is now." Azim opened the desk drawer and picked up three bundles of American currency. "Thirty thousand dollars, and of even more value, I bestow upon you the honor of being my Right." He waited as Rajah's face brightened, and a smile escaped before he continued. "Today, you and your family shall move onto my estate and live in your own house under my protection." This time, *he* took Rajah's hand and kissed it.

"Your kindness has no limits. Praise be to Allah."

"Praise be to Allah, my friend ... my brother."

Rajah bowed as he backed into his chair. Delia and the other two men stood and kissed his hand, repeating their praise to Allah. Once seated, Azim called Barhim forward. "Barhim, my old friend."

Barhim's hand trembled as he reached out to kiss Azim's hand. Azim could smell the fear emanating from him. As he accepted the kiss and praise, he fought to keep his anger from spewing forth.

"Look at me!" The trembling man slowly lifted his gaze. Once his eyes met Azim's, he could not control the quivering that passed through his body. "You, my friend, I'm not so happy with. You have not only let me down, you've also let Allah down, praise be his name."

"Azim, please, I'm sorry. I give you my word it will never happen again."

Azim continued as though he didn't hear the man's apology. "Because of your carelessness in executing the diversion, three of my best men lie dead at the hands of Israeli dogs."

"Azim, please ..."

"Would I not be just in requiring your blood for theirs?" Azim once again reached into his desk drawer, but this time he pulled out a small boning knife and held the thin blade up to the light. He looked to see the others in the room avert their gaze. His bellowing command caused the others in the room to jump. "Look at Allah's justice being carried out!"

Barhim could not stop the tears from flowing. "Please, have mercy!"

"Allah's justice ... *and* mercy."

Barhim froze as he let the words sink in. Overcome with joy and relief, he showered Azim with praise and thanks. Azim, in a quiet yet resolute voice, commanded, "Your hand, Barhim, place it on the desk."

Barhim's smile quickly faded. "My ... my hand?"

"Place it on the desk."

Once again, the quivering invaded his body and whimpers escaped his lips as he obeyed, laying his hand on the desk, palm down.

"Now, spread your fingers."

Barhim looked away as he spread his fingers apart. "No, Barhim, you must witness Allah's justice and his mercy." The sobbing man turned to see Azim place the blade against his left pinkie. Azim did show mercy, making the cut quickly. The mercy, however, did not keep him from screaming in agony.

Azim wiped the blood from the blade with a towel sitting on the desk. He then picked up Barhim's finger and wrapped it in the towel. Barhim clinched his bleeding stub in his fist and stood there, whimpering, sweat flowing from every pore in his face.

Azim handed the wrapped finger to Barhim. "The surgeon is waiting for you in his office, my friend. Take this to him and return to my side when you're ready."

Barhim didn't speak. He simply bowed his head slightly and disappeared through the door. Azim then turned his attention to the third man. Sofian sat paralyzed in his seat, afraid to break eye contact with Azim. When Azim called him forward, he reluctantly rose from his chair and shuffled to his master's desk.

Azim held his hand forward, and Sofian quickly took and kissed it as he bowed in submission. "Sofian, my friend. Today I've chosen you above all to be my Left. Your faithfulness and eagerness to serve hasn't gone unnoticed. As you've seen today, I expect unquestioning loyalty and obedience, and I reward those who serve well. Are you willing to pledge yourself to me as I seek to carry out Allah's will on earth?"

Without hesitation, Sofian stepped up to the side of the desk and knelt before Azim, clasping Azim's hand between his. "Whatever you say, wherever you send, I will serve Allah through you."

Azim stood and lifted Sofian to his feet. With a smile, he leaned in and kissed his new Left on both cheeks. When he pulled back he said, "Your first duty is to find out what Dr. Michael Sieff has discovered regarding the Samson Effect. He fooled me once; I won't be fooled again."

\*     \*     \*     \*

Thomas settled into the room Michael had assigned to him. He put the few clothes his host had provided in the closet before freshening up in the adjoining bathroom. He was drying his face with a towel as he stepped back into the bedroom. When he removed the towel, the sight of a woman sitting on his bed startled him.

"Good morning, Dr. Hamilton."

"Good morning." Thomas looked at the open bedroom door. "May I ask if you always make a habit of entering a man's bedroom unannounced?" Though he tried to sound annoyed, her beauty softened his voice.

She smiled, uncrossing her long, tanned legs and stood with an extended hand. "I'm sorry, Doctor. I knocked, but there was no answer. Before I thought, I opened the door and stepped in."

Thomas took her soft hand gently in his. "Please, Thomas."

"Okay Thomas. I'm Hanna."

"You're the stewardess on the plane."

She broke into laughter and clasped his hand in both of hers. Thomas looked at her quizzically, but before she could say anything, Michael walked into the room. "Ah, good. I see you two have met." When Hanna began laughing again, he asked, "Did I miss something funny?"

Thomas smiled. "I take it Hanna isn't the stewardess on your uncle's plane."

"Good heavens, no. She's my uncle's public relations director and closest adviser." Thomas felt his cheeks tingle. He turned to her and stammered out an apology.

She smiled. "Don't give it another thought." She looked into Thomas's eyes, neither speaking nor attempting to break away.

Michael cleared his throat. "Yes, well, if you two will follow me, we'll catch Hanna up on the Samson Effect and I'll show you both the parchment I found."

They followed Michael down a hall and into a sparsely furnished office. Other than a single bookcase and desk, Thomas only saw one rectangular folding table with a portable halogen light sitting on it. Michael instructed them to take a seat at the table while he removed a box from under his desk.

As Michael set the box on the desk, Thomas asked, "At the sake of sounding rude, may I ask what Hanna's role in all this is?"

"As you know, my uncle is financing the search for the Samson Effect. As much as he trusts me, he trusts Hanna more. This is his way of ensuring he stays in the loop."

"Which begs the question, Michael," Hanna interrupted. "What exactly is the Samson Effect?"

Michael and Thomas exchanged glances. "Go ahead Thomas, tell her."

Thomas took in a deep breath and turned to Hanna. "A little over a year ago, Michael and I found a scroll hidden in one of the caves outside of Hebron." Michael took an ancient scroll from the box and placed it before her.

She looked at it with a puzzled expression. "What is it?"

"It's an account written by King David's scribe."

Hanna's eyes grew wide. "*The* King David?"

"Yes. To summarize, it's David's royal edict to destroy what we call the Samson Effect. However, the scribe and the guardians of the Samson Effect thought it would be blasphemy to destroy this great gift given by God. Instead of destroying it, they hid the secret. It remained safe until the Egyptian Pharaoh Shishak came up against Solomon's son, King Rehoboam, and looted the treasures of Israel."

"Pharaoh took it?"

"No." Thomas pointed to another scroll. "This one tells us that in the invasion, Pharaoh's army killed the guardian of the Samson Effect. The scroll was written by his handpicked successor. Unfortunately, the guardian died before he passed on its hiding place."

"So, it's been lost to history since then?"

Michael and Thomas exchanged glances again and smiled. "Until now," Michael said.

Pent-up frustration spilled from Hanna. She looked to each man. "So, what exactly is the Samson Effect?"

Michael took over the explanation. "You're familiar with the history of God's people, I assume."

"Somewhat, as long as I'm not tested on it." She looked at Thomas and shrugged. "Haven't exactly kept up with my religious studies."

"But you're probably familiar with the times when the Spirit of the Lord came upon men when Israel needed deliverance. The men could do extraordinary things. Superhuman things."

"Like Samson."

"Maybe the most notable of the men. Apparently, a select group of priests and rabbis possessed an elixir, or food substance—we're not yet sure—but something that allowed the human body to perform miraculous feats. These priests would pray to God when Israel was oppressed by its enemies; and when they felt they knew God's choice of a deliverer, they would introduce the Samson Effect into his diet."

Thomas looked to Hanna. He could see by her expression that she was struggling to take in the information. She finally asked, "Why did King David order it to be destroyed?"

"The scroll tells us he blamed King Saul's insanity on the substance. While in hiding from Saul, the guardians of the Samson Effect sided with David. He ingested it and began to perform amazing feats. However, he also fell into a deep depression. Thoughts of suicide began to surface. When he set up his southern kingdom in Hebron after Saul's death, he removed the substance from his diet and eventually came out of his depression. Convinced of its maddening side effects, he ordered all knowledge of the substance destroyed and forbade its use ever again."

Hanna stood and walked to the window overlooking the courtyard. The men waited for her to process the information. She finally turned to them and said, "You said it was lost to history until now. You have the Samson Effect?"

"Not exactly," Michael said. "But we're close. The parchment I found yesterday gives its location, but I can't decipher its meaning. That's why I brought Thomas here. As a biblical archaeologist, he's at the top of his field."

Hanna smiled at both men, failing to hide her giddiness. "Well then, let's look at the parchment and go find the Samson Effect."

Michael let out a sigh. "I wish it were as simple as that. The Palestinians are strong in Hebron, and one of them knows about the Samson Effect and is determined to find it before I do."

"Who?"

"Azim Ebadi."

The blood drained from Hanna's face. Thomas finally broke the silence. "Obviously this Azim character is a pretty bad guy."

Hanna stepped toward Thomas until she stood face to face with him. "Bad, Dr. Hamilton, isn't the word for him. He's evil, pure evil."

A burst of machine-gun fire outside the walled estate broke the tension in the room. Michael grabbed the phone and punched an extension. "What's going on?" He listened. "Dear God, sound the alarm now. Eli … Eli …"

Michael slammed the phone down as sirens began wailing throughout the compound. He turned to Thomas. "Grab the scrolls and parchment! I'll get the box!"

As Thomas picked up the scrolls, he asked, "Michael, what's going on?"

The two followed Michael through the door and down the hall. "I believe you're about to get your first experience with Azim."

They ran into the dining room, where a security guard met them. "Two down, and the wall has been breached."

The guard ran from the dining room into the kitchen. "Clear!" The three followed to the back of the kitchen and through the door leading into the garage. The guard jumped behind the wheel of Michael's sedan and started the engine.

As soon as everyone was in the car, the guard pushed the garage door button on the remote. The car tires squealed, and Thomas was sure the car roof was going to hit the rising door. He squinted and then sighed when the car raced safely from the garage.

The car spun to a stop as the driver lined up for the gate. Outside, Thomas watched men exchange intense fire. Without warning, one of the invaders jumped next to his window. Thomas found himself staring into the barrel of a machine gun. Before the car could pull away, Thomas heard the burst of the machine gun and saw the blood-splattered, shattered window. He closed his eyes and felt the car lunge forward.

He was waiting for the pain to hit or to lose consciousness, but all he felt was the wild bucking of the car. He opened his eyes to see the bullet-riddled, blood-stained window next to him. He whipped his head around to see the invader lying dead in the driveway. He reached to his head, finding it dry and with no wounds.

Michael grabbed him by the arm and pulled him to the floorboard. "Get down. The windows are bulletproof, but certainly not indestructible."

The car accelerated and the sounds of war echoed around them as they kept their heads down, praying to find safety. Then, a new sound rolled into the chaos. Thomas heard what sounded like beating chopper blades. "I hope that's the cavalry."

Michael squeezed his shoulders. "I'm sure it is. The Israelis would have shot down anything flying into a military zone. Still, you'd be wise to keep your head down for a while."

Thomas needed no convincing. He hunched down even tighter as they continued their escape away from the attack. All he could think about now was the warm, cozy, campus coffee shop where he stretched out in his sock feet and engaged in lively, albeit not deadly, debate. He could hardly fathom just how much his life had changed in the course of a few short hours.

The car skidded to a stop. The driver turned and shouted, "Everyone out! Move!"

Thomas poked his head up with the others. The compound was nowhere in sight, but a military truck sat a few yards in front of them. Soldiers holding their rifles stood watch, guarding from assault in all directions.

Michael raised his head, confident the immediate danger had passed. "It *is* the cavalry. That's an Israeli vehicle."

They spilled out of the car as the driver, now bodyguard, ushered them forward. A man wearing a major's uniform jumped from the truck and stepped forward to meet them. He extended his hand and took Michael's in a quick, firm greeting. "I've been sent to take you and your friends to safety." The major turned and marched toward the truck. "Follow me, please, quickly."

Thomas gestured for Hanna and Michael to move, and then fell in behind them. Their own guard backed his way to the truck, his gun swinging left and right. When Thomas climbed into the back of the truck, he scooted to make room for their guard, but the major jumped in and yelled for the driver to go. Michael reached forward and grabbed him by the shoulders. "Wait, Eli's still out there."

The major shrugged Michael's hand off of him. "Get your filthy hoof off of me, Jewish pig."

Michael stumbled backwards, his wide eyes frozen in a mix of fear and confusion. All three looked out the window just as the Israeli soldiers filled Eli's spasmodic body with bullets. Before he hit the ground, the soldiers jumped onto the rear bumper and the vehicle sped off.

# CHAPTER 4

THOMAS SCRAPED HIS cheeks against the dirt floor as the soldiers threw him and his companions into a cell. He reached up and yanked off his blindfold. Behind, he heard the heavy wooden door slam and the lock bolt the cell securely. He stood, brushed himself off, and helped Hanna to her feet. "Anyone hurt?"

Michael and Hanna both shook their heads. Thomas scanned the barren cell. He kicked his foot at a gray hairball and a half-rotted rat corpse rolled over. He looked up to see a three-inch slit at the top of a stone wall that allowed a sliver of light to provide the only illumination. A metal plate covered the slit on the door.

The box, the scrolls, and, more importantly, the parchment, had been taken from them. Michael slid down one wall and buried his face in his hands. "Hanna, Thomas, forgive me. I'm so sorry."

"It's not your fault," Thomas said. "I don't see how you could have anticipated this, let alone avoid it."

Hanna smiled. "Your uncle's a powerful and resourceful man. He'll find a way to get us out alive."

Hours passed and the sunlight coming through the slit faded. They had not talked to anyone since being imprisoned. Thomas felt hunger pangs and assumed the others did too, although no one complained. More intense than his hunger, though, was his thirst.

Michael and Thomas stripped off their shirts, using them to wipe the sweat from their necks and faces. Hanna, struggling to show some modesty, unbuttoned her white cotton blouse down to just below her bosom. She seemed to cope with the ordeal as stoically as the men did. So well, in fact, that Thomas feared he would show cracks of stress before she did.

The light slowly disappeared, throwing the cell into darkness. Thomas's tongue felt like a swollen sponge filling his dry mouth. No one spoke for hours.

The darkness brought a perceptible break from the heat, though not enough for either man to put his shirt back on. The stench from their oil and sweat became more bearable the longer they were exposed to it. Thomas didn't feel at all self-conscious when Hanna scooted next to him and wrapped her arms around his. Her touch caused increased heat to radiate from her body, yet it still felt overwhelmingly wonderful. He clasped his hand over hers, slowly rubbing her delicate arm with his other hand. Without saying a word, she leaned over and put her head on his chest. For the first time, Thomas felt comfort in the darkness. Enough so, that he had no problem falling asleep.

The unbolting and creaking of the opening door woke Thomas. He felt Hanna lift her head from his chest, and an oil lantern bathed the cell in light. Thomas squinted, trying to make out the details of the two silhouettes behind the light. One man emerged from the light and yanked Hanna up by her wrist. Thomas leaped to his feet; but when he cried out for the man to stop, only a hoarse, cracked sound emerged.

The man threw Hanna to his companion carrying the lantern. He shouted something in Arabic while he grabbed Thomas by the shoulder with one hand and sank the other into Thomas's stomach.

Thomas collapsed to the floor, trying to suck in air, but his swollen tongue filled his mouth, making it difficult for the air to reach his lungs. As quickly as it had appeared, the light disappeared as the door slammed shut. Thomas felt Michael's hand glide over him and pull him to a sitting position.

"You okay?"

After a few deep breaths, Thomas was able to force out a response. "Fine … Hanna?" Michael's silence tore at Thomas's heart. He closed his eyes and bowed his head in helplessness.

"Thomas, we can't allow Azim to discover the Samson Effect."

"What can we do to stop him? He has everything, even the parchment."

"The parchment …" Michael pushed away his discomfort to force himself to keep his mind active. "It mentions that the priest hid the Effect in the belly of the devil."

"The devil?"

"I've wracked my brains trying to discover its meaning. All I know for sure is that the Effect must be hidden in, or around, Hebron. The priest goes on to write that early the next morning he reported to King David he had destroyed it."

The two men quit talking when their words grew gravelly. Thomas fought to stay awake, but exhaustion won the battle, and he soon slipped into unconsciousness.

✳     ✳     ✳     ✳

Thomas awoke as sunlight filtered through the slit in the wall and burned onto his cheek. He sat up, hungry, and his lips cracked from thirst. He looked over at Michael, still asleep against the wall. When Michael began to stir, Thomas crawled to him. He pulled himself into a sitting position and let out a sigh. "We're going to die here, aren't we?"

"I don't know, Thomas. Much more of this, and we may welcome death."

They both looked at the door when they heard the bolt slide from the other side. When it opened, a woman stepped into the cell carrying a tray of food and water. Her coal-black hair flowed around her shoulders, framing her smooth face and dark complexion. Her wide, bright eyes commanded Thomas's gaze, but the woman seemed not to notice him at all. She and Michael silently stared into each other's eyes. Thomas was about to shake his friend from his trance when she set the tray down and turned to leave without saying a word.

Ice rattled as Thomas picked up the pitcher and poured crystal-clear water into two glasses. They drained the glasses and poured more. Thomas couldn't believe how quickly the water revitalized him. After his third glass, he turned his attention to the two plates on the tray.

Each plate had a slice of grilled ham and two pieces of toast. Thomas, with dirty fingers, picked up a piece of ham and tore into it. Michael picked up a piece of toast, savoring it as much as Thomas did the ham.

"Try the ham. It's got to be the best I've ever had."

"You can have mine."

Thomas bit off another piece. "You're kidding. You'll need it to build your strength."

Michael held his plate forward. "I'm Jewish, remember?"

Thomas stopped chewing. "Of course. I'm sure Azim did this on purpose." He handed his two pieces of toast to Michael. Some sense of guilt, however, kept him from eating the double portion of meat, at least for now.

Before they finished, the woman returned to the cell carrying a brown paper bag. She looked at the ham left on the plate, then at Michael. "Feeling better?"

Michael nodded as Thomas asked, "Where's Hanna?"

"She's safe for the moment. Her safety, however, depends in large part on how cooperative you'll be with my brother."

"And who's your brother?"

Michael answered before she had a chance. "Let me guess. Azim?"

She smiled. "Perceptive, but please don't confuse his disposition with mine. In many ways, we're quite different people." She stepped over to Michael and held out the bag to him. "For you."

Michael cocked his head and warily took the bag from her hand. He opened it and reached in to pull out a turkey drumstick. When he started to eat it, Thomas reached for Michael's ham.

"The reason I'm here is to tell you Azim will be meeting with you in a few minutes. Please, for your safety and that of your friends, don't refuse him."

Michael let etiquette fall by the wayside and spoke with his mouth full of turkey. "Refuse what?"

"You'll find out soon enough." The woman paused before stepping through the door. "Oh, and please don't mention the turkey to him. He'd be very angry with me if you did."

*    *    *    *

Fifteen minutes later, Thomas and Michael stood before Azim with their arms tied behind their backs. He sat behind his desk scanning the headlines of the Tel Aviv newspaper. They quietly waited until Azim finally put down the newspaper and looked at them. He shook his head with a solemn expression. "So sad … the authorities believe you are dead."

He pointed to the headline: *Dr. Michael Sieff And Companions Dead In Terrorist Attack.*

"The story says your auto was destroyed by mortar fire and your bodies were burned beyond recognition."

Michael shook his head. "So, you can kill us now, and no one would ever know."

"I suppose that's true, but I'm hoping that won't be necessary. I do so much hate violence."

"Right. I'd need a computer to keep track of all the people you're responsible for killing."

One of the men standing next to them drove the butt of his rifle into Michael's gut. Thomas leaned toward Michael, but the other man grabbed his shoulders, holding him in place.

Michael tried to catch his breath. From his knees, he looked up at Azim. "No, you're not a man of violence."

The man with the gun raised the butt above Michael's head, but grunted and relaxed when Azim waved him off. "Do not touch these men again without my command."

Azim walked over to Michael and bent to help him up. Michael shrugged his shoulders away. "I'm fine."

Thomas pulled against his bonds, trying to break free to help Michael to his feet. In frustration, he spun around to face Azim. "What exactly do you want from us?"

Azim returned to his desk. "Ah, Dr. Hamilton. You're an old college acquaintance of Dr. Sieff, aren't you? It's unfortunate you've become mixed up in all of this." He paused and shook his head. "And I believe you're wanted for murder in the United States, aren't you?"

Thomas felt rage burn through him but stopped himself from lashing out at Azim. Instead, he stood straight and remained silently stoic.

"Very well, I have a proposition for you. We both want the Samson Effect found. Maybe we can work together and each get something we want. I, of course, will have the Samson Effect. You will have your lives and the life of the woman."

Michael smiled. "No offense, Azim, but I value a filthy swine more than I do your word." This time, the blow from the rifle butt crashed into the back of Michael's neck, collapsing him to the floor.

Azim's teeth clenched as he got up and walked over to Michael. He balled his hand into a fist and struck the man behind Michael across the cheek, drawing blood from the corner of the man's mouth. He spoke with an even, restrained anger. "I told you not to touch them without my command. Next time, it will not be my fist that strikes you."

Trembling, the man bowed his head in submission. Azim's next words barked through the office. "Delia, come."

Thomas turned toward the door as the dark-haired woman who had fed them earlier entered. She escorted Hanna into the office, bound, gagged, and stripped to her undergarments. Hanna's eyes were wide and full of terror. Thomas tried to step toward her, but the guard restrained him.

"Enough of the pleasantries. Dr. Sieff, you and Dr. Hamilton will help me find the Samson Effect, or I assure you that your friend will suffer long before she dies." He stepped to a bookshelf and pulled off a leather briefcase, handing it to Delia. "You'll find copies of all the scrolls and parchments we've found concerning the Samson Effect. My sister will accompany you on your search. Should she fail to report back to me at prescribed times, your female friend will begin her journey of terror to hell." With a wave of his hand, one of the guards grabbed Hanna by the arm and dragged her from the office.

Thomas strained against the man holding his arm but couldn't move an inch toward Hanna. Delia stood between him and the door. "Dr. Hamilton, as long as you obey my brother, you've nothing to fear. However, please don't test him. He is a man of his word. Isn't that right, Barhim?"

The man nodded and lifted his bandaged hand. Thomas saw the bloodstain where his pinky finger should have been. Barhim then stepped to Azim and whispered into his ear.

Azim returned to his desk. "All things have been made ready. Dr. Sieff, you have two weeks to find the Samson Effect. If you can't find it by then, your usefulness to me will be suspect."

"Thomas and I have spent over a year searching for the Samson Effect. You can't possibly believe we can find it in two weeks.

Azim narrowed his eyes. "Perhaps you've not been sufficiently motivated." Before Michael could respond, Azim flicked his hand in a dismissive wave.

Delia turned to Michael and Thomas. "Gentleman, I suggest we begin our search immediately." The guards blindfolded them again and led them out of the office.

# CHAPTER 5

THOMAS FELT EVERY bump under the delivery truck as he sat next to Michael against the wall. He rubbed his head on his shoulders to remove his blindfold. From the light coming through the cracks around the back door, he could see that he and Michael were the only cargo in the truck. When Michael removed his blindfold, he threw his head against the wall and uttered something Thomas was sure was a Hebrew curse.

The truck bounced along for fifteen minutes before Thomas broke the silence. "Options?"

Michael sighed. "As I see it, we can save ourselves and assure Hanna's death, which I'm sure will be as horrific as Azim says it'll be; or we can work with Azim to find the Samson Effect, which I'm sure will eventually lead to all three of our deaths."

"There has to be another option."

"I agree, but I can't think of one. Can you?"

"Not yet, but one will come to us."

"Okay, then we agree to work on finding the Samson Effect with Delia's help until we find the opportunity for all three of us to escape?"

"Agreed."

Thomas listened to the sounds outside the truck, but he only heard the rumble of the truck and its engine. He then thought of the woman driver. "Michael, when we were in the cell and Delia first entered with the food, you two looked at each other as if you've known each other. What's up with that?"

Michael looked like a caught liar about to deny the obvious and then relaxed. He parted his lips and looked away. Just as Thomas was about to press him for an answer, the men glanced at the door as they felt the truck roll to a stop. A few seconds later, it swung open. "Hope the ride wasn't too uncomfortable for you," Delia said.

Neither man responded as they struggled to their feet and walked to the door.

"Now, gentlemen, we'll be working closely for the next couple of weeks. I'm sure it will be more comfortable if we're all civil to each other."

Thomas jumped from the truck and stepped up to Delia. Until he had come to Hebron, he had never once thought of harming anyone, let alone a woman. Now, he knew he could strike Delia with no remorse if his hands were free. "It's not mine or Michael's civility I question." He turned his back to her and joined Michael.

Delia nodded. "I don't blame you for your unwillingness to accept me—"

Thomas interrupted with a smirk. "That's very kind of you."

"—but as I said, you'll find me much different from my brother." She stepped up to Thomas and glared at him. "And I promise I'm the best chance for you, Michael, and Hanna to remain safe." She turned her back and walked to the building next to the truck. "If you'll follow me, we can get started now."

Delia led them from the street where the truck was parked to the threshold of an old block-long building that looked to be an apartment unit. Curious bystanders cast their gaze away when their eyes met Thomas's. He sensed fear in them. "Michael is known here. What if someone recognizes him?"

Delia held open the door. "As long as we stay within Palestinian neighborhoods, no one will say a thing or molest you in any way. My brother has made sure of that."

Delia unlocked an inner door across from a staircase. They stepped into a large room with three twin beds and two desks. Maps of Hebron and southern Israel hung on the walls. Each desk had a computer, which shared a printer. Off to the side, an open closet displayed Palestinian clothing. An open door at the back of the room led to a bathroom.

Delia spread her arms as each man claimed a bed. "This, gentlemen, is where you'll live, eat, work, and breathe for the next two weeks except when we work on site. The computers are connected to the Internet, and you'll find your user IDs and passwords in the center desk drawer. I'm sure I don't need to tell you every keystroke will be monitored." She gestured to the young man who appeared in the doorway. "This is Fahd. If you need anything at all, Fahd will make sure you have it."

Delia nodded to Fahd. He pulled a knife from the sheath on his hip and stepped behind Thomas. Thomas held his breath, but relaxed when he felt his bonds fall away. He rubbed his wrists as Fahd stepped behind Michael.

Thomas pointed to the third bed. "And I suppose he'll sleep there to keep an eye on us."

Delia arched her eyebrows. "No, Dr. Hamilton. That's where *I'll* be sleeping to keep an eye on you."

Michael sat at one of the desks and turned on the computer. "The clock is ticking, let's get started."

Thomas rolled his chair to Michael's desk and opened the briefcase, spreading the documents across the desk. "You said the scribe hid the Samson Effect in Satan's belly; still no thought on what that could be?"

Michael walked over to the map of Hebron. "I was in the process of searching the literature on Israel's ancient geography before we fell under attack. I found nothing, but I'm positive it must be in Hebron."

"Why do you say that, Dr. Sieff?"

"Because the time between the scribe hiding it and reporting back to King David would have been too short for him to travel very far."

"Unless," Delia continued, "he sent it with someone else. If he did, it could be anywhere in Israel."

"First, my gut tells me he wouldn't have turned it over to anyone else. He was very protective of the Effect. In fact, he was committing a capital offense by disobeying the king's edict. Second, we don't have time to search all of Hebron, let alone all of Israel. We must focus our efforts here unless we come across compelling evidence to search elsewhere."

Thomas joined Michael at the map. "I agree. Since we know it was still protected under Solomon's reign, I feel confident his father's priests didn't move it north to the kingdom of Saul's son. If he did, the tide may have changed in Israel's first civil war."

Delia joined the two men at the map. "The belly of the devil ... it must be a cave. Correct me if I'm wrong, but didn't the Israelites use caves extensively to hide everything from sacred writings to soldiers?"

Michael smiled at Delia. "I'm impressed; you seem to know your Jewish history well."

"I took a few courses in college, Doctor."

"We're going to be working closely for a while. Call me Michael."

She brushed her hair from her eyes and smiled. "Okay, Michael."

Thomas rolled his eyes. "If we can forgo the pleasantries, I suggest we stay focused on finding the Samson Effect." He glared at Michael. "I, for one, have not forgotten this woman's brother is threatening to kill your uncle's assistant."

"Thomas—"

He glared at Delia. "And it's *Dr. Hamilton* to you."

Michael sighed and shrugged his shoulders.

"It's all right, Michael. No one can blame him for being upset. I think I'll prepare some tea for us. If you'll please excuse me."

As soon as Delia closed the door behind her, Thomas yanked out his chair and dropped into it. "What's gotten into you, Michael? If you're not careful, your hormones will lead you down the same path they led Samson when he met Delilah." Thomas's eyes grew wide. "There's a coincidence, Delia and Delilah. Hmmm ..."

"Stop it, Thomas. Don't you ever accuse me of betraying Hanna." Michael squeezed his hand into a fist when Thomas rolled his eyes. The two men stared at each other until Michael relaxed his fingers and sighed. "You've been a friend for a long time, and I love you like a brother. We've got to make it through the next two weeks in order to have a prayer of saving Hanna, and that woman may be our best ally in doing so."

Thomas stared at the only bare wall in the room. After a few moments, he closed his eyes and bowed his head into his hands. Michael walked up to him and squeezed his shoulders. "I'm as frustrated as you are, my friend."

"You're right."

Delia returned with three cups of tea. She set the tray on one of the desks and handed a cup to Michael. She brought another and handed it to Thomas. "Dr. Hamilton."

Thomas took the tea and smiled. "Thanks." He looked into his cup. "Sorry we got off on the wrong foot."

"You've nothing to apologize for, Doctor."

He looked up and extended his hand. "Please, call me Thomas."

She shook his hand and nodded. Michael walked over with his tea. "If we can move past the pleasantries, I believe we have work to do."

Delia smiled and sipped her tea. "I recall while growing up in Hebron a mountain with three narrow peaks. We used to call it *Satan's Pitchfork*. Perhaps the Samson Effect is somewhere around there."

"Nice guess," Michael said, "but the image of a red Satan with horns, a pointed tail, and a pitchfork is a relatively new Western image of him. The pitchfork would've meant nothing to the ancient Jews."

"Then what did they think he looked like?"

"The Jews believed he was an angelic being cast down from heaven."

"I take it angels didn't look like chubby little cherubs with wings and a bow and arrow."

Michael laughed. "Hardly. When they appeared, they looked like any other man."

"But there must've been some unique characteristic about the hiding place which identified it with Satan."

Delia's question struck a chord with Thomas. He tuned out the ongoing conversation, and his mind went back to a dig he was on last year outside of Jericho. His team had found a stone idol dating around 1300 BC, a few hundred years before the establishment of David's kingdom. The idol was a Canaanite deity, but one of the interns pointed out the irony that its image was also that of the Hebrew devil.

The answer struck Thomas like a bolt of lightning. "Michael, I'm disappointed in you." Michael and Delia turned to Thomas. He pounded the desk with his fist, unable to keep his smile from growing. "How quickly you forget what your mother taught you. 'Now the serpent was more subtle than any of the beast of the field which the Lord God had made,' Genesis 3:1."

Michael's eyes grew. "I think that may be it! We're looking for a snake or a serpent!" He glanced at his watch. "It'll be dark in less than an hour. I propose we research the geography tonight for a field expedition tomorrow morning."

Delia jumped to her feet and made a beeline to the door. "I'll make arrangements for a day trip tomorrow."

Thomas took a sip of tea. "Maybe we ought to ask ol' Fahd to break out a bottle of champagne."

"Not so fast. It *may* be a serpent we're looking for. Even if it is, we don't know how much the landscape may have changed in three thousand years. And might I remind you we only have two weeks to find what no one has stumbled on in over three millennia."

Thomas plopped down on his bed. "You can sure bring someone down."

"I prefer to call it managing expectations." Michael walked over to the map. "However, if we *are* on the right track, I know just where to start looking tomorrow."

*     *     *     *

The sound of hushed giggling woke Thomas. He rolled his head to see the clock's red digital numbers flash 3:15. He lifted his head and leaned on his elbows to see Michael and Delia in their respective beds, lying on their sides and conversing in hushed tones. He lay down and listened to them carry on as though they were lifelong friends.

He closed his eyes and tried to ignore the sounds. He hated himself for letting even the slightest bit of fondness for Delia slip into his mind. Michael had told him she was suspected of carrying out a number of assassinations against Israelis. She was cold-blooded and more than likely would step aside when his and Michael's usefulness was through. He forced his mind back to Hanna. What was Azim doing to her right now? Was she in pain? Was she humiliated? He thought of Delia, whose aim it was to gain his trust. Hatred began to push away any fondness that had snuck in. He could be just as cunning as Delia. He could let her believe she had his trust.

Another giggle from Michael broke his thoughts. Delia shushed him and then responded with her own muted giggle.

Something wasn't right. Michael had a good head on his shoulders. He would never jump into such a ridiculous relationship, especially so quickly. Tomorrow, he wouldn't let anything keep Michael from giving him a straight answer.

Thomas closed his eyes, convincing himself repeatedly that Michael, too, must be displaying his cunning.

*     *     *     *

Thomas awoke at 6:00 a.m. to the sound of a commode flushing in the adjoining bathroom. Its occupant stepped through and flipped on the bedroom lights.

"Sorry for waking you," Michael said as he stepped into the room.

"No problem. Time to get up anyway."

Delia entered, already dressed and ready for the trip into the desert. With a slight, silent gesture of her hand, she dismissed Fahd. She glanced at each man with a smile. "So, where are we off to this morning?"

Michael walked to the map of Hebron and took a pen from his shirt pocket. "First light, I want to be on this hill." He circled an area on the map repeatedly.

Delia stepped to the map. "Why there?"

"If my hunch is correct, terrain with the features of a serpent will be easier to make out from an elevation. This hill will give us a great panoramic view of the whole area."

Delia raised an eyebrow and nodded. "Good. Can you be ready to leave in thirty minutes?"

Thomas grabbed some clothes and headed to the bathroom. "I'll be out in fifteen."

"Thomas …"

He stopped and turned to Delia.

"Please choose a tunic from the closet. My brother's influence is great here, but we should still try to blend in as much as possible."

He looked at the closet and then turned to Delia. "I'll put it on over my own clothes."

Michael laughed. "Trust me, my friend, come this afternoon you'll be sweltering with all that clothing on."

Thomas reluctantly pulled a tunic from the closet. He tossed his clothes onto the bed and slipped into the bathroom, shaking his head. The first thing that commanded his attention was the rust-stained toilet. It was on par with some of the worse truck stop toilets he had seen. A freestanding iron tub rested against the wall. "Great, no shower."

Thomas leaned into the tub and plugged the drain with the rubber stopper. He turned on the hot water and walked to the sink. A minute into brushing his teeth, Thomas walked over to the tub and dipped his hand into the water.

Cold.

He spit into the sink, grabbed a washcloth, and shut off the water in the tub. He stripped and plunged the cloth into the cool water, ready to take a sponge bath.

The sound of automatic gunfire and shattering glass in the bedroom startled him, forcing his nude body against the icy floor. Thomas heard Delia scream in the bedroom. He crouched, yanking a towel from the rack and wrapping it around him. He eased to the door and cracked it open.

Glass covered the bedroom floor. Michael lay over Delia with his face down and buried under his arms. Blood was splattered over them and the bed next to them.

Thomas heard screeching tires and ran to Michael and Delia, losing his towel behind him. He grabbed Michael by the shoulders, shaking him and yelling his name.

# CHAPTER 6

THE JEEP SPED away from the apartment less than fifteen seconds after the attack through the bedroom window. The streets were empty, giving the driver and the gunman a clear escape route. A few sharp turns later, the driver pulled through an open gate, which two men awaiting his arrival immediately closed.

The driver skidded to a stop and killed the engine. He and the gunman flew from the jeep and jogged through a doorway into their rabbi's home. The doormen slammed and locked the door behind them as they strode down a hallway into the room at the end. An elderly man behind the desk stared unblinkingly at them.

"Well?"

The gunman stepped forward. "It is done, Rabbi."

The rabbi simply nodded once then whispered, "Good, Judas."

He placed his frail, wrinkled hands on the desk and pushed his chair away. His arms trembled as he struggled to pull himself from the chair. Judas and the driver, Simon, slipped around the desk to help him up.

The rabbi reached for the cane propped against the desk and hunched his weight over it, beginning the slow, arduous journey across the room. Simon and Judas waited patiently for the rabbi to reach the bookcase. He leaned his cane against a wall and grabbed a shelf with his left hand. His trembling right arm reached up and pulled a thick volume from the shelf. His arm began to shake under the weight of the book. Judas started toward him.

The rabbi reached with his left hand to grip the book, stabilizing his hold on it. He slowly turned to see Judas behind him.

"Rabbi, let me carry that for you."

The rabbi shook his head. "No, but you can help me back to my seat." He turned to the driver. "Simon, please bring my cane."

A few eternal moments later, the rabbi was back at his desk with the book lying before him. He looked each man in the eyes then took a breath. "It's time for me to decide. You've both served Yahweh well." His eyes came back to the driver. "Simon."

Simon approached the desk. "Rabbi."

"Simon, faithful Simon. I know you will be faithful to the Lord's call until death."

"Yes, Rabbi."

"And I know you will serve Judas as faithfully as you've served me."

Behind, Judas's eyes widened for a moment and then relaxed as he glanced to the floor. He prayed his hands would not betray his nervousness.

Simon turned to his new rabbi and smiled. "I will serve him faithfully until death." He held his gaze for a moment and then turned back to the elderly rabbi.

"I know you will." The rabbi opened the book and pulled out a small bottle from its hollowed-out pages. He lifted it in his trembling hands and then called Judas to him. Judas walked past Simon, slowing just enough to squeeze his friend's shoulder before walking up and kneeling before his rabbi.

The rabbi pulled the cork from the bottle and swiveled his chair until he faced Judas. He lifted the bottle over Judas's head and slowly poured the thick oil. Judas remained frozen, accepting the anointing from his mentor.

"Judas, the Lord anoints you to carry out his work, searching out and protecting his sacred strength. May he be with you in life, in death, wherever he calls you to go." When the bottle was empty, the rabbi set it on the desk. "Rabbi Judas, arise."

Judas lifted from his kneeling position and mouthed a silent prayer. The rabbi turned to Simon. "I have much to discuss with Judas. Please, leave us alone."

Simon nodded and backed his way from the room and shut the door. When the two were alone, the rabbi nodded for Judas to take a seat across from the desk. He sighed before revealing the ancient secret he possessed.

"Judas, you know most of my life has been devoted to protecting a great secret of our God. Today, unclean gentiles and Jews who have left their faith have jeopardized that secret."

Judas looked into the sunken eyes of the frail, wrinkled man. In his youth, Judas remembered the strength that exuded from this man. The secret he was protecting had exacted a heavy toll on the rabbi.

The rabbi continued. "I'm old. My body cannot keep up with my mind's fervent desire to continue the search and to protect the secret. Over four thousand years of sacred history now falls on your shoulders to protect until the day when your frail body entrusts the service to another."

Judas felt the weight of responsibility, and yet, at the same time, felt the exhilaration that tensed every muscle and sped his beating heart. "Rabbi, I'm ready to die for my God." He shifted his eyes away, hesitant to hasten the rabbi's disclosure. However, he looked back at the old man and drew in his breath. "Please, tell me the secret of the Lord's Strength."

The rabbi smiled. "Yes, my son. It's time for you to know. You must swear not to reveal to anyone what you are about to hear. Not even to Simon. The secret must be yours until you choose your successor."

Judas's eyes fixed on the rabbi. He reached for the old man's feeble hand, gently clasping it in his. "On my soul, I swear to keep this secret."

*     *     *     *

Thomas looked at the blood splattered over Michael and Delia, but he could not find the source of the bleeding. After what seemed an eternity, Michael slowly lifted his head and rose to his knees.

"Delia, are you all right?"

Delia blinked and pushed herself to her knees, wiping the blood from her face. "I think so. I don't feel any pain."

With Thomas's help, the two slowly stood. Once on their feet, the three found the source of the splattered blood. A severed pig's head rested at the foot of Michael's bed. Delia grabbed Thomas's shirt from his bed, wiped the blood speckles from her arms, and stormed into the bathroom.

Thomas grabbed his pants and threw them on while Michael sat next to him at the foot of the bed. The door to the room opened. Fahd ran in with a pistol pointed at them. He looked scared. "Wh—what you done?" he cried in broken English.

The two men held up their hands, waving their open palms before their face. "Fahd! Put down the gun. Delia's okay. Please!"

Fahd's eyes darted from man to man to pig's head. Thomas could see his white knuckles wrapped around the trigger. The muzzle of the gun shook in rhythm with the boy's trembling body.

"What you done?" the boy cried out again.

Then Thomas saw the trembling die as a stone-hard look came over Fahd. His eyes no longer showed terror, but resolve and hatred. "Delia," Thomas yelled, "now would be a good time to get in here!"

The bathroom door opened and everyone turned to see Delia walk through the door. "Fahd, it's okay. Put down the gun."

Thomas turned to see Fahd's anger melt into overwhelming joy. He lowered his pistol and put it into his waistband.

Delia sat at the desk and picked up the phone. In a few seconds, she was speaking in her native tongue. Thomas strained to find one familiar word, but he found no context in the conversation. Then, abruptly, Delia hung up the phone and looked up at them.

"Azim is sending men over now to clean the place. He's made arrangements for us to finish getting ready before we leave this morning to find the cave—"

"What?" Thomas cried. "Delia, your brother can't seriously expect us to go out today." He waved his hand at the pig's head. "Whoever did this knows who we are and what we're looking for. It'd be a suicide mission."

"That's exactly what Azim expects us to do. He'll find out who did this and he'll take care of them. Until then, he'll post guards to watch over us at a distance."

"But—"

"No *buts*; it's not negotiable." Delia stood and stepped to the door. "Collect your belongings and come with me. The building's owner lives directly above us. He's waiting for us now." She grabbed a duffel bag and stepped to the door. "Fahd, wait here until the men arrive to clean this place."

Fully heartened he wasn't facing cold-blooded murderers, Fahd nodded and pulled out his pistol. Delia looked back to Thomas and Michael. "Well?"

They looked at each other and then began collecting their belongings. They then followed Delia out the door and up a flight of stairs. She knocked on the only door on the second floor, and a tall, muscular Palestinian man dressed in khakis and a plaid shirt opened the door. He stepped aside for her to pass. The man's burrowing eyes, however, locked onto Thomas. As he passed into the room, Thomas bumped into the man and swallowed hard, feeling as if he had bumped into a mountain. The man, at least a head taller than him, stared down with narrow eyes and a mouth turned down into a frown.

Once inside, Thomas saw three other men at least as big as the doorman. All were dressed in similar Western clothes, and all wore the same expression that told Thomas they would as soon gut him as speak to him. That was all the encouragement he needed to remain silent.

A plump, elderly woman appeared and examined Delia's blood-stained top. She gripped Delia's arm and led her out of the room and down the hall. Thomas and Michael looked at each other, then around the room. Neither man dared to speak a word. Michael stepped to a sofa and silently watched for any prohibition against sitting. The three men held their hard gaze, but didn't stop him from sitting.

Following his slow, deliberate lead, Thomas edged over to the sofa and sat next to Michael. While they waited for Delia to return, Thomas scanned the room. It wasn't exactly what he expected to find in a Hebron home. In the middle of this unfamiliar, foreign, desert country, the room was an oasis of his Western home. The couch, coffee table, and chairs were Victorian French design. Mounted on the rich mahogany wall was a plasma television and stereo unit attached to *Bose* speakers. Nothing in the room hinted of his image of the Middle East.

A booming voice startled Thomas. He and Michael turned in unison to see the man who had just entered the room. "Welcome to my home, gentleman. May I offer either of you something to drink?"

The man was obviously Palestinian by complexion and accent, but Thomas noted his English was fluent and educated. True to his surroundings, he wore a navy blue Armani, a Rolex, and a single gold-nugget ring on a perfectly manicured hand. His smile was warm and inviting, but Thomas was wary of the leopard's spots under the sharply dressed exterior. He was, after all, an acquaintance of Azim.

The man stood at a fully stocked bar that had been hidden behind a panel in the wall. "Come now, gentlemen. Please allow me to extend my hospitality to you." He waved his arm toward the bottles. "Wild Turkey, vodka, a martini, perhaps? Dr. Hamilton, I even have the finest imported American beer."

Thomas looked at Michael, who rolled his eyes and shrugged. "Brandy?"

The man smiled warmly and reached for a bottle. "Frapin—my favorite. Your choice compels me to join you. Dr. Sieff?"

Michael's response had a cold edge to his tone. "It's a little too early for me, thank you."

"Very well, Doctor. If you change your mind, you need but ask."

He brought two glasses to the couch and handed one to Thomas. Thomas avoided Michael's eyes as he accepted the drink, hoping it would take the edge off his guilty conscience.

The man sat in the chair across from the sofa and took a sip of his drink. "Please allow me to introduce myself. My name is Umar. Welcome to my home."

Michael ran his fingers through his hair and glanced at his watch. Before the silence became too awkward, Thomas lifted his glass and tipped it slightly in Umar's direction.

Umar's friendly demeanor did not wane. "I'm so thankful neither of you were hurt this morning." He leaned forward and, for the first time, his smile melted from his face. "I assure you, we'll find out who did this." Umar did not blink. Thomas felt the icy presence of the killer he knew hid beneath the chic, Western clothing. Before his trembling hands could rattle the ice in his glass, Thomas tipped it back and gulped.

This time the silence was awkward. Thomas dared not try to fill in the void. He didn't trust the strength of his voice. His lips parted, and then sealed shut as he looked into his swirling brandy.

A familiar voice broke the deafening silence. "Uncle!" Delia glided across the floor and hung her arms around Umar.

Umar stood and held Delia at arm's length. "Are you all right, child?"

As he examined her, Delia nodded. "I'm fine. Irritated, but no injuries."

"Uncle?" Michael asked.

Delia looked at Umar and smiled. "I'm sure you extended the appropriate hospitality to our guests."

Michael stood and walked over to Delia. "He's been decent to us."

Umar put one arm around Delia and the other around Michael, squeezing both into his chest. "It's my pleasure your brother has entrusted your safety to me. From now on, you will have nothing to worry about." Umar turned to Michael. "Doctor, are you sure I can't interest you in something to drink?"

Michael extricated himself from Umar's embrace. Whatever he was about to say changed when he glanced at Delia. "I guess I could have a Coca-Cola."

Umar beamed. "Fine. Why don't you come with me while I fix you a glass."

Delia noticed Thomas's glass was empty and reached out to touch his arm. "Do you need a refill?"

Thomas pulled his arm away. "I don't know how you've been able to bewitch Michael so quickly, but don't think it will work with me."

Her cheeks reddened more, and her brows turned angry. "It's clear that we don't like each other, but at least I've attempted to act civil. If you want me to, I can be the ruthless assassin you think I am."

Her soft eyes turned cold and passed their chill through Thomas. "You are what you are and nothing I do or say will change that."

Thomas turned to the bar to see Umar and Michael engaged in a deep conversation—at least one side of a conversation. It seemed Umar was doing all the talking. In a few moments, the two men returned.

"Delia, I don't know what your brother's business is with these two men, but he's impressed upon me its urgency. You'll find your truck fueled and ready to go." He nodded to the three well-dressed killers. "Don't worry about your safety. You will be in no danger."

Delia kissed Umar on the cheek and thanked him. As she, Thomas, and Michael walked out the door, Thomas looked at the muscle-bound doorman and smiled. The doorman returned his smile with an expressionless stare. Thomas leaned in and whispered to Michael. "I feel much better knowing he's on our side."

"Don't get too cozy with that thought. Alliances are fluid. One minute he'll be watching your back, the next he'll be putting a knife into it."

# CHAPTER 7

THE TRUCK RUMBLED through the city and out to the southern outlying area of Hebron. Thomas stole glances through the window and door-mounted mirror for any signs of Umar's men. Either they were good at subterfuge, or they weren't skilled at trailing. He couldn't decide if he should worry more about Umar's men or the men who attacked them this morning.

Delia followed Michael's instructions to a rocky, desert location and parked the truck at the base of the tallest hill. "This is where we start."

They got out of the cab and walked around to the back of the truck. Michael opened the door and removed the backpacks tethered to the side railing.

Thomas flung his over his shoulder as he shut the door. "I must say the ride in the cab was much more comfortable than the ride back here."

Delia slung her pack over her shoulders. "I'm sure it was. As long as you don't give me a reason, you'll not have to ride back there again."

Thomas stepped away without acknowledging her statement. He knew the "can't we all just get along" chorus was an act. As soon as he could get Michael alone, he would find out what's going on. Michael's peculiar behavior toward her was beyond what was needed to help keep Hanna safe. As for himself, Thomas refused to be a lamb led to the slaughter, and he would do everything in his power to keep Michael from being one too.

He watched Michael help Delia on with her backpack. They smiled warmly at each other. Michael stood behind her and placed a hand on her shoulder. She didn't flinch, nor did her smile disappear. With his other hand, he pointed out their route up the hill.

Thomas tightened the straps on his backpack, his eyes following Michael's finger. "Why did you choose this place to start?"

Michael dropped his pointing hand, but his other remained on Delia's shoulder. "Old Hebron was south of the modern city. Figured we'd start at ground zero to look for the serpent landscape." He nodded to the hill. "We'll have a nice panoramic view from up there."

Thomas removed his hat and wiped his brow with his sleeve. "You'd have to pick the hottest day to go rock climbing, wouldn't you? Delia, I'm almost sorry I didn't wear that Palestinian man-dress you wanted me to wear." He took out his canteen and swallowed a couple of gulps of water.

"Careful," Delia said. "You'll want that water a lot more this afternoon than you do now."

Thomas looked up the hillside. A few hundred feet could hardly be called a mountain, he thought. He stepped up on his tiptoes to stretch out his calf muscles. His months of tennis and indoor rock climbing had kept his body in top shape. This would be a piece of cake. If he couldn't play Michael in a game of tennis, then he'd grab a victory from him by beating him to the summit. He waited for Michael to take the first step up the hill. When Thomas beat him to the top, he didn't want Michael hastily dismissing his victory. After Michael was five feet up, Thomas set out for the summit.

He caught up with Michael's leisurely pace and set the competition in motion with a single phrase. "Either move it or get out of the way."

Michael looked over his shoulder and smiled. "I'll have the water waiting for you at the top." His leisurely pace morphed from casual strides to the scurrying of a four-legged spider.

Thomas kicked up his pace but quickly realized that real rocks didn't always provide the grip that the rock walls he had climbed at home provided. He stretched his fingers to a small cleft at Michael's feet and hit pay dirt. His biceps bulged as sheer strength propelled him up until he and Michael climbed side by side. Neither slowed their pace as they approached the summit.

"Good. You've caught up with me. Now it's a fair race."

Sweat rolled down Thomas's forehead as he began to overtake Michael. "Looks like the years have slowed you down."

"I'm just getting warmed up."

Somehow, Michael found a way to accelerate his ascent. A hairline crack emerged in Thomas's smug confidence. The closer they came to the summit, the steeper the hill grew; but it seemed the climb was becoming easier for Michael.

Thomas pushed his aching muscles to move him faster. His fingertips grew raw as he willed them into the solid rock surface. But nothing he said or did to motivate himself stopped Michael from slowly pulling away from him.

To make matters worse, Delia approached on his left. A faint sheen upon her skin glistened in the sun as she apparently decided she could hang with the boys. When she started to pull away from him, Thomas strangled the tiny crevices in his hands and ground his teeth in utter contempt for yet another loss to Michael.

With one last burst of energy, Thomas surged past Delia and pulled himself upon the flat summit. He collapsed on the ground and heaved gulps of air into his lungs. Delia crawled next to him and oozed onto the ground with rubbery arms. As his breath returned, Thomas heard the sound of shoes scuffing on the surface and coming to a stop next to his head. Michael bent down with his promised canteen. "Sorry, couldn't find a glass."

Thomas pulled himself up and took a swig from his own canteen. He wiped his mouth with his sleeve and asked, "How can you not be winded?"

"Oh, I don't know. I guess it's because the years haven't slowed me down too much."

Thomas didn't understand. He and Michael were both in shape, but Michael never let his body keep him from doing what he set his mind to do. Thomas did, however, find a sliver of hope when he spotted a vein in Michael's neck throbbing in step with his own racing heart.

When they caught their breath, they began scanning the landscape with their binoculars. After forty-five minutes, they settled on three locations that by some wild stretch of the imagination could possibly be their snake-caves. Michael sketched the missing snake features on the landscape into a notebook, resulting in three snakelike images.

Delia studied Michael's artwork and wrinkled her brow. "I don't know; the pictures just don't look like the landscapes. I see it on paper, but not out there."

"I agree you'll have to use some imagination. But remember, the terrain may have changed in three thousand years, or the scribe may have done what early astrologers and sailors had done with the constellations—take a few points to build an elaborate picture."

"You're assuming," Thomas said, "the scribe's 'snake' was a rock or cave. For all we know, it could've been a symbolic reference known only to a select group of scribes. I mean, it could be a statue in Jordan, for all we know."

"True, but we only have two weeks to find it. The way I see it, we have to take an educated guess and focus there. Unless ..." Michael turned to Delia. "Azim could be persuaded to extend our search."

Delia shook her head. "When the time comes, I'll try to secure more time for us, but unless we've made considerable concrete progress, I know what his answer will be. His unyielding demand for obedience in the face of all obstacles is what ensures unquestioning loyalty from everyone who answers to him."

Thomas took another swig from his canteen. "That settles it, then. Let's drive to Snake Cave Number One and see what we find."

*       *       *       *

The rabbi explained to Judas the secret of the Lord's Strength given to man, dating as far back as the day when Moses first received it.

"Moses entrusted its protection to his nephew, Nadab, a priest," the rabbi explained. "However, he and his brother, Abihu were struck down by the Lord for offering strange fire to him. Since the priesthood was new to Israel, Moses and Aaron feared the Lord would continue to show his displeasure against the priests whenever they failed to obey him fully in their sanctified role.

"So they chose an honest, humble man from the tribe of Gad. He became the protector of the Lord's Strength, and he established the code we follow to this day."

Judas listened, spellbound by the rabbi's words. So many questions were struggling to burst from his lips, but he held them in check until an appropriate time. The rabbi lifted himself from the chair and grabbed his cane. "Come with me."

Judas accompanied the old rabbi at a snail's pace, which gave his teacher ample time to explain where they were going.

"Sometime after Solomon's reign, the protector chosen was a man of great wealth and influence in Judah. He was also a man of pure heart and devoted to his calling. He built a modest dwelling in Hebron to serve as home for the Lord's Strength. That dwelling is its home to this day."

The rabbi led Judas down the hall and into his bedroom. Judas marveled at how little a man of the rabbi's age had collected in his life. The house itself was simple, but the bedroom was nearly barren. An opened closet contained clothes on only five hangers. The bedroom had only three pieces of furniture. A simple, small, square table and a stool sat on one wall. A cup of Bic pens and a writing tablet sat on the table. A king-size bed, which seemed so out of place in this humble little home, sat in the center of the room.

The rabbi shuffled into the room and slowly eased onto the stool. "This, Judas, is the dwelling place the protector built. Through Christian crusades and

Muslim occupations, the Lord has seen fit to keep this small home in the hands of the Jewish protectors. That, my student, is one of the greatest miracles indeed."

"Rabbi, I don't understand. How could this home have survived all the centuries of warfare and bloodshed? And, forgive me, but this home was built in the twentieth century."

"Judas, Judas, it's not the walls of this house that has survived. I have no idea how many times they've been destroyed and rebuilt. No, the true dwelling place is there." He lifted his cane and pointed at the bed.

Judas stared at the bed and looked tentatively back to the old man. "Rabbi?"

The old man smiled. "Slide it against the window and tell me what you see."

Judas obeyed, straining every muscle to slide the mammoth bed inch by inch. When he finished, he stood next to the bed, examining the bare area it had covered. "I don't see anything."

"Ah, now take my cane and go into the closet."

Judas obediently followed the rabbi's instructions.

"Now, remove the rug and look for a chip in the floor. Place the cane in the hole and turn it until it locks into place."

Judas inserted the cane and turned it until it felt snug. "Now rotate the cane clockwise until it stops."

He turned the cane with relative ease. In the bedroom, where the bed had been, he heard a grinding sound and saw a thin rectangular crack emerge as part of the stone floor began to sink away. His heart beat faster as a hole in the floor appeared.

"The seam has remained invisible all these centuries because each protector makes only two trips down in their lives; once when they're anointed and once when they show it to the next anointed."

For the first time since he had known the rabbi, Judas saw in his eyes an almost childlike giddiness. After a few minutes, the rectangular stone had submerged and slid out of the way. The cane found resistance and stopped turning. Judas removed it and went to the rabbi.

The rabbi took the cane and pointed it at him. "The iron foot on the cane— that's the key. Place it on any rod you wish. Now, help me up."

Judas helped him to his feet and the two walked over to the hole. Steps led down into the blackness. The rabbi reached into his pocket, pulled out a lighter, and handed it to Judas. "Go down and light the lamp on the wall to the right and then come back and help me down."

"Rabbi, the steps are narrow. It might not be safe for you to go down."

"The last time I made the trip down was over forty years ago. I've dreamed of this day since. Try to stop me."

"Okay, okay." Judas smiled. He took the lighter and descended fifteen steps before reaching the bottom. He found the lamp and lit it, revealing a room about fifteen feet square. A golden altar sat against the back wall. Two small, gold tables stood on both sides of the altar. The back two tables were about three feet tall while the two tables in front stood about two feet tall. Golden candlesticks, each with twelve unburned candles, sat on the tables. Imbedded in the walls sparkled every type of precious stone imaginable. Judas stared at everything, lost in the room's beauty.

The rabbi's feeble yet determined voice snapped him from his trance.

"Rabbi, it's beautiful."

"I know it is. Now come back for me right now or my blood will be on your hands when I try to come down myself."

"Yes, Rabbi." Judas helped his teacher down, and soon both men stood transfixed. When Judas turned to the rabbi, he saw tears streaming down his teacher's cheeks.

The rabbi grabbed Judas's arm and slid to his knees, bowing his head before the altar. Judas followed his example and knelt next to the rabbi, who began a prayer of praise and thanksgiving, followed by a petition to be with and to guard the new protector.

When the prayer ended, Judas felt tears in his own eyes. He straightened his back and drew in a deep breath. "Rabbi, thank you for bringing me here. I'll keep this secret until the day I die. I swear it."

The rabbi patted him on the back. "Judas, dear Judas. I've watched you grow from a child to a man. I was sure you'd protect the secret even before I asked, as you must be when you choose your successor. But this," the rabbi said with a wave of his arm, "this is not the true treasure. Are you ready to see the true treasure, the Lord's Strength; the strength of Moses, of David, of Israel's ancient judges, of Samson?"

"Yes, rabbi."

"I'm sure you are." He handed Judas the cane. "Put the key into the hole in the center of the altar, but don't turn it yet."

Judas did so and awaited further instructions.

"You must never forget the following sequence. If you do, it is said the key will be crushed within the altar and you'll be the first protector in history to lose the precious strength of the Lord."

Beads of perspiration ran down Judas's forehead. He never trusted his memory for important things; however, he cleared his head and waited for the sequence.

"Face the altar and turn the back left candlestick a quarter turn clockwise. Turn the front left a quarter turn counterclockwise."

Judas did so and felt gears within the tables clicking as they turned.

"Now, the right side. Rotate the back candlestick three-quarters turn clockwise and the front one a half turn clockwise."

When he finished, he wiped the sweat from his palm onto his thigh and chanted the sequence silently in his head. The rabbi interrupted his chant, setting off panic alarms in his mind.

"Ready?"

He wiped his hands dry again, deciding to wait until he went back up the stairs to get the sequence from the rabbi again. He nodded.

"Good. Now turn the key clockwise."

He wiped his hands dry one last time and started to turn the cane. A section of the wall behind the altar began to recess. Euphoria swept through his body when he did not feel the key crush within the altar.

When the recessed section of the wall was back far enough for him to slip by, the rabbi stopped him. Judas flicked the lighter, slipped into the room, and found an oil lamp sitting on a chiseled square stone about chest high. The room was only eight by eight with no jewels or gold. It was a plain rock room, roughly hewn. Judas saw a laboratory beaker on the center of the rock cube. The rabbi slipped in behind him and pointed to the beaker.

"There it is, the Lord's Strength."

"The beaker? How old is this secret?"

The rabbi laughed. "The containers have changed over the centuries, but the content has remained preserved since the days of King Solomon." He walked over, picked up the beaker, and handed it to Judas.

Judas looked inside and saw a finely chopped substance that looked like burgundy oregano. The rabbi took back the beaker and removed the cork. He measured out a third of the substance on a sheet of paper and replaced the cork. He then removed a flask from his jacket pocket and set it on the stone.

"Judas, my hands aren't as steady as they once were. Would you mind pouring this into the flask?"

Judas rolled the paper and funneled the substance into the flask. Following the rabbi's instructions, he replaced the cap and shook the flask.

The rabbi let out a sigh. "It takes one ounce. There are only two ounces left—enough for two more men. If no one finds the lost seeds, the Lord's Strength will be lost to mankind forever." He paused for a moment and stared at the beaker. Judas waited for him silently, patiently. The rabbi finally turned to him, tears back in his eyes. "I pray your search will find more success than mine." He looked at the flask. "I was told if it was freshly cut, the result would be even more amazing and longer lasting." The rabbi still stared at the flask, licking his lips. He finally turned to Judas with a sigh. "Drink, my friend."

Judas didn't move. He trusted the rabbi explicitly, or so he thought. What kind of drug was this? What was going to happen to him? He swirled the flask and looked at the rabbi. "Perhaps we could take it upstairs and—"

"Drink it now, boy, or I swear I'll rip it from you and drink it myself!"

The rabbi's voice reverberated in the tiny underground room and almost caused Judas to drop the flask. The old man's eyes nearly popped from his head. Every vein in his neck and forehead burst to the surface, throbbing with every beat of his heart. For the first time in his life, Judas was sure he was experiencing a demon possession.

Then, as abruptly as the rabbi's outburst came upon him, he returned to his gentle self. "Forgive me Judas. My heart is broken knowing I'll never again experience what you're about to experience." He looked through Judas, his mind lost somewhere in the memories of the past. "Please, drink it."

He did.

# CHAPTER 8

AFTER A SHORT drive from the hill, Delia pulled the truck next to Snake Cave Number One. The men unloaded the tools they would need in the cave. Up close, everyone admitted the rock formation looked nothing like a serpent. They approached the opening, which corresponded to a snake's eye on Michael's sketch. The entry was just wide enough for them to crawl through comfortably.

Thomas's flashlight cut fifteen feet to the back wall. He scanned his light back and forth and saw another hole. "Not a bad place to start. Looks like a passageway extends through the hill. Perfect place to hide something."

A smile burst onto Michael's face. "Imagination's pretty good, huh?"

Delia took a small pickax from her backpack and stepped into the cave. "We'll see." In a few seconds, she disappeared through the small opening in the back. Thomas walked over to Michael and shook his head. "What's going on, Michael? I know you're trying to get on her good side, but you've been flirting with her since the day she entered our cell. *Our cell*, Michael! You haven't forgotten we're still technically her prisoners, have you?"

Michael smiled and shook his head. "No, but I do think I could fall for her."

"You what? Come on, Michael. You're Jewish; she's Palestinian. You guys hate each other."

"Why, that's a pretty prejudicial thing to say. Thought you were above that."

"*I* am, but what do you think dear old brother would think of you even touching his little sister?"

"How's he going to know?"

"How's he going to know?" Thomas counted off the reasons with his fingers. "First, her uncle has three goons out there watching us. I may be wrong but my hunch is they'd love to bring back this juicy tidbit of gossip to him. Second, don't you think your girlfriend may not be as interested in you as you are in her? You come on too strong and she'll have big brother take care of you for her. Heck, I bet she'd enjoy spilling your guts herself."

"Look, she does have feelings for me." He put his hand on Thomas's shoulder. "Trust me, my friend. I'll be careful."

All Thomas wanted to do was wring Michael's neck and shake some sense into him. However, he knew if he lost his cool, he'd drive a wedge between them. Instead, he took a breath and spoke in the kindest voice he could muster. "I know you'll be careful, but what about her? All she needs to do is utter one careless, innocent word at the wrong time and you'll be dead."

"She's smarter than that—"

Thomas waved him off. "Yeah, I know, I know. It's obvious you have your mind made up. Just promise me *you* will be careful. Remember, I'll probably suffer collateral damage from anything aimed at you." He rolled his eyes at Michael's sheepish grin.

"I'm going to tell you something I hope will help you feel better, but I don't want you to make a big deal about it in front of Delia, okay?"

"What?"

"You remember when I praised her for being a good student of Jewish history?"

Thomas nodded warily. "Yeah."

"Well, I know because she took the course from me. Apparently, her brother wanted her to take the ancient Hebrew language course I was teaching in Jerusalem." Michael looked out toward the horizon. "That was last year, and she was only there for a semester, but we got to know each other pretty well in that time."

"How well, Michael?"

"Let's just say we became close friends. She seemed fascinated with me and my work. We spent the evenings talking about class, visiting museums, and sharing our hope of peace between our people."

"It's obvious why she was so fascinated with you. She was preparing for this day."

"It was more than that. There's no doubt in my mind she'll do what she can to help us." He picked up a small spade and walked toward the cave. "She's afraid of him, you know."

Everything fell into place for Thomas: the turkey leg, the giggling, and her eagerness to be part of the team. "I bet. He strikes me as the type of guy who wouldn't think twice about killing his own sister if she dishonored him." They made it to the mouth of the cave and dropped to their knees. "Just be careful."

Michael nodded, his eyes thanking Thomas for his understanding.

"Oh, don't thank me. I think this is by far the dumbest thing you have ever done." Thomas extended his hand toward the opening. "Shall we, or would you prefer a few moments alone with her?"

Michael slipped in front of him. "Don't start with me."

As they entered the cave, they heard Delia's shrill scream echo past them. On impulse, they both scurried into the cave, Michael calling her name. From the hole in the back, they saw Delia's feet and legs backing out. Sharp, heavy breaths replaced her screams. Once out, she crawled to Michael and melted into his arms. Thomas shined his light on them. She was shivering and violently swiping her hands through her disheveled hair and at her shoulders.

"Get them off! Get them off!"

Michael frantically looked over her body from head to toe. "Get what off?" He gripped her shoulders. "Delia, look at me. Get what off?"

Her shivering died away as she turned her head to the hole. "Snakes."

Michael and Thomas stared at each other. "There's a brood of snakes in there. Hundreds of them."

Thomas shined the light at the hole. "I didn't think snakes traveled that far into caves."

"Well, if you don't believe me you can crawl in and see for yourself."

"Oh, I believe you." He shined the light back to Michael. "Why don't you go and check it out?"

"Me? Why me? I hate snakes."

"So do I. Besides, this cave was your pick."

"I'm not sticking my head into that hole."

"Fine," Delia interrupted. "I'll have Azim send men to clear out the snakes. We can start on the next cave."

"You know," Thomas said, "I don't understand why a hardened killer shrieks over a few snakes."

Delia rolled her eyes and crawled out of the cave. By the time Michael and Thomas caught up with her, she had already made her phone call. They returned their equipment to the truck and opened their packed lunches. Thomas wiped the imported Miller Light across his forehead, thankful it was still cool.

"So," he said, "Michael tells me you two are quite an item."

Michael choked on his cheese. Thomas was sure his reddish tint was from anger rather than asphyxiation. "Thomas …" The words caught in his throat. Thomas's smile did not exactly help matters.

Delia's eyes widened more than Thomas could have imagined. Then they narrowed as a sweet smile blossomed upon her face. "Michael, you're not ashamed of me."

"Delia, I'm sorry. I didn't mean to—"

"Don't be sorry. It feels good not to have to hide our feelings around Thomas."

Thomas laughed. "Hide? If you've been trying to hide your feelings, we're as good as dead. I take it your brother or uncle doesn't know."

"Are you kidding?" Michael asked. "They'd draw and quarter me if they did."

"He's right. I'm afraid even blood wouldn't keep me safe from Azim's wrath."

"I suggest, then, you two be a little more careful than you've been. Remember good ol' Fahd? I don't think he'd think twice about outing you. And your uncle's men may have their eyes on us as we speak."

"We know the risk," Delia said, "and we're no fools. We don't have a death wish."

"Tell me, what do you expect from a relationship with Michael?"

"Thomas," Michael said. "Please don't do this—"

"I want to know. What would Israel's number one enemy want from the nephew of the ambassador to the United States?"

"You want to know? Fine. The truth is I hate what my brother has turned me, his baby sister, into. I'm ashamed that I'm afraid to refuse him. I can kill a man without blinking, but I can't capture a man's heart. Not until Michael came along.

"So yeah, Doctor, I may be a cold-hearted assassin, but it feels good to be able to shriek when I see snakes. Michael is the only man who has made me comfortable being a woman."

Thomas looked from Delia to Michael, who hung his head and shook it slowly. Thomas then turned back to Delia. "I'm sorry, I guess I—"

"I don't want your pity. I don't even want your support or your blessing. I just hope, for Michael's sake, you can give us a chance. We already have the world against us."

They finished their lunch in silence and then drove to the second site on Michael's map. All along the way, Delia had one hand on the steering wheel and the other on Michael's thigh. Thomas huffed and looked out the window. The two of them did have a death wish, he thought. The freedom they felt by him knowing about their relationship was making them a little too confident.

A flash of light caught his eyes. He looked across the valley to the ridge on the other side. A man stood on it, following their truck through a pair of binoculars.

∗          ∗          ∗          ∗

Judas and the rabbi sat at the table in the humble little kitchen. They shared a meal of milk, soup, and bread. It had been about an hour since Judas had taken the mixture. He didn't feel sick and his mind seemed clear. He waited, not sure for what, but for something to happen to his body.

"Rabbi, I'm embarrassed to tell you this, but I've forgotten the sequence of the candlesticks. May I ask how you've remembered it after all these years?"

"Sure." The rabbi took a sip of milk. "Remember the notebook in my bedroom? It's been written in there since the day I entered the altar room."

Judas felt the blood tingle in his cheeks. "Do you mind if I look at it?"

The old rabbi smiled and nodded. "I was wondering how long it'd take you to ask about the sequence. Me, it took three days before my pride was broken enough to ask." The rabbi glanced at his watch. "Would you like something else to eat?"

"No. Everything was delicious."

"Delicious may be too strong a word. Adequate, yes. Well then, let's go back to the bedroom."

Once in the bedroom, Judas stepped over to the desk and laid a hand on the notebook. "May I?"

"Before you do, would you mind setting my bed back in place?"

Judas let out a silent groan. "Of course, Rabbi." He walked over to the bed and bent over the center of it. Thankfully, he had a strong back. He tensed his muscles and pushed.

The bed flew across the room and crashed into the wall, leaving a hole half filled by the bed. A curse slipped from Judas's lips before he had a chance to think. He looked from the wall to the rabbi.

"Rabbi, I … uh …"

The rabbi cackled, his whole body jiggling as he leaned on his cane. "Don't worry Judas. You should have seen me forty years ago when my rabbi showed me the strength. He pretended his car tire rolled onto his foot and yelled for me to help. I pushed so hard the car rolled three or four times. Needless to say his prank backfired and he was quite angry." He looked at the bed sticking out of the wall. "A wall, I can laugh about."

Judas pulled the bed from the wall and set it in place. Luckily, the bed remained intact. He promised to fix the wall and then asked about the sequence.

"The notebook is yours." The rabbi picked up the pillows and climbed into bed. He propped the pillows against the headboard and leaned back on them. "Judas, sit at my desk. There are things I still need to tell you."

Judas sat down and flipped through the notebook. Its yellowed pages were full of entries about the Lord's Strength.

"The Lord has bestowed upon you a great responsibility and privilege. You will be judged in the afterlife by how you carry out this responsibility. First and foremost, you must never give in to the temptation to return to the altar room until the time you pass your responsibility to another. It's not your place to be a deliverer. If you are the one who finds the lost seeds, the Lord will guide you to his deliverer. Understand?"

"Yes."

"Very well. Nearly everything you need to know about the seeds and how they were lost are in that notebook. It also contains all the clues we have as to where they are hidden. Finding them is your second greatest responsibility.

"Be careful Judas. Two enemies are also searching for the seeds. More bloodshed may happen under your protection than has happened during the last thousand years. Dr. Michael Sieff is a Jew who cannot be trusted. Azim Ebadi is also seeking the sacred seeds. You must not let them find the seeds."

"I understand."

"I pray you do." The rabbi yawned. "Now, enjoy your strength, but don't draw undue attention to yourself. Let the experience fuel your desire to remain true to your calling." Judas nodded and stepped toward the door. "One more thing. Your strength will only last approximately two weeks before it suddenly departs. Do not, Judas, give in to the temptation to reenter the altar room."

"That I swear, Rabbi." Judas grinned. "Nor will I cut my hair for the next two weeks."

"Read his Word, Judas. You'll find Samson's strength wasn't in his hair, but in the Lord. When *he* departed, Samson's strength left."

Judas nodded. "You said *nearly* everything I'll need to know about the seeds is in the notebook. What else do I need to know?"

"This, you cannot write down. You must commit it to memory. It's the only way to ensure no one misuses the Lord's Strength." The rabbi explained the final secrets of the Lord's Strength to Judas and sent him home to rest.

Judas flipped through the notebook as he walked the two blocks to his own home. In spite of what the rabbi had told him, he still decided not to cut his hair for the next few weeks.

He couldn't wait to show off his strength to Simon. He knew he wouldn't be able to explain, but he didn't see the harm in demonstrating his strength to Simon. He arrived, unlocked the door, and stepped into the home he shared with Simon.

"Simon, you home?"

No answer.

He tossed the notebook onto a table and walked to Simon's bedroom. He stopped at the door and lightly rapped on it. "Simon?"

Still, no answer. He reached for the handle and slowly turned. When the door cracked open, he called out Simon's name again. He then opened the door and stepped in.

It felt as if every ounce of his great strength had fled. He stared at his friend's bullet-filled body and at the swine's head that rested upon his chest as he lay on the bed.

Judas knew who had done this.

He marched from the building and down the street, oblivious to everything around him. His mind was focused on one thing: finding Azim. The Lord, he reasoned, had given him two weeks to avenge his friend's death. It would not take that long. He'd be done before he sat down for his evening meal.

From behind, he heard his name being shouted. He kept marching forward. Ahead, two teenage Palestinian armed youths patrolled the street corner. Judas looked them dead in the eyes, silently daring them to try to stop him. He didn't veer around them or slow his pace. His eyes never broke from the bearded one.

About ten feet ahead, the two kids stepped directly into his path and put their hands on their shouldered rifles. The bearded one took a couple of steps toward him and ordered him to stop.

Judas kept marching, staring defiantly at the boy. When they were within a couple of feet of each other, Judas silently reached out and with lightning-quick reflexes, bent the gun's barrel up in a ninety-degree angle. Then, as he resumed his march, he stiff-armed the boy into the wall of the cafe. Customers sitting at the sidewalk tables stopped their conversations and watched in stunned silence as he marched on.

Judas looked at the second boy. The boy's eyes swam in terror. He looked at his gun and then released his grip on it as though it had just come from a furnace.

He scurried out of Judas's path, his eyes fearfully pleading for Judas not to harm him.

Judas kept marching. He heard his name being called again. This time, he stopped and turned.

One of the rabbi's gatekeepers caught up with him. Winded, he stopped and drew in deep breaths. "Judas, please. You mustn't put yourself in danger. Tobin is getting the car."

The second gatekeeper drove up and skidded to a stop next to them. Aaron, the other man, held out his hand and urged Judas to get into the car.

Judas felt the rage flowing through his body. "You don't know—"

"Yes, Judas, we do know. The rabbi has sent us. Please, get in the car before the guards call for others and regain their courage."

The man's impatient, pleading expression overcame Judas's immediate urge. They both slid into the back seat, and Tobin pulled away. Judas looked at Aaron. "You know what happened to Simon?"

"We saw him. We were on our way to the rabbi when Tobin saw you walk into your house. We rushed in and told the rabbi what had happened. He ordered us to bring you to him immediately. He said your life was in danger; so, we ran to your house, but you had just left."

"Tobin. Stop the car!"

Tobin looked into the rearview mirror, but kept driving.

"I said, 'Stop the car,' now!"

The man in the back seat sighed. "Please, Judas. The rabbi has ordered us back."

"Which is exactly why I want out. He'll try to talk me out of doing what must be done."

"Tobin and I know the time is coming when you'll be our rabbi, and we'll serve you in serving the Lord. Please, be our leader now by not acting on impulse. Give us confidence in whom we'll serve."

Judas closed his eyes and let his silence be his answer. A few minutes later, they pulled through the rabbi's gate and parked next to the front door. The two men left the car to secure the gate while Judas entered the house. The rabbi was seated at the kitchen table.

"Judas, sit."

Judas paced wildly. "You know what they did to Simon—"

"I said, 'sit!'" The rabbi's eyes drilled through Judas. "Am I still your rabbi?"

Judas quit pacing and slid into his chair. "Yes, Rabbi." He wiped his tears with his sleeve. "It's just … Simon …"

"I know, my son."

The two quietly grieved together. "Judas, I believe it was the Lord's will for you to experience his strength when you did. He's given us two weeks to eliminate those who would take and profane his gift."

Judas's pain eased. This wasn't exactly what he'd expected to hear from the rabbi. In fact, he felt sure he might have misunderstood. "Rabbi?"

"Listen to me, Judas. The next two weeks won't define your service to the Lord, but the years that follow will. If we avenge Simon's death, we must do it in a way that won't compromise your ability to perform your greater service. Understand?"

"Yes, Rabbi."

# CHAPTER 9

THOMAS NUDGED MICHAEL with his elbow. "I think we have company."

"What company?"

Thomas nodded at the window. "Up there, on the ridge; see him?"

Michael ducked his head and stared out the window. "I see him."

Delia removed her hand from Michael's thigh. "See who, Michael?"

"There's a man with binoculars watching us. Three to one it's one of your uncle's men."

"I'm sure he is."

"Now will you two take things more seriously? If that man has seen your hand on Michael's thigh, we're all dead."

"You're right, Thomas." Michael turned his head to Delia. "You know he is, too. Let's make it through the next two weeks. We'll focus on us then."

"Michael, who are we kidding? It'll never be safe for us to be together. There's no place we can run where we won't be constantly looking over our shoulders."

Even Thomas could feel the weight of the silence. He knew Michael's academic mind was crunching all the numbers and running all the equations for an answer on how he and Delia could safely be together. No matter how many times he did, Thomas knew he would always get the same answer.

Delia parked near the next cave on Michael's sketchpad. The three silently gathered their tools and approached the cave. Thomas broke the silence. "I'll go in first. Just leave me a clear path for a few minutes in case I run into any snakes."

Michael worked to lighten the mood. He smiled and slapped Thomas on the back. "If you do see snakes, yell for me. I'll come running, and we'll have a foot race."

"What are you talking about?"

"I know how badly you want to beat me in something. Having snakes behind you may be your best chance."

Thomas felt the competitive juices starting to bubble in his veins. It was bad enough he had come to Hebron looking for his first victory over Michael; now Michael was taunting him about it. "Don't worry about my motivation. Before I leave Israel, you'll be licking your wounded pride."

"Oh, is that what one does when one loses? I guess I've never been in the position to know."

"Boys, am I going to have to cause both of you to lick your wounded pride?"

Thomas eyed Michael and let the smile spread across his face. He dropped to his knees and shined his light into the opening. The passageway was narrow and ended a few feet back. Thomas couldn't see around the wall on the right to tell whether the passage continued or if it just opened into a larger room. At least he didn't see any snakes.

He inched his way along with a pick in one hand and the flashlight in the other. When he reached the back, he poked his head around the corner to see a passageway descending sharply into the black void. He pointed the beam down the tunnel, but the tunnel continued beyond the light. From what he could see, it looked like the passageway descended at a forty-five degree angle.

He shined the light around until he found a rock about the size of his fist and tossed it down the passageway. It rolled out of sight. Thomas could hear slight echoes from it well beyond the light.

As he began to turn around in the narrow passageway, he felt something slither under his left pant leg and onto his calf. At the same time, he heard the unmistakable hiss of a snake.

He was about ten feet down the passageway, violently shaking his left leg, before Michael's laugh sunk in. Thomas tried to stop himself from sliding farther, but the loose gravel and the steep incline made for a bad combination. He slid on his knees, palms, forearm, and then his chest as he disappeared into the darkness.

Shouts of his name replaced the laughter. He wasn't sure how far he slid, and somewhere along the way, he had dropped his pick and flashlight. Every part of his body that made contact with the tunnel floor felt numb.

Thomas smacked into the cave wall and bounced down the tunnel as it made a sharp left turn.

"Michael!" His voice was strong—a good sign.

In the distance he heard, "I'm coming."

When he stopped sliding, he lifted himself to his hands and knees just as pain morphed from the numbness. He moved his limbs; nothing broken, thank goodness.

Everything was dark. Very dark. Pitch black.

Thomas raised his hands above him and slowly lifted to his knees. He felt nothing above him, so he slowly stood. He looked up the passageway. About twenty feet up, he saw light dancing in the shadows and the sharp curve he painfully remembered from the trip down. He heard Michael's controlled slide toward him. A few seconds later, his friend stood at the curve, blinding him with the light.

"Thomas, you're all right!"

Michael half surfed, half galloped his way down until he was standing next to Thomas on the level surface. For the first time, Thomas was able to see the scrapes and cuts through his ripped shirt and pants. He reached up to his face, wincing at the touch to his injuries. Blood from his face and forehead stained his fingers.

Michael had picked up his flashlight on the way down and handed it to Thomas, who turned it on to see his friend's terrified expression.

"Thomas, I'm ... I'm sorry. I didn't mean for this to happen. It was a joke. You okay?"

Thomas stared at him.

"Thomas?"

He drew back and punched Michael in the jaw, sending his friend staggering and then falling to his knees.

"Yeah, I think I'm fine." He shook his hand, secretly fearing he had broken a finger or two.

Michael rose to his feet, rubbing his jaw. "Finished?"

Thomas felt a deep, warm contentment and nodded.

"Good."

They both turned when they heard Delia coming down after them. She turned the curve and called out, "Thomas, Michael!" When she took the next step, her feet slipped out from under her, and she made the rest of the trip down on her bottom.

She sprang to her feet. Michael was caressing his jaw. Thomas was massaging his right hand and was covered in blood. "Oh, Thomas." She reached her hand gently to his forehead.

Thomas winced and pulled away. "I'm sure it looks worse than it is." He glared at Michael. "Except for my hand, that is."

Delia stepped to Michael. "I told you not to do that!" With no warning, she drew back and punched him in the arm. Michael's hand left his jaw and began massaging his upper arm vigorously.

"Why does everyone keep hitting me? You can't possibly think I meant for this to happen."

Thomas felt good. With a bounce in his step and a smile on his face, he walked over to Delia and put an arm around her shoulders. "I am *really* starting to like you."

Delia spent the next few minutes using pieces of Thomas's torn shirt and a little of her own spit to clean his wounds while Michael crawled up the tunnel with his flashlight until he came to the curve. When Delia finished, Thomas shined his light up and saw Michael running his fingertips along the wall. "Michael, what do you see?"

Michael paused for a moment, contemplating his observation before yelling back. "I think, my friend, when you ran into the wall, you may have unwittingly uncovered a clue."

"What kind of clue?"

"I believe I see the remnants of *the mark*."

Thomas forgot his aches and pains. "You're kidding!" He flew to his feet and ran full speed up the incline. When he reached Michael, he dropped to his knees and looked at the part of the cave wall illuminated by Michael's flashlight. He slowly ran his fingertips along the chiseled image.

"Well, what do you think?"

"I don't know. Looks like it may be it. Half the image must've been chipped away." Thomas craned his neck to see Delia carefully climbing up to them. "Delia, stop!"

She froze at the command. "Why? What?"

"There's a very important, very thin, rock chip that may be under our feet. If it is, it's crucial we don't break or crush it." He shined his light in front of her feet. "Carefully step up. Make sure you push the loose gravel out of your way with your foot before you step on it."

In a couple of minutes, Delia stood next to the two men, who were on hands and knees examining the stones beneath them. Michael shook his head. "I don't know, Thomas; you came down pretty fast. If you chipped it off when you hit it, it may be pea gravel by now."

"And it might not be. Keep looking. We've got to find out if it's *the mark* or not."

"Uh, gentlemen, what are you talking about?"

Neither Michael nor Thomas stopped sifting through the loose gravel, and neither answered her question.

"I asked you a question! What about a mark?"

Michael stopped sifting and looked up at her and then to Thomas.

"Don't do it, Michael." Thomas watched his friend struggle to keep quiet.

"At every site—"

"Michael, shut your mouth. It's the only thing we have over Azim."

"We've no choice, Thomas! We either tell her everything we know and trust she'll work with us, or she'll eventually find out on her own."

Thomas felt a headache coming on when he saw the look in Michael's eyes. Michael was going to play the only trump card they had. Thomas held his breath and squeezed his lips tightly, keeping the arguments from escaping. Then he reached the point where his lungs were going to expel the air. When it happened, he was surprised at what came out.

Laughter.

"Go ahead and tell her, Michael. Might as well."

Delia's eyes fell on Thomas. They were soft and reassuring. "Thomas, please trust me. Let me help."

Thomas's laughter died away and his smile slowly faded. Looking into her eyes, he simply nodded.

Delia went to Michael, who shined his light onto the cave wall. "See this picture?"

"Yes."

The light revealed a carving, or at least part of a carving. Michael traced an image onto the cave floor with his finger. "This is the image recorded on the parchment I found."

"I remember."

He traced another image onto the floor. "And this is the one Thomas and I found a year ago on another parchment written about the Samson Effect."

Delia looked at the two images and then to the wall. Michael beamed at the speed comprehension spilled from her. "Separate, the images are commonplace: a crescent moon and a diamond. Together, they form a unique image."

"Very good." He traced the complete image on the cave wall with his finger-tips, filling in the missing parts. "This image was found at every site where we found a manuscript. The parchment that Caleb," Michael's voice quivered at his friend's name, "—a friend found was the only piece of writing that bore both images together. That's how we knew it was authentic."

"What does the mark mean?"

"We've no idea. We just know it's present when we've found anything about the Effect."

Delia looked down and pushed the loose rocks with her toes. "And if we can find the missing chip with the matching image, then we can confirm someone who knew about the Samson Effect has been in here."

"Uh, guys." Delia and Michael turned to Thomas. "Want to look at this?"

They both looked at the stone chip Thomas held. He lifted it to the wall and placed it above the image. It fit like a piece of a puzzle in its only place. The top and bottom points of the diamond touched the top and bottom points of the crescent moon.

Delia gasped.

Michael looked at Thomas. "It's in the cave."

Thomas felt the impending discovery deep within his gut. A quick look at Michael told him his friend felt it also. Delia looked different. The feeling in Thomas's gut slowly turned queasy. She was hiding something.

"What's wrong, Delia?"

She gazed hypnotically down the tunnel as a tear rolled down her cheek. The words spilled out as though she was in a trance. "Have you wondered why Azim is willing to kill so quickly for the secret?"

Thomas thought he did. "Because it can give an ordinary man great strength."

She smiled but didn't break her hypnotic gaze. Under her breath, Thomas thought he heard her say, "He's going to kill me."

"Oh, Dr. Hamilton, the Samson Effect is much more powerful than that … much more."

\*       \*       \*       \*

Sofian felt sick to his stomach. Azim had given him a simple command: find out what Dr. Sieff knows about the Samson Effect. However, Azim also tasked him to work with Umar in avenging the attack on Delia. Less than twenty min-utes after the attack, a few Hebron residents who had witnessed the attack volunteered to share what they saw. The man who threw the pig's head was easy to find and kill, but the gunman had disappeared.

Until now.

He looked at his fingers, wincing at the memory of Barhim's screams. He had kept his men outside his office until he overcame his sick feeling. That was the last thing he wanted to get back to Azim.

He took a cloth from his jacket, dabbed the moisture from his face and neck, and then took a few deep breaths until his stomach had settled. He rose to his feet, squared his shoulders, and walked over to open the door. His men filed into the office.

"I just talked to Azim. He's given us the honor of eliminating the rabbi and his men and of finding the source of his student's strength." His eyes passed over each man. One, and one alone, had steady eyes and did not avert his gaze.

"Jabir, are you willing to be Allah's agent, praise be his name?"

Without hesitation, the young man stood. "I will live and die to serve Allah."

For the first time since hearing he was given the "privilege" of eliminating a man who could bend a rifle muzzle with no effort, Sofian felt calm. "Good. You have command. Do you have any questions about what needs to be done?"

"No. The four Jews will be dead before the sun sets."

One of the men in the room sprang to his feet, shaking his head adamantly. "Please, Sofian, you did not see this man. I did. He had hate in his eyes. And his strength …" He scrunched his brow, searching for the right words. "His strength was not of this world. You can't send us against him—"

"Enough! You will carry out Azim's orders—"

"But, Sofian—"

"I said 'enough'!" Sofian's eyes burned into Jabir. "If any of these men disobey, kill them on the spot." He then stared at each man. "If you die, so will your wives. And if Jabir 'mysteriously' dies, so will your wives." He paused to let his words sink in. "Now, are there any questions?"

The room was silent.

"Good." Sofian's demeanor softened. "When you carry out Azim's orders, I assure you, his favor will shine upon you."

Sofian returned to his desk and spoke in a low, resolute tone. "Now, go."

When the men filed out, Sofian gave in to the quivering that invaded his body. His lips silently, rapidly, mouthed a prayer to Allah. He thought of Azim's warning about the extent of the strong man's power, and his stomach felt sick again. If it were true, what power on earth could stand against the rabbi's student?

# CHAPTER 10

SILENCE FILLED THE cave as the two men hung on Delia's words. Uneasiness flooded through Thomas. From what he knew of the Samson Effect, it could wreak havoc if used by the wrong people. Thomas saw in her eyes that she truly believed the Effect was more powerful than he or Michael had imagined. If she believed it, then so did Azim.

Michael took her hands gently into his. "What do you mean the Samson Effect is more powerful than we thought?"

Thomas could see she was struggling between telling and not telling them. Fear, however, seemed to be winning out. She looked away and shook her head. "Michael, please, I can't tell you." Her head shook with resolution. "If I did, Azim wouldn't think twice about killing me."

She looked into Michael's eyes, silently pleading for his understanding. She then looked at Thomas with the same pleading in her eyes. Thomas shined his flashlight back to the entrance of the tunnel, making sure they were alone. He then turned back to Delia. "If you really love him, then you must trust him. His life is on the line. I'll leave you two alone, but, please, tell him what we're up against."

He lowered his flashlight and began descending to level ground. Before he made it half way down, Delia called out to him. "Thomas, wait." He stopped and turned his flashlight on her, praying she hadn't rejected his request outright.

"I love Michael." She looked into Michael's eyes and gently caressed his cheek with her hand. "Enough to die for him." Their gaze lingered, and then she turned to Thomas. "And I know he loves you like a brother. If he trusts you, so will I."

She leaned against the wall and sighed. "Azim has kept some of the scrolls from you. He doesn't know about the mark you've found, so he's not 100 percent sure all the scrolls refer to the Samson Effect. However, there's one in particular that's caused him to pursue it at any cost.

"A friend found it in Iraq and knew Azim collected ancient artifacts. He contacted Azim and arranged to bring it, and other items, to Hebron to see if Azim was interested in buying them."

Thomas knew immediately the scroll must have been written during the Assyrian or Babylonian empire, but he failed to see its connection to the Samson Effect. No historical evidence existed that placed the Effect anywhere but in Israel.

Delia continued. "The scroll was written in Hebrew. When Azim had it interpreted, the author claimed to be the Protector of the Lord's Strength, the title used consistently in others that are linked to the Samson Effect."

Michael must have been thinking the same thing Thomas was thinking. He interrupted Delia, shaking his head. "But why would the Protector take the knowledge from Israel?" Then his eyes grew wide. "Unless he was among the captives led away from Judah by Nebuchadnezzar." The realization seemed too much for him. He dropped to his knees with a pained expression on his face. "It could be anywhere in the world."

Delia's tone was quick and excited. "No, Michael, he's also found scrolls written centuries later by the Protector of the Lord Strength. All have been found around Hebron."

Michael sat on the cave floor and took out his canteen. He took a drink and looked up at Delia. "What did the Babylonian scroll say?"

"It talks of three Jewish men who were, by order of the king, thrown into a giant kiln."

"Shadrach, Meshach, and Abednego," Thomas said.

"You're familiar with the story, then. As you know, Doctor, the flames didn't harm the three men. The Babylonian scroll attributes their safety to the Lord's Strength."

Thomas and Michael remained quiet. Delia's voice shook them from their thoughts. "You can see, then, why my brother is so determined to find the Samson Effect."

"I'll say," Thomas said. "If the biblical text and the Babylonian scroll are correct, the Samson Effect could make a man nearly indestructible."

"Come on, Thomas," Michael said. "Think about what you're saying. Granted, I thought the Effect might be some super herb that stimulates the production of adrenaline or something, but the notion it has the ability to turn someone into Superman is more than I can buy into."

"I agree, but I think we need to be open to the idea it may have a more powerful effect than we assumed."

"You think my brother is powerful now, just what do you think he'll be like if the Babylonian scroll is correct?" She embraced Michael and leaned her head onto his shoulder. "I've had nightmares about that since the day he told me about the Babylonian scroll."

Michael held her head to his chest. "That's why we're going to find it first." He looked up at Thomas, who simply nodded.

Michael kissed the top of Delia's head and pulled her from his chest. "I think it's time we find out what we can about the mark we've found down here."

All three whipped their heads around and looked up the tunnel when they heard the loose gravel fall.

\*     \*     \*     \*

"They'll try to kill you, you know." The rabbi looked without expression across the table at Judas. "What you did to the two Palestinian guards will make them fearful."

Judas knew he had compromised his greater duty by acting so foolishly in front of so many people. He couldn't imagine how bad it would have been if he hadn't listened to the two men the rabbi had sent to bring him here. He had no idea how to proceed, but he trusted the rabbi's wisdom. He sat silently and waited for the rabbi to help him choose the correct course of action.

"Judas, help me to the stove. My water's boiling."

"Let me get it for you."

Judas rose to his feet, but the rabbi waved him off. "I'm not a total invalid. Just help me to my feet."

Judas obeyed, knowing it was futile to argue with the old man. He walked next to the rabbi until they reached the stove. The rabbi reached out a trembling hand and turned off the burner. The excited water slowed until steam gently rose from its calm surface. The rabbi gripped the handle with both hands, lifting the small pan from the stove. It trembled in his hands. Judas was afraid the splashing water would land on the rabbi's hand, causing him to drop the pan and burn his thin, wrinkled skin. He reached his hand to the pan, but the rabbi rebuffed him with a stern, "No. You may, however, get my cup for me."

Judas reached to the stove for the rabbi's cup, hoping the rabbi wasn't going to ask him to hold it while the feeble man filled it with hot water. Just as he gripped the cup, the rabbi grunted and threw hot water into his face.

Judas dropped the cup and stammered backwards, screaming and rubbing his face with his hands.

"Judas, Judas!"

Judas quit rubbing and waited for the pain to hit.

It never did.

It felt like cool water splashed from a faucet onto his face. He was confused, still waiting for the pain to hit.

"How do you feel?"

Judas rubbed his face again. "I don't know, rabbi, I—"

"Of course you know. Are you burned?"

"I don't think so."

"Here."

By reflex, he reached down and caught the pan the rabbi tossed to him. He looked down to see the faintest bit of steam still rising from inside. When his brain registered he was holding hot metal, he released the pan.

"How about now? Are you burned?"

He opened his hands and looked at his fingers and palms. He felt no pain and saw no redness. Abruptly, the confusion left him, replaced by the realization that it must be the Lord's Strength. He wiggled his fingers and smiled. "Why didn't you just tell me instead of scaring me to death?"

"Tell you, huh?" The rabbi turned to the stove and brought the burner flame to high. "Okay, Judas, the flame won't hurt you. Stick your hand into it."

The smile slowly left Judas's face. "Are you serious?"

"Very. Your experience should tell you you'll be safe. Come on, put your hand into the flame."

Judas looked down at his slowly wiggling fingers. His pace to the stove made the rabbi look like an Olympic runner. The rabbi patiently watched until he reached the stove.

He turned to the rabbi. "Go ahead, Judas."

Judas lifted his left hand, looked at it, and mouthed a silent prayer. Then, before he had time to change his mind, he screamed and thrust his hand into the flame.

He held it there for three seconds, watching the blue flames dance around it, before involuntarily yanking it to safety. He turned it palm up and waited.

No pain.

No burn.

He looked at the rabbi, unable to keep the grin from stretching across his face. He thrust his hand back into the flame and held it there. After thirty seconds, the rabbi turned off the flame.

"This is just the beginning of what you'll be able to endure over the next two weeks."

"Tell me, Rabbi!"

The rabbi held out an arm, and Judas helped him back to the chair. "Your bones cannot be broken, nor can your skin be pierced, by knife, by arrow, or by bullet. The Lord, my friend, will confound your enemies as much as he did Samson's enemies." The rabbi held his hand toward the chair. "Sit."

Judas sat down, admiring his hand. Then he thought of Simon and slowly dropped his head to the table. As the rabbi sat, he said, "Please, tell me how I can avenge Simon and still continue to be the Protector."

"Over time, Judas, people will forget what they saw you do. Until then, you must remain quiet and do nothing to bring attention to yourself. You must use your gift in secret and wait until the opportune time to act. When you do act, you must then slip back into obscurity."

"Yes, Rabbi." Judas thought about the crowd of people who saw him bend steel. "Are you sure people will forget?"

"They'll forget. Trust me, the more time that passes, the more they'll doubt what they saw. Soon, it will seem too fanciful for them to believe and they'll relegate it to an active imagination. All except Azim."

Judas clenched his fist. "I'm not afraid of him."

"Not now, my impetuous friend. But what about when the Lord departs from you, as he did from Samson?"

Judas remained quiet. Finally, he answered. "That's why I must take care of him soon."

"Yes, while not giving everyone else in the city another image to fortify what they've already seen."

The two gatekeepers appeared at the doorway. Tobin stepped forward. "Please forgive us for interrupting, but we have—" Tobin stopped and looked at Judas. He bowed his head and continued. "We have Simon. What would you like us to do with him?"

Everyone looked at the rabbi. "Tonight, we'll bury him in the courtyard." The two men reverently nodded and started to leave. "Wait. I think it's time for you two to join us. Judas and I were just about to plan out how to avenge Simon."

Tobin clenched his teeth. "Whatever it is, count me in."

"Me too," Aaron echoed.

The four men sat around the table and planned their attack on Azim. Judas and the rabbi, though, did not share their plan on dealing with Dr. Sieff, nor did they mention the Lord's Strength. They each soon had their specific duties defined. At the rabbi's insistence, they all agreed not to venture out of the house until morning.

What Judas did not tell them, however, was that he would begin his part of the plan that very evening.

# CHAPTER 11

JABIR SAT IN the passenger seat and slipped the clip into his handgun. Behind, he heard the clicks of two more clips. He turned to the driver and glanced at his gun. "Hamid, get your gun ready."

Hamid pulled his handgun from beneath his jacket and stared at it. Jabir handed him a clip. He took the clip and pause before clicking it into place. He glanced in the rearview mirror at the two men stoically waiting for orders, and then turned to find Jabir's eyes still on him.

"Jabir, please, listen to me—"

Jabir held up a hand and shook his head. "Not another word."

"But you didn't see him. He bent the gun with his bare hands like it were nothing to him." He turned to the two men in the backseat. "You saw it; tell him."

Jabir turned to see the two men cast their gaze down, but they remained silent. "Well, did you see this *superman* bend steel?" Neither man answered. He looked back to Hamid and chuckled. "Please, Hamid, you're better than this. This is no different from any other job we've done."

"But—"

"Look, Sofian is one step closer to Azim, which means we are one step closer to Azim." He patted Hamid on the cheek. "Besides, when didn't one of your bullets stop a man?"

"I have a bad feeling about this one."

Jabir's smile grew into a frown. "Enough. We'll carry out Azim's orders, and we'll quit talking about your superman. Understand?"

Hamid didn't answer. He bowed his head and closed his eyes. Jabir pointed his gun at him and nudged his temple. Hamid opened his eyes and slowly turned to see the barrel staring him in the face.

"Understand?"

Hamid nodded. Jabir pulled the gun away and spoke loud enough for the two men in the backseat to hear. "We all know the four men we're after. When Sofian calls, we'll enter the rabbi's house and execute him along with anyone else with him." His glare burned into Hamid. "This is just like any other order we've carried out. Those filthy swine dared to lift a hand against Azim's sister, so they deserve to die." He heard strong agreement from the two men in the backseat.

Jabir and Hamid stared at the cell phone when it rang. Jabir pushed the button and held it to his ear. Fifteen seconds later, he ended the call. "Sofian confirms the Israelis are out of the area and all four men are in the rabbi's house." He opened his door and the others followed him out. "Allah's justice will be carried out."

The four men walked down the quiet alley behind the rabbi's house. Discarded crates were piled next to the shop doors across from the house. Through the cast-iron gate, Jabir could see three men in the window sitting at the kitchen table. The blinds on all the other windows were turned at just the angle where he could not see in. He waited until the fourth man returned to the table before lining the rabbi in his sights. Each man drew his gun and found his particular target. They all waited for Jabir to give the order.

＊          ＊          ＊          ＊

Thomas, Michael, and Delia stared up the tunnel, fearful of whom, or what, was on its way down. Delia and Michael pulled away from each other and stood on opposite sides of the tunnel. Thomas prayed whoever it was didn't overhear their conversation, but the echoes caused by the rolling stones left him with a bad feeling.

Thomas saw the outline of a man emerge from the darkness. The man called out something in Arabic, and Thomas thought he heard the word "Delia." Delia responded in Arabic, and Thomas was sure he detected relief in the deep voice that responded. Soon, a mountain of a man stood next to them.

Delia and the man, who Thomas recognized as one of Umar's men, carried out a conversation in Arabic. Thomas looked to Michael and asked, "What's he saying?"

Michael shushed him and held up a finger while he listened intently to what they were saying. After a few minutes, he turned to Thomas. "I'm far from being proficient in Arabic, but I think I've got the gist of what he's saying. He said we've been down here a long time and they began to worry, so he came to make sure we were all right."

Thomas waited for the rest of the interpretation, but Michael remained silent. "That's it? All that talking, and that's it?"

"I told you it was just the gist." Michael thought for a moment and then added, "He did say something that doesn't make sense. He said he feared the light and scared the darkness away to hell."

"Not bad, Doctor." The two men turned to Delia, who stood with a grin. "You're right about him checking on us, but the other thing he said was that none of them had a flashlight so he had to make the trip with only the light from his cell phone. He said the shadows it cast made him feel like he was descending into hell." She looked to the man and smiled. "He's glad to see us and says he'll stay with us until we go to the surface."

"Does he speak English?" Thomas asked.

"Only what he picks up around Umar."

"Then …"

"I believe we're quite safe."

They spent the next two hours searching the tunnel for any signs pointing to new information about the Samson Effect. Thomas was pleasantly surprised that Delia and Michael put on a good show for their guest. If he didn't know better, he would have thought their relationship was purely professional.

The man said something to Delia, who nodded. "He said he thinks we better be getting back up now. It's late and someone else will soon come down if he's not back up."

Michael sighed. "Might as well leave. We've been to the end of the shaft and searched the floor and walls for any signs of a chamber or something buried. Nothing." He looked at the stone chip in his hand. "I don't understand why the mark is here."

Thomas put his hand on Michael's shoulder. "Whatever was down here has obviously been removed. Let's just hope it wasn't the Samson Effect itself."

On their way up, Thomas learned that Azim hired men to clear the snakes from the first cave. He sensed it bothered Delia that the men claimed there were only seven snakes in the nest, considerably less than the hundreds she estimated. He found it funny until they volunteered him to be the first one down. He found himself having second thoughts about the exterminators' thoroughness.

Once out of the cave, they picked up their tools and headed home, planning to revisit the first cave in the morning.

*        *        *        *

A car pulled around to pick up Umar's man from in front of the cave's entrance. They began following Delia's truck to make sure the three arrived home safely. The man who entered the cave turned to the man in the backseat and said, in perfect English, "When Umar calls, tell him I need to speak with him. It's about Delia and Dr. Sieff."

*        *        *        *

Thomas wasn't looking forward to spending the night in the room again. The window had been replaced, but he found comfort when Delia told them her uncle had placed men in one of the buildings across the street to keep watch over them twenty-four hours.

He let the other two enter first and found Michael sitting on *his* bed. "You're not sleeping in my bed."

Michael gestured toward the bed that the pig's head had landed on. "I think they replaced the bed. Look at it. It looks brand new."

"Good, then you won't mind getting off my bed, will you?"

"Come on, Thomas. You know I'm Jewish."

Thomas looked at the bed and cringed. "Fine, but if I even think I smell bacon, I'm taking my bed back and you can sleep on the floor, for all I care."

Michael smiled and lay down on his back, stretching his arms behind his head. His smug look was almost enough to make Thomas walk over and flip him out of bed. Instead, he reached down and yanked the covers from his new bed. The sheets were clean. A cursory examination turned up no signs of pig blood. Thomas shuddered at the thought of lying down on the bed and decided he had better not look at it too closely.

"You remember why I studied biblical archaeology, don't you?"

Michael rolled on his side and thought. "I remember. You wanted to become an MD, but you couldn't stand the sight of blood." Michael smiled until the meaning behind Thomas's question dawned on him. "There's no blood on that bed, and besides, *my* reasons are spiritual. You wouldn't want to be responsible for a stain on my soul, would you?"

"When's the last time you've been to a synagogue?"

Delia stepped between them. "Boys, boys. As much as I hate pigs, for biological and spiritual reasons, I may add, I'll sleep on the bed if it'll keep you two quiet."

Thomas felt appropriately chastised. "No, no; I'll take the bed." He looked at Michael, preparing to fight over the bed, but Michael closed his eyes and smiled. He plopped down on the bed and bit his tongue.

The door opened and the man who was with them in the cave stepped in. He spoke to Delia, who relayed the message to Michael. "My uncle wishes to speak with you, now." They both stood and stepped to the door, but the man stopped Delia with his arms and said something to her. She looked at Michael. "Alone."

✳      ✳      ✳      ✳

Umar sat in the chair across from the sofa and coffee table casually sipping his wine. When Michael entered, he stood and extended his hand toward the sofa. "Dr. Sieff, please be seated. May I offer you a Coca-Cola?"

Michael eased onto the sofa and crossed his legs. "Actually, I'd prefer what you're having, if you don't mind."

"Not at all; my pleasure." Umar walked over to the bar and reached for a bottle. "Tell me, Doctor, was your expedition today profitable?"

"We managed to do all right for ourselves."

Umar poured the wine and headed back to Michael. "Would I be out of line in asking what it is you're looking for?" He handed the glass to Michael and sat down.

Michael swirled his wine as he carefully chose his words. He smiled and glanced to Umar. "Maybe you'd better ask Azim. I mean no disrespect, but I don't want to tread where I don't belong."

Umar narrowed his eyes. "Interesting choice of words."

The words flowed like molasses from Umar's lips. Michael felt uncomfortable in the ensuing silence as Umar stared at him. He sipped his wine and adjusted himself on the couch.

Umar cracked the silence with his jovial voice. "No, I guess you wouldn't. Azim will tell me in his time."

Again, silence smothered Michael. Umar contentedly sipped his wine and smiled, never taking his eyes off Michael. When it seemed apparent Umar wasn't going to speak, Michael set his glass on the table. "I'm sure you didn't ask me here to have someone to drink with or to just find out why Azim's working with us."

The smile didn't fade from Umar's face. "Perceptive, Doctor." Umar downed the remaining half glass of wine and set his empty glass next to Michael's. When he leaned back in his chair, his smile was gone and his forehead pinched in anger. His voice became heavy, and every syllable caused Michael's muscles to tense. "Do you remember what we talked about at the bar this morning, Doctor?"

Umar's flaming eyes unnerved Michael. He slowed his breathing in an attempt to keep his body from betraying his fear. "Of course. You made yourself perfectly clear."

"Apparently, I didn't. I told you I love my niece, and I would have no hesitation in killing anyone who harmed her. Do you remember that, Dr. Sieff?"

Michael controlled every biological sign of nervousness except for the lone drop of sweat that ran from his forehead to the tip of his nose. He replied calmly, "I remember."

Umar leaned back and gripped the chair's arm. When he did, his jacket pulled away, revealing a chest holster and gun. "Then what are the stories I hear about you putting your filthy hands on my niece, and ..." Umar brought his hand to his mouth to suppress a vomit. He squeezed his eyes shut and wiped his face with his hand. The next words fell from his mouth like individual buckshots. "And ... put ... your ... lips ... on ... her?"

More sweat drops joined Michael's lone drop. He reached for his glass, but he couldn't prevent the wine in it from vibrating. In a fraction of a second, a battle raged in his mind on whether to deny the accusation or to seek forgiveness. Consciously, he had no idea what his brain had chosen until the words fell from his lips.

"I love her."

*No ... oh please, no!*

It was too late. All he wanted to do was to stretch out his arms and corral the words back to him. Umar's dark, leathery skin turned crimson. He stood and towered over Michael, speaking through clenched teeth. "You are a fortunate man, Doctor. I love Delia too much to let this get back to Azim, and I very well can't kill you or I'd have to answer to him. However, I will teach you to never defile her again."

With a sharp nod, he ordered his men to Michael. One man pulled him from the sofa by his hair while another locked his arms behind his back and held him steady.

＊          ＊          ＊          ＊

Thomas was standing by the map when the door flew open and Umar marched in followed by two men dragging Michael by the shoulders. Both of Michael's eyes were bruised and swollen shut. His nose looked like it was broken, and blood was caked on his face. Delia cried out his name and raced toward him as the men threw him onto the bed.

Before she could reach him, Umar grabbed her hair and roughly yanked her to a stop. She turned in time to catch her uncle's backhand across her cheek. Her legs gave way, but Umar's hold on her hair kept her from falling.

Thomas rushed to Michael's side and then to the bathroom for a damp cloth. When he returned he gently dabbed the blood away, and Michael began to moan.

"Dr. Hamilton, you and Delia will continue Azim's work until Dr. Sieff regains his strength." He dragged Delia by the hair to the door. "Fahd, you'll now be sleeping in this room." He forced Delia's face to his. "One word from you and I swear I'll turn you over to Azim!"

Before he left, he turned to Thomas. "Dr. Hamilton, don't give me any reason to display my wrath toward you. I'm not sure I'll be as controlled next time."

# CHAPTER 12

MOVEMENT IN THE alley caught Tobin's eyes when he glanced through the kitchen window. He squinted and then his eyes flew open. "Everyone down!" He dove to the floor as bullets crashed through the window.

Judas's reaction was swift. So swift, in fact, that he flew to his feet and placed his body between the flying bullets and the rabbi before Tobin hit the ground. He felt the rapid, gentle thumps of the bullets on his back before he eased the old man away from the window.

As abruptly as the gunfire started, it ended. Judas looked over to the men. Only Tobin was hit.

"It's just my arm. How's the rabbi?"

Judas turned to see the rabbi's head slumped to the side and his eyes closed. Dread swept through him as he slowly pulled the rabbi away. A large bloodstain covered his chest. Judas shook his head and then lifted the rabbi in his arms and carried him to his bedroom.

"Judas?"

Judas didn't answer Tobin. The two men followed him to the bedroom. He gently laid the rabbi on his bed. Tobin forced his way to the bed and began examining the rabbi. Judas stepped back, praying Tobin's paramedic training would help.

It didn't take long. Tobin didn't pound on the rabbi's chest or blow into his mouth. He just looked up at the two men and shook his head. For the first time since taking the mixture, Judas felt weak. The other two men looked at him, waiting for him to speak. The weight crashed down on his shoulders. He was now their rabbi.

He did not want this. Not now, not like this. He wanted, no, he needed, the rabbi. Nevertheless, he was gone. The rabbi had chosen him for this moment. Judas didn't understand why, but, by faith, he believed the rabbi acted in wisdom when choosing him to be the next Protector.

Right now, two men needed a leader. They needed one more than they ever had before. This was his lot, his burden alone. Therefore, he decided to lead, to do the only thing that had to be done at this moment.

He knelt with the two men and prayed.

$$* \qquad * \qquad * \qquad *$$

Thomas slept in the desk chair he placed next to Michael's bloodstained bed. He awoke every hour or so during his friend's fitful sleep. This time it was two hours from dawn, and he feared the opportunity to sleep had fled for the evening. At this moment, he felt alone. What had been an adventure in search of a holy grail was becoming deadly. He thought of Clifton and then of Caleb and Hanna. Now it was Michael.

He couldn't get the expression on Delia's face when they had dragged Michael into the room out of his mind. Any lingering doubts he had about her love for Michael were wiped away at that moment. Now, even she, the enemy, was not here to comfort him and Michael; there was only Fahd, snoring away with his pistol next to his pillow. He was about to begin his third day under house arrest, and no one of consequence knew where he was.

Michael grew restless again. Thomas watched him, holding onto the thin strand of hope he refused to release. His mind traveled to the coffee shop where he met friends and laughed, to his sanctuary, the place where he was never alone.

$$* \qquad * \qquad * \qquad *$$

Thomas was awakened by a slap to the face. Umar towered above him; and by the look on his face, sleep had not softened his anger. "Get up. You have fifteen minutes to get ready."

Thomas stood and looked at Michael. His friend's eyes were open, but he grimaced at the slightest move. "Take it easy, Michael. How do you feel?"

The words blew gently across Michael's cracked lips. "Delia?"

Umar grabbed Thomas by the hair and thrust him toward the bathroom. "I said get ready!" He then swung around to Michael. "If I ever hear her name from your lips again, I'll personally cut out your tongue." He said something in Arabic to one of the men with him, marched through the room, and stomped his way up the stairs. The man remained behind, folding his arms and watching Thomas.

Thomas resigned himself to the fact that he was in the final two weeks of his life. He picked up his clothes and stepped into the bathroom, shutting the door behind him. A few seconds later, the door opened and he saw Umar's man standing in the doorway shaking his head. Apparently, he had lost his privacy as well.

Fifteen minutes later, Umar was back. In the open doorway, he saw two other men escort Delia down the stairs. She had no bruises or cuts that showed. Thomas wasn't surprised. After all, she was Azim's sister.

She paused at the door and looked at Michael. Her lips quivered, and, for an instant, it looked as if she was about to take a step into the room. However, Umar barked out something, and the man behind her pushed her forward. He then turned to Thomas. "Dr. Hamilton, don't forget what I said last night about not giving me a reason to display my anger toward you."

Michael sat up on the edge of his bed, holding his ribs. "I'm going with you." He shifted forward to get off the bed, but he clutched his chest tighter and moaned. "Thomas, help me up."

"Lay back down, Michael. You need to rest."

Michael shook his head. "No, I'm going."

Umar walk to the bed and backhanded Michael across the cheek. "Enough of this." He turned to Thomas and grabbed his arm. "Doctor, go!"

Thomas watched Michael endure pain by crawling across the bed and reaching for the window shade. The effort he exerted on the simple task of opening the shade nearly caused him to pass out. Thomas witnessed Michael and Delia's eyes connect, each reaching a hand to the other. Delia displayed no inhibitions about openly weeping in public.

Then the window shattered.

Thomas dropped to the floor as bullets whizzed by him. There were no screams. The outburst of gunfire lasted no more than five seconds. Three men wearing black boots, white baggy pants, and white tunics ran into the room. All Thomas could see of them were their eyes through the slit in a cloth that covered their faces. The men fanned out back to back and quickly examined the dead men on the floor.

Thomas remained petrified. A pair of black boots stepped next to his face. Above, he heard, "Dr. Hamilton?"

He responded without moving. "Yeah."

"Get up, quickly, and follow me."

Thomas did as he was told. Michael had his arms around the shoulders of two of the men. Umar lay next to him with a carefully placed bullet in the center of his forehead, staring blankly at the ceiling. The other two men were not as neat. Fahd was draped over his bed with a chunk of his neck missing. The man Umar sent to watch Thomas lay in a pool of blood. In his American clothing, he reminded Thomas of one of the guys he saw in a picture of the mob's St. Valentine's Day massacre.

Outside, Thomas saw six more men dressed the same way as the three who had escorted them out, brandishing their weapons in every direction. The two men with Delia were also dead, but she was standing, untouched, against the building at gunpoint.

Michael struggled with pain to get the words out. "Across the street." He pointed to the window where Delia had told them Umar had men planted to guard them.

Above, two military helicopters hovered low. A van screeched to a halt in front of them. The men ushered Thomas into the van, but Michael resisted. He nodded toward Delia. "The girl."

"Dr. Sieff, please, get into the van."

"The girl."

The man yelled something to the one guarding Delia, who nodded and led her to the van. Once in, the door shut and they sped away.

✳     ✳     ✳     ✳

From the time they had arrived at the military hospital, Thomas and Delia had sat alone in a waiting room under guard. No one would talk with them, and they could only leave the room by escort to the restrooms. Two hours passed before a doctor entered the room.

"Your friend has been pieced together and wishes to see you. Please follow me."

They followed the doctor to another room, which also had two armed soldiers guarding the door. They entered to see Michael leaning back in the inclined bed, sipping water through a straw. Delia hurried to the bed and leaned to kiss him. Michael's moan drew her back. She wanted to touch him, but she didn't know where.

Ambassador Ben Hur sat in the chair next to Michael's bed. His eyes grew wide when he witnessed Delia's affection toward his nephew. He cocked his head, opened his mouth, but then blinked and shook his head.

Thomas stepped to Michael's bedside. He looked his friend up and down and smiled. "You look terrible."

Michael rolled his eyes, barely moving his lips when he spoke. "Thanks."

"I take it back. Actually, under the circumstances, you look pretty good." He looked at Michael's bandaged chest. "How many ribs broken?"

Michael chose to hold up three fingers instead of speaking.

"And how long are you going to have to wear the mask over your nose?"

Michael shrugged.

"Broken jaw?"

Michael shook his head. "Four broken teeth."

Thomas winced but did not ask his friend any more questions.

The ambassador stood and nodded toward Delia. "Thomas, I'd like to speak with you and Michael alone."

"Ambassador, I assure you it's safe to speak with her too."

Michael nodded.

"I really think it's best we talk alone."

Thomas turned to Delia and raised his eyebrows. She smiled and walked to the door. Before she left, she blew Michael a kiss.

As soon as the door shut, the ambassador's eyes grew wide again. "Do you know who the devil that woman is?"

"She's Azim's sister," Thomas said matter-of-factly.

The ambassador froze, except for a couple of blinks, and then asked, "And that doesn't bother you?"

"Look, I wasn't easy to convince, but I'm convinced now. How much do you think her life is worth now that she has fled with the enemy? She risked everything to be with Michael."

With pained effort, Michael also stood up for her. "Uncle Ben, you know me. Please trust me on this."

They looked at each other for a moment until the ambassador finally shook his head. "Forget she's Azim's sister; she's not Jewish, for goodness sakes."

Michael slowly threw the deathblow. "Neither was grandmother."

The ambassador was silent. He finally turned his head and spoke. "The doctor said that within a month's time you'll be able to go back to work."

Mentioning a time frame forced Thomas's eyes open and set his heart racing. "Hanna! Azim has her and will kill—"

The ambassador held up his hand. "We sent a second Israeli Special Forces team for her. She's safe."

Thomas felt a weight lift from him. He couldn't suppress a smile. What a difference twelve hours could make. Though deprived of a good night's sleep, he felt exhilaration spread through his body. "Ambassador, I have a couple of questions that trouble me."

"What are they?"

"I'm sure the Special Forces knew who Delia was; why didn't they kill her?"

"They almost did. Apparently, her and Michael's behavior right before the attack gave the team's leader just enough doubt. However, her guard was given the order to kill if she so much as blinked the wrong way."

Thomas nodded and then asked his other question. "And before we were loaded into the van, Michael mentioned the Palestinian guards in the building across the street. I don't understand why they didn't fire back."

The ambassador smiled. "We knew about them. They were neutralized before the rescue was carried out."

"I see." He ran his fingers through his hair and turned to Michael. "I'll make sure Delia is taken care of while you recover."

Michael smiled and nodded.

"Oh, Ambassador, I was wondering if you could arrange a meeting between Hanna and me?"

"Funny you should ask; she's requested a meeting with you. You'll have the chance to see her soon." He held out an envelope. "In here, you'll find everything you need to make yourself legal in Israel: passport, driver's license, diplomatic credentials from my office, and money. Just stay away from the American embassy for the time being. I'm still working on that."

Thomas took the envelope and nodded. "Thanks."

The ambassador stepped up to his nephew, smiled, and shook his head. "Michael, Michael. You do look terrible." He rubbed his chin and pursed his lips. "Tell you what, I'll let Thomas introduce me to Delia and give it an open mind."

Michael nodded and closed his eyes.

Thomas said good-bye, and they left. When they took a few steps down the hall, the ambassador stopped. "Thomas, things are not good. I need your help."

Thomas looked back toward Michael's room. "He's hurt, isn't he?"

"Don't worry about Michael. I assure you, under the circumstances, he's quite well."

Thomas exhaled. "What is it, then?"

"I need you to go back to Hebron and continue your search. I need you to find out everything you possibly can about the Samson Effect."

"You must be out of your mind if you think I'm going back there. Just how long do you think I'd survive?"

"I can arrange to have soldiers protect a perimeter around you wherever you need to go and have a combat chopper assigned to patrol your area."

"No, thanks. Your Israeli soldiers seem to be called away every time Azim shows up."

"I assure you, this will be different. These men will be solely assigned to you with orders not to leave under any circumstances."

Thomas shook his head. "I'm sorry, Ambassador, but the answer is no." He took a few steps down the hall and then stopped and turned to the ambassador.

The ambassador stood with his hands in his pockets and his feet firmly planted. "I think someone's already found it."

Thomas approached warily. "What do you mean?"

"Eyewitnesses saw a man, a Jew, bend the barrel of a gun with one hand. They also saw him throw a man through a cafe wall." The ambassador reached into his jacket pocket and pulled out a photo. "This is the cafe."

Thomas stared at the photo. "I don't understand. If you think the man has it, what good would it do for me to continue the search?"

The ambassador put the photo back into his pocket. "I want you to meet a man tomorrow. I believe he's the only other person in Israel who knows about the Samson Effect. Talk with him. If, after that, you're still not convinced, I won't ask you again."

Thomas squinted. "Why me?"

"Because you and Michael are the only men qualified to find it, and because I trust you."

"*If* I do this, I'll have a couple of conditions."

"What? Name them."

"First, we wait until Michael's well, and he and I work together."

The ambassador shook his head. "I'm sorry, but that's why we're out here. If he knew what I was asking, he'd kill himself to go with you. You'll learn tomorrow why we don't have the luxury to wait until he's better."

"I'll table that condition, but the others are not negotiable."

"Go on."

"I expect to know everything you know about the Samson Effect."

"That's what your visit tomorrow is for."

"I'm serious, Ambassador. If I learn you've kept anything from me, I'm through."

"Anything else?"

"Just one more thing. Delia works with me."

The ambassador forgot he was in a hospital. "Out of the question!"

"It's nonnegotiable."

"No!"

"Then I guess my visit to your friend will be pointless, won't it?"

A crimson tint swept over the ambassador's face. "If that's what you want, fine. Just know she's the one person I can't protect you from."

"I understand the risk—"

"No, you don't."

The queasiness came back to Thomas's stomach. "But she's the one who called to let you know we were still alive and how to find us." Thomas's voice was not as strong as it was a few seconds ago. "You'll see when you meet her."

"I've no intentions of ever meeting that woman, and you'd be wise to stay away from her. She's shrewd; she and Azim have probably planned this to get closer to the Samson Effect." He abruptly turned and began to march away, but stopped to turn and point a finger at Thomas. "Wait until you see her dossier of suspected crimes; it'll send a chill through your spine. It's only a matter of time before she rots in an Israeli prison ... or worse."

# CHAPTER 13

"IF IT'S A jihad the Israelis want, I say let's bring it to them!"

Barhim added his agreement with Sofian, emphasizing it by pounding his four-fingered fist on Azim's desk.

Azim's expression did not change. He stared at each man one at a time until his eyes rested on Rajah. "And what do you say?"

Rajah didn't hesitate. "A jihad would be foolish. It's taken more than a decade for Israel to give our people the control we now have over Hebron. We'd give up everything we now have if we act rashly."

"Allah will be with us!" Barhim cried.

"Yes, Allah is always with us, praise be his name. But a jihad must be to his glory, not to satisfy our own egos." Barhim rolled his eyes and looked away, but Rajah continued without missing a beat. "Azim, what they did to you deserves punishment. You'll look weak in the eyes of the city leaders if you don't do something, and that may be tough to overcome. My counsel is that you take care of this matter quietly, not by calling our brothers together through a jihad."

Azim drew in a breath and exhaled. "A jihad doesn't make sense now, but I will avenge my uncle and sister." He again looked at each man and then narrowed his eyes. "And if Delia is not returned safely to me, the one responsible for her death will taste my wrath." He nodded to Sofian. "Take Barhim and finish your work with the rabbi. Before you kill them, use whatever means are needed to have them tell you everything they know about the Samson Effect."

Sofian spread his hands apart, palms up, and curtly bowed. When Azim gestured for him to leave, he and Barhim slipped through the door, leaving Azim and Rajah alone.

Azim slammed his fist on the desk. "How could this happen? Tell me that; how could our security have been so lax that the Israelis could walk in and take everything from us? Answer me!"

"Our security wasn't lax. I lost four men in the raid, and Palestinian security lost three. It happened so quickly, we had no time to call for reinforcements."

"How did they find out where Sieff was? And why was my uncle not protected?"

"Azim, we placed extra guards on them. I'm at a loss. It's almost as if ..."

Azim narrowed his eyes. "As if what?"

Rajah closed his eyes and pressed his fingers against his forehead. "Someone's been passing information to the Israelis."

Azim's eyes drilled into Rajah. He said nothing for a full thirty seconds. Never once was there a traitor among his men. People had died for his cause rather than sell out to infidels. It had to be something else.

"The computer; Sieff or Hamilton must have sent a message through it."

"No, we monitored everything they did on it. It wasn't the computer or any other means of communication."

"Then who?"

Rajah eased back into his chair and placed his interlocked fingers into his lap. "I have one idea."

Azim's heart began racing. He leaned forward and in a controlled voice asked, "Who?"

"Sofian told me one of his men was terrified to go against the rabbi's student. In fact, he was forced at gunpoint to carry out your orders against the rabbi. He may have done anything if he thought it would keep him from confronting the Jew."

Azim nodded. Barhim's missing finger would be nothing compared to what he would do to someone who had betrayed him.

"Would you like to speak with the man?"

"Not yet. Have Sofian watch him. I want you to pull all phone records on any line he had access to. If he acted out of fear, he may have done something stupid."

"As you wish."

The idea that someone could betray him kept lingering in his mind. What if it was Barhim, taking vengeance for his finger; or Sofian, or even Rajah, his most trusted adviser? The city leaders respected Rajah. Perhaps corrupt men had influenced him.

"And have the records for the last three days from every phone associated with you, me, Sofian, Barhim, Umar, and anyone associated with us delivered to my office. You and I will go over them personally. Perhaps, as I said, the traitor may have done something stupid."

"I'll have them tomorrow."

"Good. I also want you to find someone to continue with Dr. Sieff's work. We must find the Samson Effect."

Rajah bowed his head, stood, and left the room. A few seconds later, Azim buzzed his chief bodyguard. The man immediately entered and stood before Azim with his gun drawn and four men following behind.

Azim dismissed the four men. "I want you to heighten your alert for the next three days. Be wary of everyone, even those closest to me."

＊    ＊    ＊    ＊

When darkness fell, Judas insisted on digging the two graves alone. Tobin and Aaron watched through the narrow slits in the blinds. Judas finished the first grave in a little over fifteen minutes and started on the next immediately. It felt like he was using a child's toy shovel on the beach.

He slowed his pace on the second grave, not from exhaustion, but to give himself time to think about Simon and the rabbi. He also thought of his fleeting strength. He knew the other two men would be digging his grave right now if it were not for the mixture.

Then he thought of the attack. As powerful as he was, his hesitation cost the rabbi his life. He thrust the shovel into the earth. If he were a split second quicker, the rabbi would be alive. Before he knew it, he was tossing the dirt over his head. This grave was at least eight feet deep.

He jumped flatfooted and landed on the ground next to the grave. He looked through the open blinds at the two gawking men. Judas nodded and they stepped onto the porch, where two plywood caskets sat next to each other.

Aaron's eyes were still wide when he stepped forward. "Judas, I mean rabbi, how—"

Judas held up a hand and shook his head. "Please understand, I'm bound by an oath not to reveal to anyone the secret we're protecting."

"But you dug those graves quicker than I could have if I used a bulldozer." He stepped behind Judas and tugged on his shirt. "And there are at least six bullet holes here, yet you have no wounds."

"Let it be enough that you've been allowed to witness the awesome, powerful gift the Lord has entrusted us to protect." His eyes shifted to the other man. "Not many men have witnessed what you two have witnessed."

Judas stepped up to the caskets, signifying he wasn't answering any more questions. Tobin ran his fingertips over the rough homemade caskets and sighed. Without a word, he and Aaron stooped to pick up Simon's casket. Judas shook his head and waved them away. "I'll get them."

He bent down and effortlessly picked up Simon's casket and set it on the rabbi's. He then stooped and placed a hand on both sides of the casket by the rabbi's head and lifted. He led the two men to the graves and lowered the caskets into their holes.

Judas let the men mourn in silence for a few minutes before sending them back into the house. He then filled the graves and raked the excess dirt into the surrounding soil. When he finished, only two flat stepping-stones marked the head of each grave.

He returned to the house and stepped into the rabbi's bedroom, where he picked up the notebook and pulled the metal foot from the rabbi's cane. He then went into the rabbi's office and rummaged around the desk until he found a legal-size manila envelope. He placed the two items into the envelope and sealed it, reinforcing the seal with staples.

When he came back to the kitchen, Aaron and Tobin ended their hushed conversation. After a short silence, Tobin said, "Rabbi, Aaron and I were talking about Azim." He looked toward Aaron who nodded. "His security will make it nearly impossible for us to touch him. We both want nothing more than for him to pay for what he's done, but we're afraid if we act so quickly after their deaths, we'll end up acting foolishly."

"I agree. That's why I want you in Jerusalem tonight."

"Why?" Tobin asked. "Without you?"

"I'll meet you at the old synagogue in two weeks." He handed the envelope to Tobin. "If I'm not there in two weeks, I want you to open this."

Tobin took the envelope with his free hand and tucked it under the arm in the sling. "Rabbi, we don't want to leave you, we just—"

"I need you two to be safe. The envelope contains everything you need to know about the great honor the Lord has given us. Tobin, should something happen to me, what's in the envelope is for your eyes only."

"But what are you going to do?"

"I'm going to carry out my role as Protector of the Lord's Strength."

"But Rabbi—"

"Tobin, the matter's settled. You're to follow my instructions in full."

"Yes, Rabbi."

"Good. I want you two to leave within the hour." They looked at their watches and nodded. "And I don't want you to draw attention to yourselves. Just wait for me, and above all, don't let anyone have that envelope. *Anyone.* You're to destroy it before that happens."

*          *          *          *

Thomas slipped between the two guards and entered the hospital room he and Delia had been given for the evening. She was seated in a chair next to the window, but stood when he entered. "How's Michael?"

"Resting." He kicked off his shoes and sat at the foot of the bed. "Why don't you try to get some sleep and we'll check on him in the morning."

"I'd rather spend the night at his side."

Thomas reached out and grabbed Delia's forearm as she passed. "I don't know how safe it'd be for you to roam the hallways alone."

Delia stared at him with a questioning look. She gently pulled her arm from his grasp. "What's that supposed to mean?"

Thomas avoided her eyes, answering in a noncommittal tone. "I don't know. I mean, you're a Palestinian in the middle of an Israeli military hospital."

Delia stared at him for a moment before continuing to the door. "I'll take my chances."

"Delia, wait."

She let go of the doorknob and faced Thomas. "What's going on, Thomas? The truth."

He still couldn't look her in the eyes. "It's Ambassador Ben Hur. I don't think he likes you very much."

Delia smiled and rolled her eyes. "No kidding. What did you expect? My family is not on the best terms with the Israeli government."

"I know, but I think it's personal with him. He doesn't exactly approve of your and Michael's relationship, and I don't think he'd think twice about using his power to see to it you and Michael are permanently apart."

"He told you this?"

"Not in as many words." He finally found the fortitude to look her in the eyes. "He thinks you're waiting for the perfect time to betray us."

He couldn't stop his eyes from dropping away. He felt ashamed that the ambassador planted the seeds of doubt now taking root, resurrecting his past suspicions. Her quiet, gentle voice pained him.

"You believe him, don't you?"

It would be much easier if she responded harshly, in anger, but she didn't. He knew his delay in answering her cast a shadow of doubt on his sincerity. "No, I don't believe him. In fact, I insisted you and I …"

"You and I what?"

Thomas sighed. "Sit down."

He told her what the ambassador had said about him continuing the search for the Samson Effect and how he had no intentions of meeting her. The only thing he kept back was the damning dossier the ambassador promised to produce. He finished by asking, "You do agree it's best we not tell Michael about the Hebron trip until he regains his strength?"

She stared past him out the window as she nodded. She then looked at him and placed her hand on his. "I'm afraid the whole Israeli army couldn't protect me from my brother if I went with you to Hebron. In fact, I really don't know where I can be safe." She squeezed Thomas's hand. "Thank you for standing up for me."

"Listen, why don't you just stick with me or Michael until these people get comfortable with you being around? You can go with me tomorrow to meet a guy I'm supposed to see."

Delia shook her head. "I'll stay with Michael tomorrow. In fact, I'd appreciate it if you'd walk me to his room right now."

Thomas slipped from the bed and walked with her as the soldier escorted them to Michael's room. Michael was awake, flipping through television channels when they entered. He endured the pain, and against Delia's insistence for him to lie down, embraced her. Thomas took a few steps back, feeling more confident about her as he watched their embrace. Neither noticed when he left the room.

On his way back to his room, he took out the name and address of the man he was going to visit tomorrow. A phone number, marked "Taxi," and a street address were at the bottom of the paper. He turned it over but found nothing else written on the paper.

When he arrived at his room, he called the operator to get the number for the address on the paper. The operator told him the number was unlisted. He hung up and crawled into bed. Exhaustion came out of nowhere and devoured him. He closed his eyes without taking off his clothes or turning out the light. Just as he was about to fall asleep, he heard a scratching sound at the door. One eye opened, and he reluctantly turned toward the door.

Someone had slipped a white eight-by-ten envelope under the door. Curiosity beat out exhaustion, and he rolled out of bed and picked up the envelope. The only thing on it was the word "Interpol" stamped on the front. Obviously, the ambassador was in a hurry for him to read up on Delia.

He took the envelope back to his bed and lay down. It was heavy; there must be a lot in there on her, he thought. He slipped his finger into the opening above the seal, but paused before ripping it open. Did he really want what was in there to cloud further his judgment about Delia? If there was anything with even the slightest bit of evidence, he knew she wouldn't be walking around as freely as she was now. He then removed his finger, placed the envelope in the nightstand drawer, and turned off the light.

# CHAPTER 14

THE NEXT MORNING, Thomas took a taxi to the Christian quarter of Jerusalem. The driver stopped in front of a small Protestant church. He turned to Thomas and smiled, pointing to the meter. "Fare, please."

Thomas unfolded the address and held it before the driver. "Are you sure we're here?"

The driver pointed at the address on the paper and then at the church. "Yes, yes, yes. Fare, please."

Thomas shook his head and pulled out his wallet. When he paid his fare and stepped out of the taxi, the driver sped away. He looked around at the buildings and the heavy traffic along the street. He then looked at the church, trying to find a street number. Certainly, a church would not have an unlisted number, he thought.

"Dr. Hamilton?"

Thomas looked to his right to see an elderly man approach. "Yes. You must be Arnold Willingham." He reached out to shake the old man's hand. "Name doesn't sound Jewish to me."

"Oh, it's not." Arnold smiled. "Born and raised in Las Vegas."

"An American? What made you leave Sodom for the holy city?"

"It's a long story. The short version is that I left home in the sixties and eventually founded this church."

"You're a pastor?"

"Was; retired now. My son has taken over the reins. I'm just around as an adviser, more or less." Arnold nodded to the church. "Care to come in?"

"Sure."

Thomas followed the old man into the church. He opened a door off to the side of the sanctuary, and they went down a flight of stairs. Thomas looked around at what appeared to be an apartment under the church. "You live here?"

"Yes. Hard to pass up free rent." He waved his hand around the room. "Only thing I don't like about it: no windows."

Sure enough, the only things Thomas saw on the walls were bright landscape paintings and mirrors. He looked at a picture on an end table of a younger Arnold Willingham, a woman, and a boy in his teens.

"That's my wife and son. He's much older now. The picture is over twenty years old. My wife, rest her soul, is with the Lord."

"I'm sorry to hear that, Mr. Willingham."

The old man smiled and casually waved off the sympathy. "Oh, don't be. She died years ago. I'm confident and comforted we'll one day be together eternally."

"I'm sure."

Thomas was about to bring up Ambassador Ben Hur when Arnold preempted him. "So, you wish to discuss the Lord's Strength, or Samson Effect, as you call it." He chuckled. "Samson Effect. That's good; creative."

Thomas was flabbergasted. He wasn't quite sure what to say or believe. Before him stood a Christian pastor from Las Vegas who spoke casually about what he thought was one of the greatest mysteries of antiquity. He leaned in and whispered, "You know about the Samson Effect?"

This time, Arnold's chuckle caused his solid girth to jiggle. "Oh my, yes. And no need to whisper. We can speak freely down here."

Thomas felt the same excitement he felt when he unearthed an ancient artifact. "What exactly do you know about it? Do you know what happened to it?"

Arnold held out a hand. "Slow down; first things first. Let me tell you *how* I know about the Samson Effect." He chuckled again when Thomas's title for the Lord's Strength slipped from his lips. Thomas nodded and patted his pockets. Arnold shook his head. "Don't worry about writing it down. Just listen."

Thomas reluctantly agreed and sat on the couch across from Arnold, who stroked his trim silver beard. "I suppose it was forty-some years ago when I first visited the newly created state of Israel. I was awestruck visiting the places I read about in the Bible. I was young, about twenty, and traveling alone. I met a rabbi who agreed to show me around, and we quickly became friends. I ended up staying in Israel a month longer than I had planned, and he invited me to his home in Hebron."

At the mention of Hebron, Thomas felt himself grow rigid. He literally had to remind himself to breathe.

"He introduced me to his teacher, a strange old recluse who had very little to do with me. They shared a home, but I rarely saw the old man. One day, my friend told me I had to spend the evening in Jerusalem. He didn't offer any reasons, and I didn't ask. When I came back the next day, he seemed different."

"What do you mean, different?"

"I couldn't put my finger on it then, so I shrugged it off; but three nights before I was to return to the States, I went to the kitchen for a late-night snack. My friend was sound asleep at the table, and a notebook was open before him. I poured a glass of milk, sliced some bread, and sat at the table. Without thinking, I pulled over the notebook and began reading it."

Arnold abruptly stopped his story. "I'm sorry, Dr. Hamilton. Speaking of bread, may I offer you something to eat or drink?"

Thomas didn't try to hide his impatience. "No, no. Please, continue."

"Very well, then. The notebook contained the history of what you call the Samson Effect and the responsibility of its Protector. As I finished, my friend awoke. When he saw me reading his notebook, well, let's just say he wasn't too thrilled. I honestly thought he was going to throw me out on the street then and there.

"Then, I began laughing. I told him that it was the best piece of fiction I'd ever read and that he ought to get it published. At first I thought he was going to take a swing at me, but then he sat back in his chair and began laughing too. I guess we got carried away, because his teacher yelled from his bedroom for us to be quiet. He took the notebook and went to his room.

"Neither of us mentioned it again; and when the day came for me to leave, he drove me to Jerusalem. He denied it, but to this day, I'm convinced he ran into the ditch on purpose. We got out and looked at the car. There was no way we were going anywhere without a tow truck, but he just looked at me and smiled. Then, before my eyes, he grabbed the bumper and pulled the car to the road as though it were a cardboard cutout."

Thomas slowly smiled and tried not to insult the pastor. "Do you want me to believe someone already has the Samson Effect, the Lord's Strength, if you will? That goes against everything we found written on the subject."

"Then how do you explain, Dr. Hamilton, my knowledge of it?"

"Now there's where I'm stumped. I know you're friends with the ambassador. Everything you told me could've come from him."

The old man laughed pleasantly. "Ah yes, Benjamin." He shook his head. "Isn't it strange how, in the most divided city on earth, a Christian pastor could become friends with an Orthodox Jew and an Israeli politician?"

"I'm afraid I don't quite understand," Thomas admitted.

"My family and I returned to Israel in the eighties and founded this church. I rekindled my friendship with the Jewish rabbi and met Benjamin when he was a major in the Israeli Air Force. Now that he's an ambassador, we don't see each other quite as often, but he manages to swing by for coffee every now and then."

Thomas fidgeted in his seat. He began to wonder how much truth was behind the pastor's words. The man seemed sincere, but Thomas still had trouble believing someone had the Samson Effect when all manuscripts claimed it had been lost to history. "Tell me, Mr. Willingham, how did you and the ambassador begin discussing the Samson Effect?"

Thomas could swear the pastor had a glint in his eye. "Why, because of you, Dr. Hamilton."

"Me?"

Arnold stood and motioned for Thomas to follow. "Yes. Let me show you what I mean."

Thomas followed him to a small office. It actually looked like a walk-in closet, framed with shelves, floor to ceiling, and packed with books. A card table, which served as a desk, and a chair sat in the center, leaving just enough space for one man to walk around it to retrieve books from the shelves.

Arnold walked directly to a shelf in the back corner and pulled out a binder with the name "Dr. Thomas Hamilton" written on the spine. Thomas watched in anticipation, wondering what the folder contained.

Arnold turned toward the door. "Let's move to the kitchen, where we'll have more room."

A few moments later, the two men sat at the table with the binder open. Thomas immediately recognized the photocopied cover on the first page as the issue of *The Journal of Biblical Archaeology* in which he and Ellen had copublished an article.

Arnold flipped through a few pages of handwritten notes until he came to Thomas's article. The title blazed across the top of the page in block letters: "Mental Illnesses and the Old Testament Characters."

Thomas pulled the binder to himself. "Ah yes, it received mediocre interest."

"Oh, not by me, Dr. Hamilton. Based on what you wrote and what I read in the rabbi's journal, I formed a supposition that linked the Samson Effect to the behavior exhibited by those great men in the Old Testament."

"You mean to tell me you believe all the great men in the Old Testament used the Samson Effect, and it was responsible for their mental illnesses?"

"Yes. Well, not all the men, of course. The notebook claimed Moses was the first to be given the Samson Effect. Last year, I was casually discussing your article with Benjamin over dinner one night, and eventually we both realized the other knew of the Samson Effect. He's continually pressed me to reveal my sources; but because of my word to the rabbi over forty years ago, I could not."

"Then why tell me?"

The glint faded from Arnold's eyes. "Because my friend was killed yesterday, and I'm worried sick the secret will fall into the wrong hands."

Thomas intuitively knew Arnold was speaking of Azim. "But you said the Samson Effect wasn't lost; your friend had possession of it. Everyone I'm aware of who knows about it assumes it's lost and is looking for it."

"But it *is* lost. My friend was the protector of the secret and of the very small sample that has been guarded by centuries of protectors." Arnold sat back in his chair and folded his arms over his belly. "Did you, by chance, hear about the incident in Hebron where a Jew reportedly bent the barrel of a gun barehanded?"

"Ambassador Ben Hur mentioned something to me about it last night."

Well, last night I figured out the man was my friend's student. Now he's the new Protector."

"How did you learn all this?"

"Because two of his students came to me last night. They knew their teacher and I were friends, and they needed a place to stay for a couple of weeks. They told me about the rabbi's death, and Benjamin told me about the man who bent the gun. From that, it was easy to figure out the rest."

This was as close to the ancient secret as Thomas had ever been. His muscles tensed as he realized he was about to take a giant leap forward toward the object of his two-year quest. "Where are they? May I talk with them?"

"They're at the Wailing Wall. They should be back soon. But, Dr. Hamilton, we dare not admit knowledge of the secret to them."

Thomas leaped to his feet. "Why not? Together, we can find the Samson Effect before Azim does." He shuddered at the thought of that madman finding it first.

"We can't. They have no idea about the details of the Samson Effect; only the protectors have the full knowledge. Neither do they know me like the rabbi did. They're serious about their responsibility, and they wouldn't hesitate to kill either one of us if they felt we were a threat to their duty."

Thomas dropped into the chair. "Then I'm back to square one. It seems every time the Samson Effect is within reach, someone picks it up and moves it further from my grasp."

"Patience, Dr. Hamilton. If the Lord has meant for you to find it after it's been lost for three thousand years, you'll find it. If not, then there's nothing you can do."

Thomas held his tongue, not wanting to offend the pastor. He knew if some powerful miracle drug existed, probability and chance could care less if it was him or Azim who found it.

Arnold folded his hands on the table and narrowed his eyes. "Dr. Hamilton, may I pose a theological question to you?"

"About the Samson Effect, sure."

"Let's assume you find it and let's also assume it gives you great power, but it costs you your mental health—drives you to depression, thoughts of suicide, paranoia—what would you do with it?"

Thomas considered the question. It cast his theories of the mental health of the Old Testament characters in a new light. As unlikely as he thought the correlation between the Samson Effect and degenerative mental health was, he had to admit it was, indeed, a possibility.

"I thought you said this was a theological question. Sounds more like an ethical one to me."

"Ethics is based in theology. I believe the Lord used the substance to fulfill his will and guarded it through the protectors to preserve its purpose. Now if the Lord no longer wishes to use it and removes his protection from it, do you really believe you should step into his shoes and determine who uses it and for what purposes?"

"I still don't think it's a theological issue. You said yourself if the Lord wants me to find it, I will. Besides, and please don't take offense, I don't quite know if there is a God. For all we know, the substance is a product of nature, one with amazing side effects, albeit, but a product of nature, nonetheless."

The old pastor rested his chin on his hand, and it appeared to Thomas the glint was back in his eyes. Thomas sighed, thankful his comment had not angered the pastor. "I believe, Dr. Hamilton, based on everything I've read about you, that you're a good, moral man. I also believe, whether you do or not, that the Lord may be working through you to find this because he knows your heart. He knows you'll do the right thing if you find it."

"And what would be the right thing?"

The pastor's smile grew even broader. "I really don't know. But if given the opportunity, I'm sure you'll figure it out. I just want to make sure you take into consideration all the consequences."

The two stared at each other for a moment until Arnold slapped both hands on his lap. "Well, I suppose you'd like to see my old rabbi friend's notebook, wouldn't you?"

Thomas felt a chill grip his body. "You have the notebook?"

"Not the original, but I do have one I've recreated as best I could from memory. It doesn't contain everything, but you'd be surprised at what's in there."

"You don't know how much I'd appreciate seeing it."

Arnold rose from his chair and walked toward the office. "Wait right there while I get it." He stopped and turned to Thomas. "Before I give it to you, you must promise that if you find the Effect, you'll bring it here for me to see."

"If the notebook leads me to it, you have my word."

A grin spread across Arnold's face as he turned and disappeared into the office. He returned with a blue spiral notebook. Thomas stood before him and received the notebook as ceremonially as a mayor bestowing an award to an honored citizen. He felt a lump in his throat as he reverently pulled the notebook to himself.

The solemn atmosphere shattered as both men turned their head to the squeaking stair steps. Two men stared back at them with angry eyes. One man had a manila envelope tucked under his arm; the other knelt down, pulled up his left pant leg, and drew the six-inch dagger strapped to his leg.

# CHAPTER 15

MICHAEL ROLLED OFF his hospital bed and stepped gingerly to the closet. As he passed by the mirror, he glanced at his reflection, staring at the bruises created by the morning's oral surgery procedure. He groaned and turned his head away. He did look as bad as he felt.

When he reached the closet, he pulled out a dress shirt and struggled to force his arm through the sleeve. The bandages around his ribs were tight and did little to keep the pain at bay. He finally swallowed his pride enough to look at Delia, who sat chiseled in her chair with her face turned away from his.

"The least you could do is help me get dressed."

Delia remained silent for a few moments before she whipped her head toward him. "I told you, you're being foolish! You're in no condition to leave your room, let alone join Thomas and me in Hebron."

"If you think I'm going to just lie in this hospital room while you two search for the Samson Effect, you're nuts."

Delia opened her mouth, but closed it and looked away. "Thomas was right; I should never have told you."

Michael started buttoning his shirt and then let out a quiet groan. Every movement sent fire through his ribs. "Well, it's good you did. I would never have forgiven you if you hadn't."

Delia turned to him and shook her head. "You've got to be the most stubborn man I know." She rose from her chair and stepped up to him. She gently reached out her hand and started buttoning his shirt. "You can't even dress yourself. How do you think you'll be able to handle things in Hebron?"

Michael leaned in and kissed her on the forehead. "Because I'll have you there to protect me."

Delia rolled her eyes and lightly punched his side. The fire from his ribs ignited every synapse around his injury and nearly brought him to his knees. "Take it easy, will you?"

"If you can't handle a love tap, then you're in trouble."

Michael bit his tongue and stepped back into the closet for his pants. Behind him, Delia asked, "Do you need help with your trousers?" He stepped out of the closet, slid into a padded chair, and glared at her. "I think I can manage myself."

He fought to show no signs of pain as he bent one leg up and slid his foot through the pant leg. As nonchalantly as he could muster, he looked at Delia and nodded curtly. When she giggled, he felt the fire spread through his cheeks; but before he had a chance to say a word, she slinked toward him and slid to her knees. Without saying a word, she leaned forward and touched her lips lightly to his side.

"I'm sorry. I know you're in pain." She rolled her eyes to his and moistened her full lips. In a whisper, she asked, "Forgive me?"

Michael looked down at her and ran his fingers through her hair. He knew beyond any doubt he'd always love her. He closed his eyes and nodded. She laid her head into his lap and kissed his thigh.

"Good gracious! What's going on here?"

Michael opened his eyes to find his uncle standing in the doorway. His uncle's wide eyes and stunned expression were too much for him to handle. He burst out laughing as Delia sprang to her feet and smoothed her blouse and skirt with her hand.

He alternated between laughter and groaning before he finally caught his breath. "Uncle Ben, haven't you heard of knocking?" Delia punched his side before he saw it coming. The pain chased away any humor he found in the situation. He glared at Delia, but when he saw the stern warning etched on her face, he silently sucked in the pain.

He looked at his uncle and shook his head. "Nothing's going on. Delia is helping me get dressed."

The ambassador stepped over to Michael and looked down at him. "And exactly *why* are you getting dressed?"

Michael managed to lift himself from the chair. "I'm going to Hebron with Delia and Thomas, and don't you start in with me. There's nothing you can say that Delia hasn't already said. Bottom line, I'm going. End of discussion."

The ambassador stood silently as Michael prepared to go toe-to-toe with the best negotiator he'd ever known. He fastened his belt and waited for his uncle to make his move. What the ambassador said caught him off guard and threw up his defenses for a covert attack.

"I suppose you're right." His uncle sighed and shook his head. "If you're set on getting yourself killed, then who am I to try to stop you?"

Michael nodded cautiously. He had never known his uncle to give in this easily. He had the overwhelming feeling he was about to step into a trap. He reached to the table and picked up his wallet. As he slid it into his pocket, he kept his uncle in sight through the corner of his eye. "I appreciate your support."

"Oh, you certainly do not have my support. How someone so intelligent could be so stupid is beyond comprehension. I just know how important the Samson Effect is to you."

Delia locked her arms through Michael's and smiled. "You don't have to worry about anything. I'll keep an eye on him." The ambassador never looked away from Michael. "I'll arrange security for you. Just promise me you'll not do anything stupid and you'll stay with the men I'll send with you."

Michael allowed a small smile to give his thanks. "I promise." He turned to Delia. "Perhaps the three of us can have lunch before we meet up with Thomas."

Delia looked toward the ambassador with raised eyebrows. Again, he did not acknowledge her presence. "Sorry, but my schedule is tight today. I'll call *you* to arrange a time when you and I can get together." He turned curtly and stepped out of the room.

Michael released his hold on Delia and started after his uncle, but she grabbed his arm. "Please, let him go."

"He may not approve of our relationship, but I'm not going to stand by while he treats you like a dog."

"I appreciate that, but give him time. I'll win him over quicker if we don't antagonize him. After all, I'm starting to win Thomas over, and I have faith I'll also win your uncle over too."

Michael shook his head. "Thomas's heart wasn't corrupted with prejudice."

✳    ✳    ✳    ✳

After spending two hours pouring through the phone records of everyone associated with him, Azim found his traitor. The damning evidence sat face up on his desk. After futilely trying to rationalize away what the phone records told him, he finally succumbed to the truth and melted into his chair.

Rajah seemed equally stunned. He waited silently for Azim to come to terms with the traitor's identity.

Azim took in a deep breath and closed his eyes. "You know what must be done."

Rajah cocked his head to one side. "Forgive me, but I'm not sure I fully understand your intentions."

"My intentions?" Azim could feel every muscle in his face and neck tighten as fire pulsed through his veins. "She's responsible for Umar's death, and she has betrayed me. I will not forgive her. She must die."

"Perhaps there's an explanation. Delia may have been—"

"Do not mention her name in my presence again! How could there be any other explanation for her calling the Israelis from her room the night before the attack? Answer me!"

"Azim, I don't know—"

"You don't know because there's only one explanation." Azim grabbed the phone records in his fist. "Bring her to me alive. I want her to see my face before she feels the cold hand of my justice."

Azim clenched his teeth and squeezed the paper until his knuckles grew pale. He felt every muscle tense, and a slight tremor spread through him. The tension grew until it was focused so tightly that his body couldn't stand it. His fist exploded on the desk, accompanied by the guttural command. "Go!"

Rajah jumped to his feet and bowed as he shuffled backward and quickly slipped out the door. When it closed, Azim felt the tension fall like chains dropping from his body. His strength drained from his body, and he poured like water into the chair.

*　　*　　*　　*

Aaron descended the stairs with a dagger gripped in his fist. Thomas and Arnold froze as they watched the two men until they all stood facing each other in the tiny living room. Tobin reached out and gently took the notebook from the pastor and slipped it next to his envelope.

"What's the meaning of this, Tobin?"

Tobin's anger burned in his eyes. "If you weren't the rabbi's friend, you'd be dead right now." His eyes flashed to Thomas. "Who is this man, and what does he know about what we're sworn to protect?"

Neither Arnold nor Thomas answered. Aaron lifted the tip of the dagger under Thomas's chin and pressed until Thomas could feel a drop of warm liquid run down his neck.

"Thomas Hamilton. My name's Thomas Hamilton."

Tobin nodded to Aaron, and Aaron withdrew the blade. Thomas reached to his neck and pressed his thumb on the puncture. The pastor fished a handkerchief from his pocket and handed it to him.

"Mr. Hamilton, what do you know of the Lord's Strength?" Tobin walked to the table and glanced over the papers spread over its surface. "Oh, it's *Doctor* Hamilton, I see." He walked back to Aaron and took the dagger from him. He then stepped to Thomas and placed the tip against his chest. "Well, Dr. Hamilton, what's your business with the secret?"

Thomas tried to swallow the lump in his throat but nothing went down. The sting of the dagger tip pulled the words from his lips. "I've been following archaeological clues of the Samson Effect for over a year now."

"The what?"

Everyone turned their heads toward the door at the top of the stairs when someone knocked and then cracked it open. "Father, may I come down?"

Thomas felt the pressure from the dagger ease. Before he had a chance to think, he grabbed Tobin's wrist and hyperextended his arm at the elbow. Tobin cried out in pain and released the dagger. Thomas kicked it away and landed his fist across Tobin's jaw, knocking him through the tiny living room and into the kitchen.

Arnold grabbed a coffee table book and swung like a major-league slugger, knocking Aaron to his knees. He then jogged to a stunned Tobin, yanked the envelope and notebook from his arms, and tossed them to Thomas. "Run!"

Thomas looked up the stairs at the confused face of the younger pastor and then started up the stairs, calling for Arnold to follow. He glanced behind him when he was halfway up the steps, relieved to see the old pastor at the foot of the stairs. He froze when Arnold abruptly stopped on the second step, and his eyes grew wide.

A gentle whisper escaped the old man's lips. "Run." Thomas watched him topple from the stairs and saw the dagger handle sticking from his back.

Arnold's son thrust Thomas against the rail as he tried to squeeze by and get to his father. Thomas watched Tobin pull the dagger from the old man and look up at them. He snapped from his shock and grabbed the man's forearm as he rushed past him.

"Come on!"

Thomas felt like he was pulling dead weight. He was about to release his grip on the man when he felt the resistance ease. He hurdled the top step and flew through the door. The moment the young pastor cleared the door, Thomas slammed it shut and leaned his weight against it.

"Find something to secure the door."

The young pastor didn't make a move. His eyes fixed upon the door. Thomas feared the pastor had heard nothing as he struggled to take in what he had just witnessed. Thomas couldn't reach out and shake the man without the assassins bursting through the door.

He could feel the door rattle behind him. The doorknob turned and the door drew open, pushing his feet across the tile floor. Thomas leaned back and dug the heels of his hiking boots into the floor. The door stopped opening, but the men on the other side matched Thomas's resistance.

Thomas felt fire burn through his thighs and calves. He had no more strength to give, and what he was giving began to slip away. It was nearly imperceptible, but he felt the door slightly nudge open more. His clenched teeth began to throb.

He held the door until his strength was spent. He bowed his head and let up. As soon as he did, the door swung freely. Thomas staggered backward until the closed door stopped him. He opened his eyes to see Arnold's son digging his shoulders into the door.

"The hammer and spike!"

Thomas followed the man's gaze to a simple wooden mallet and a thick iron nail set in a crucifixion display. His mind immediately connected with the pastor's as he reached for the items and turned to the door. Almost miraculously, he felt his strength return. He placed the nail point on the tiled floor and brought the hammer down full force. The first swing cracked the tile and the second embedded the spike an inch into the floor. After three more swings, the spike's head extended just high enough to prevent the door from opening further.

The pastor stepped away, and they both stared at the door. It rattled open an inch, but the spike held firm. Thomas grabbed the pastor's arm and pulled him away. "The door won't hold long. We need to call the police."

"My office is this way."

Thomas followed, casting glances behind at the violently rattling door. When they reached the other end of the sanctuary, the pastor ran into his office and picked up the phone. Thomas stopped at the office door and turned toward the back of the sanctuary. To his horror, he watched the top and middle hinges break from the door jamb. The door folded forward, and the two men climbed out of the stairwell. He turned to the pastor. "We've got to go now!"

The pastor placed a hand on the mouthpiece. "I'm being connected now."

"They're out!"

The pastor dropped the phone and ran to Thomas. The two assassins stared at them and then charged.

"This way."

Before he could turn to follow, Thomas felt as though Samson himself had slugged his left shoulder. The force knocked him against the wall. One of the assassins was charging toward him with the dagger drawn. The other had stopped and was pointing a gun at him.

"Come on!"

Thomas turned to see the pastor standing at a side exit with the door wide open. He began running as another shot rang out. When he reached the door, he jumped the three steps to the parking lot and the pastor slammed the door closed. They turned toward the busy street out front and ran.

The door behind them burst open, and the two assassins ran full speed at them. Thomas and the pastor ran into the crowd and quickly caught the attention of three armed patrolmen. The soldiers pointed their guns at them and barked out a command Thomas didn't understand. By instinct, however, he held his hands behind his head and dropped to his knees.

The pastor, also on his knees, was speaking furiously to the soldiers, who glanced past Thomas. One soldier nodded, and the other two took off toward the assassins. Out of nowhere, countless soldiers poured into the parking lot. A soldier approached Thomas and demanded, in English, for him to produce his papers. Thomas pulled out the papers Ambassador Ben Hur had given him the night before. The soldier took the papers and ran a check on them. He returned and ordered the soldiers to stand down.

He escorted Thomas to an ambulance, where a medic removed the bullet from his shoulder and dressed his wound. Another police car skidded to a stop in front of the church. A man in a suit stepped out and, without introduction, demanded to know what was going on.

"My father was killed just now in the church." The pastor nodded at the church.

Other cars arrived, and the police were already in the process of securing the area. The man in the suit looked down at the papers handed to him and then looked at Thomas. "Mr. Derrick White, I see you're visiting from Canada. If you'll please come with me, I have some questions for you." The man turned to the pastor. "You, go with this man."

Thomas wracked his brain for some way to avoid the interrogation, but everything he thought of would only cast suspicion upon him. With resignation, he nodded, knowing he could always invoke the ambassador's name if he found himself in serious trouble.

The man gestured to the backseat door of his car, and Thomas began walking toward it. An officer approached, handed the man a sheet of paper, and whispered something into his ear. They both looked at Thomas, and then down to the paper.

The man in the suit barked out something. Before Thomas could react, two men pinned him to the ground, closed cuffs around his wrists, and then yanked him to his feet.

Thomas shook his head. "What's going on? Why are you doing this?"

The man in the suit stepped up to Thomas with a smirk on his face. "It seems you're a very popular man in the United States, *Dr. Hamilton.*"

# CHAPTER 16

THOMAS GREW NUMB from sitting on the iron bench he was shackled to. For an hour he watched policemen pass by, none even glancing his way. His fervent requests to speak with someone, anyone, were ignored.

A door opened down the hall, and the detective, the man in the suit who had brought him in, stepped out of an office, followed by Arnold's son. The young pastor's eyes met his, and his stomach tightened as he felt the pain hidden behind those young eyes.

Two small children, a boy and a girl, rushed past Thomas and threw their arms around the pastor, who knelt to receive them into his arms. The children's wails echoed through the hall. A woman rushed past and joined the grieving trio.

"Dr. Hamilton."

Thomas roused from his thoughts and looked over his shoulder. "Pastor Willingham has convinced me you're not the one who killed his father."

Thomas sighed. "No, I—"

"Silence! You may not have done it, but we both believe you are involved. I've agreed to let him sit in while I ask you a couple of questions. If I don't like what I hear, well, let's just say you'll be able to witness Israeli justice. If your words satisfy me, I'll arrange to turn you over to the American consulate."

"Please, if you'll call Ambassador Ben Hur—"

"Dr. Hamilton, I will not ask you again to remain silent." The detective nodded to a man who knelt and unlocked the shackles from the bench. "Bring him to me."

The policeman escorted Thomas down the hall to the interrogation room. He stopped before entering and looked at each member of the Willingham family, who stared back silently, except for a sniffle from the girl. When Thomas's eyes met the pastor's, he saw the moisture dammed behind the lids, ready to burst forth. His escort pushed him forward and led him to a chair in the room. A few clicks later, his shackles were firmly secured to an iron ring protruding from the wall. The detective and pastor followed and sat at the table across from him. The policeman left and shut the door behind him.

"Now's your chance to speak, Dr. Hamilton. Help me understand who you are, and what you're doing in my country illegally, while evading U.S. authorities for murder." He arched his eyebrows and turned to the pastor. "That's about it for me. Anything you want to add?"

The pastor's gentle spirit tugged at Thomas's heart. "I just want to know why my father died."

Thomas could not look at the pastor. Instead, he looked at the detective. "Please, just contact the ambassador. One call to him will clear everything up."

"What kind of fool do you take me for, Dr. Hamilton? Do you really expect me to go to my supervisors and say, 'a wanted murderer from the U.S., with a false passport and traveling under an assumed name, is asking me to contact the ambassador to the U.S. to clear up everything for him?'" The detective leaned back in his seat and folded his arms over his chest. The smirk returned to his face. "Let's stop this charade. Why don't you tell me what happened?"

Thomas snapped. He lunged forward, but the shackles held him firmly in place. Every muscle fought against the chains, fueled by the detective's calm smile. "You're making a mistake!"

The detective eased from his chair and shook his head. "It's not me who's making the mistake." Thomas collapsed into his chair. "We'll talk again when you're more in the mood to cooperate."

The detective and pastor filed out of the room, leaving Thomas shackled and alone. Thomas tugged on the chain and quickly realized there was no way in the world he'd be able to break free. He slumped in the chair and did the only thing he could do: wait.

It seemed an hour had passed before the door opened again. The detective stood in the doorway and shook his head. "You have a visitor."

The words brought Thomas to full attention. "Who?"

Ambassador Ben Hur slipped into the room and thanked the detective, who nodded and left. He then turned to Thomas and said, "Before you say anything, remember our relationship affects Israel's national security. This room is being monitored, so be judicious with what you say. Understand?"

Thomas nodded.

"Good." The ambassador took off his gloves and sat at the table. "Dr. Hamilton, I'm sorry to get you involved in this. If it's any consolation, you'll be leaving with me."

"You don't know how glad I am to hear that." He tugged at the shackles. "Can you get me out of these?"

"I'm working on that as we speak. It should only be a few more minutes." The ambassador looked at the mirror and then to Thomas. "Have you told them about the nature of our relationship, or about the reason you're in Israel?"

"No, but I was about to spill everything. They threatened to either deport me or convict me."

"I'm glad you hung on." The ambassador picked up one of his gloves and slapped it a couple of times in his palm. "So, did you get a chance to read the file I had delivered to you?"

"File? Oh, the one on Delia. Not yet."

"Why not? You've no idea how dangerous she is. She's a Jezebel who's somehow managed to entice an otherwise brilliant man."

"Ambassador, isn't it conceivable she's been looking for an opportunity to escape her brother? I really think she loves your nephew."

The ambassador leaned back in his chair and shook his head. "She's good. She has even managed to beguile you. I'll tell you this, Dr. Hamilton, it'll be over my dead body before she has a chance to betray Michael. Just promise me you'll be vigilant and keep an open mind."

Thomas nodded, realizing it would be futile to ask the ambassador to do the same. He turned toward the door as a man dressed in full military uniform stepped into the room.

The ambassador stood to shake his hand. "Colonel Yarconi, thank you for coming."

Thomas strained his arm against the shackles as he attempted to extend his hand in greeting. Colonel Yarconi beckoned with his hand before the mirror and, in a few seconds, the detective appeared. "Please remove his restraints."

"I don't think that's a good idea."

"Detective, you'll find all papers signed and in order for me to take this man into my custody. Now, please remove his restraints."

The detective peered at Thomas through squinted eyes, but followed the colonel's orders. Thomas rose to his feet and rubbed his wrists, relieved for his newfound freedom.

"May I ask, Colonel, why this man is so important to our military?"

The colonel's face remained void of emotion. "No you may not, Detective."

After a few moments of thoughtful silence, the detective stepped up to Thomas until Thomas could smell the lunch on his breath. His eyes coldly bore into Thomas's eyes. "If you so much as spit on my streets, I'll pick you up and hand you over to the American consulate before you can blink." He turned his icy contempt to the colonel. "I'm sure you'll want to know I plan on turning in a complete report to the Americans about their fugitive."

The ambassador rose to his feet and in an even tone admonished, "Do not forget who you're talking to, Detective."

"I assure you, he won't forget." All eyes turned to the white-haired man who entered the room. "You'll have no problems from my unit, Ambassador. We're happy to assist the military in whatever way we can, aren't we, Detective Hazan?"

Hazan's face reddened. "Yes, Lieutenant."

"Good. And that report you are going to file, have it on my desk tonight. I'll make the decision if it should be forwarded to anyone." Detective Hazan nodded curtly and stormed out of the room.

"Well, gentlemen, if you'll kindly vacate my station, I'm sure things will settle down soon."

The ambassador smiled and extended his hand. "Thanks, Jonas."

"No problem, my friend." The lieutenant turned to leave, but stopped and turned back to Thomas. Keeping his eyes on Thomas, he directed his comment to the ambassador. "Try to keep this man away from dead people. If another murder victim turns up around him, I doubt even our friendship can prevent a more thorough inquiry."

"Of course."

The lieutenant's eyes warned Thomas not to press his luck. He left, and the ambassador motioned for the colonel and Thomas to follow. A few moments later, they were outside and heading down the steps toward the limo parked out front.

"Dr. Hamilton, there's someone who's anxious to speak with you."

The chauffeur opened the door for the men and Thomas entered, but froze when he saw Hanna seated facing him. Her smile paralyzed him with joy, and the colonel had to tap his shoulder to urge him into the car. He slid to the other side of the limo, followed by the other two men.

"Hello, Thomas."

Thomas's eyes traveled over Hanna; his words lodged in his throat. He wanted to reach out to touch her and pull her into his arms. Her smile melted his heart. Words finally escaped his lips. "You look wonderful."

She blushed and turned her smiling face away. Thomas snapped from his trance and looked at the ambassador and the colonel. They returned his look with raised eyebrows, both fidgeting in mild discomfort.

Thomas turned back to Hanna and smiled. "I mean, you look like you've made it through your ordeal unscathed."

"Well, maybe physically unscathed. Actually, I was treated better than I expected. I hear Michael wasn't as lucky." She tenderly reached a finger to the scars on Thomas's face left from his tumble down the cave. "These look new."

"Don't ask," Thomas said. "The war story on these is rather embarrassing."

The limo began pulling away from the curb when Thomas tensed and yelled for the driver to stop. The driver's eyes peered back at him from the rearview mirror, and then shifted toward the ambassador. Thomas turned, wide-eyed, to the ambassador. "For heaven's sake, stop now!"

The ambassador nodded. "Driver, stop." He turned to Thomas. "What is it?"

"The notebook. I didn't get the notebook back."

The ambassador slid to the edge of his seat. "What notebook, Thomas?"

Thomas described the notebook Arnold had given him. Before he finished, the ambassador was on the phone to his lieutenant friend. A few seconds later, he set the phone down. "Since it belonged to Arnold, they released it to his son."

Thomas felt the knot tighten in his stomach. "If the assassins return to find that family with it, they'll massacre them all to protect the secret."

The ambassador instructed the driver to attach the diplomatic flags to the limo and race toward the parsonage next to the church. As they pulled into the parking lot, Thomas's dread deepened when he saw smoke billowing from the parsonage. He frantically scanned the property for help, but he found only a vacated crime scene. The ambassador was on the phone, reporting the fire, when Thomas opened the door and dashed toward the burning house.

"Thomas," Hanna cried. "No!"

Thomas quickened his pace. When he arrived at the front door, he pounded on it and immediately reached for the doorknob. It was locked, yet cool to the touch.

"Thomas!"

Thomas turned to the limo, seeing the ambassador jogging toward him, followed by the colonel and Hanna. He leaned down and took off one of his hiking boots. Then, standing and facing the window next to the door, he reared back and threw the boot through the window.

Thomas heard sirens in the background growing louder. He paid little attention to the jagged glass teeth around the window and found a place to put his hands so he could hoist himself through the window. As he was about to jump, a hand on his shoulders restrained him.

The colonel pushed him aside and used the heel of his dress shoes to chip away the jagged glass. He then took off his jacket and flung it over the windowsill. Thomas nodded his appreciation, and then pulled himself into the burning house.

"Pastor!"

A quick sweep of the rooms at the front of the house yielded no people. He opened the front door for the others, and then set his sights on the hall where the thick gray smoke grew intense and fire licked the walls and ceiling.

"Thomas, don't do it. The firefighters will be here any moment."

"We may not have a moment, Ambassador." Before another word could be spoken, Thomas dashed into the hall, feeling the heat increase upon his face with each step.

"Pastor!"

He flung open the first door to the right but saw no one. He looked through the open bathroom door across the hall, finding that room also empty. He fought through the heat to the next door on the right. He reached for the doorknob and yanked his hand away when pain melted through his palm and fingers.

He pounded on the door.

"Pastor!"

He steeled himself, took the doorknob into his hand again, and opened the door. The flames leapt at him with a force of their own and pushed him backward through an open door across the hall.

Thomas fell onto his back and stared up at the swirling flames which covered the ceiling. Then black smoke rolled in from both sides and covered him.

He rose to his knees, feeling the needle pinpricks of heat stab his entire body. His eyes burned from the smoke, and everywhere he turned he saw blackness. He knew the door was somewhere, but he felt as though he was locked in a cube with no way out.

"Thomas!" He turned toward the direction he thought the sound came from. He opened his mouth to call back, but smoke filled his lungs, suffocating him and allowing only coughs and heaves to escape his lips.

He gasped for air, but his lungs were again filled with the soupy smoke. His starvation for oxygen overrode the heat's pain upon his skin. He dropped to his hands and began crawling toward what he hoped was the door. The crackling fire roared in his ears as he crawled forward. He felt his chest heaving, but a strange calmness overcame his numb body.

His head bumped into something, and he felt up the surface until his hand reached a tabletop. He tried to pull himself up, but his hands landed on sheets of paper and slipped off the desk. He fell down and rolled onto his stomach.

His gasps turned into uncontrolled hacking, and he felt himself slipping into unconsciousness.

With his cheek against the carpet, he could see through the wisps of smoke hovering above the floor. He craned his neck, struggling to find the bottom of the door before unconsciousness claimed him, but the last thing he saw made him forget about everything else. As he gave up his fight, his eyes closed over the sight of the parchment Michael had discovered.

# CHAPTER 17

THOMAS AWOKE TO the sounds of screaming sirens and bumps that shook him on his cot. One man bent over him, listening to his heartbeat with a stethoscope, while another taped a needle to his arm. He groggily reached up to push the mask from his face, but a firm grip stopped him.

"Take it easy, my friend."

Thomas rolled his head toward the voice and saw Michael's face smiling back at him. His thoughts began to clear, and he attempted to lean forward on the cot. Once again Michael stopped him, gently forcing him back down.

"The fire ..."

"You're lucky Colonel Yarconi found you when he did. Looks like at least one of us is destined to always be in the hospital."

Thomas reached out and gripped Michael's arm, forcing the graveled words from his throat. "The Davidic parchment; I saw it."

Michael cocked his head to one side; his smile seemed quizzical more than joyous. "You saw it? Where?"

"In the pastor's house, before I blacked out."

"It must've been something else. I never made copies of it, and Azim has the original. It's doubtful he'd give it, or a copy, to a Christian pastor."

"I know what I saw. It was the symbol that caught my eye." He removed the oxygen mask, brushing aside Michael's attempt to stop him. One of the paramedics reached for the mask and politely, yet forcefully, encouraged him to put the mask back on.

"Just a minute!"

The paramedic looked at Michael, who stared at Thomas for a moment and then nodded. The paramedic shook his head but eased away.

Thomas leaned up, resting on his elbows and looked directly into Michael's eyes. "Someone else knows about the Samson Effect. The pastor's hiding something, and I believe your uncle is too."

Thomas felt exhaustion creep over him. He dropped his head onto the pillow and offered no resistance to the paramedic's insistence on replacing his oxygen mask. By the time the ambulance pulled into the hospital drive, he had told Michael about his visit with the elder pastor and about the notebook.

The ambulance stopped, and the paramedics opened the door and rolled him out. Michael jumped out to his side and followed him through the hospital doors. "But why do you think my uncle's hiding something?"

Before Thomas could reply, a guard stopped Michael as the paramedics wheeled him through another set of doors.

\*    \*    \*    \*

Judas had spent the last twenty-four hours finding and following his rabbi's assassins. He fought the impulse to snuff out their lives immediately, biding his time, waiting for them to lead him to Azim. Against him, he would let his fury burn.

He sat in an outdoor cafe, nursing his tea from a table where he could watch people come and go from Azim's building. Every now and then he caught himself rubbing his freshly shaven cheek and chin. With his beard gone and his black hair dyed brown, he felt conspicuous rather than inconspicuous.

Across the street, he watched a group of men step out of the building as a car drove up to the front door. Azim stepped out of the building and glanced down both directions of the street before entering the car.

Judas downed the rest of his tea and stood from the table. He watched the car pull away from the building and make a U-turn. He casually entered his car and pulled into traffic, keeping his eyes on Azim's car.

He followed them to the same building he and Simon had thrown the swine's head into. Azim's party exited the car while he found a parking space in front of a market three blocks down the road.

When the last man walked through the door, he eased out of his car and strolled toward the building. He passed without slowing, casting a brief glance while looking for any breach that would allow him entrance. He turned the corner at the crossroad and continued until he reached an alleyway behind Azim's building. Two men were sitting in a car, looking bored, but definitely there for a purpose. He kept walking and noticed the top of a structure on the roof above Azim's place. He also saw ladder rungs embedded in the building across the alley from the ground to the roof.

He turned a corner again and walked in front of the businesses that backed against the buildings on Azim's street. A grocery store stood directly behind Azim's building. He casually entered and began browsing the aisles. An elderly man sat behind the register. Every time Judas glanced at him, the man had his eyes locked onto him.

Judas fingered through cans of soup while looking over the shelves to the rear of the store. To the left he saw an open doorway with stairs leading up. On the center wall, he saw a set of double doors he supposed led to a storage area. He picked up a can of soup and made his way to the back of the store.

The door to the store opened, and Judas turned to see seven or eight men enter, laughing and filling the room with chatter. A young, clean-shaven man Judas guessed to be in his mid-twenties picked up a bottled drink from a tub of ice, downed the contents, and smacked his lips. He reached back into the tub and began tossing bottles to his friends. A sharp complaint from the old storekeeper and the ensuing conversation revealed to Judas that the young man was the store-keeper's son. Everyone's spirits lifted when the young man set a wad of currency on the counter as he leaned in to kiss his father's forehead. Cheers and laughter erupted as the young man's friends went on a shopping spree.

Judas made his way toward the stairs. He knew his best chance to slip up the stairs unnoticed would be in the midst of the boisterous customers.

One more quick glance at the storekeeper found him laughing and conversing with one of the customers while counting the crisp currency in his hands. When it seemed everyone was preoccupied, Judas eased closer to the stairway and made one more sweep of the room.

The storekeeper's son picked up an apple and bit into it. He then lifted his eyes to Judas. "My brother, come and let me buy you something to drink."

Judas froze, feeling the hairs on his neck tingle to life. The man stared at him, smiling and waving him over. Every set of eyes in the place stared in his direction, especially the storekeeper's eyes. As he was about to make his way to the young man, a ten-year-old boy swept past him and ran into the arms of his older brother. Everyone's eyes followed the young boy as they all crowded in to pat the boy on the head. Just as the man lifted his younger brother up onto the counter next to his father, Judas silently slipped onto the stairs. He quickly ascended, praying the clamorous group would mask the creaking noise coming from the stairs.

When he reached the top, he stepped into a small apartment. The window next to the ladder was across the living area to the right. He hurried to it, casting glances over his shoulder at the staircase entrance.

Once at the window, he turned the handle and pushed it open. Below, he saw the top of the car with the two men who were guarding Azim's building from the rear. He reached out and grabbed a rung of the ladder. After one more quick glance at the staircase, he pulled himself through the window and quickly made it to the roof.

Across the alley, he could see Azim's flat roof. It was one of only two areas on the block-long building that contained air-conditioning units. The structure he saw from the ground looked like a small shed with a single door on it.

Judas crouched down and, with little effort, leaped from one roof to the other. He made his way to the shed, hoping it would lead inside the building. He reached out and turned the handle, relieved to find the door unlocked. His relief turned to frustration when the shed proved to be just that, a storage unit for tools and supplies.

Judas shut the door and scanned the roof. His face brightened when he spotted the large rectangular outline of a doorway flush with the roof. As he walked over, he saw hinges on one end of the door. He reached for the handle at the other end and tugged on it, finding it locked. He scanned the roof again. Finding no one, he began slowly pulling up on the handle, increasing his force bit by bit.

With a relatively small creak, something gave way and the door flew open with ease. Below, he saw a lavishly furnished bedroom. He dropped into the empty room and stealthily eased over to the door. It opened to a hallway. From down the hall, he heard the sound of a woman crying and a man trying to offer her soothing words of comfort.

Judas cracked the door open a little more and looked down the hall, which opened into a sitting room where the backs of three men obscured the rest of the view. He was sure, however, that the man uttering the soothing words was Azim, comforting his aunt about Uncle Umar's death.

This was it. This was his chance to avenge his rabbi's and Simon's death. With the element of surprise and the Lord's Strength upon him, he knew he could kill every person in the room as effortlessly as Samson killed a thousand Philistines with the jawbone of an ass. His jaw clenched as he let the images in his mind of Simon's desecrated body and the rabbi's lifeless, bullet-filled body burn resolve into his conscience.

Every muscle in his body tensed as he prepared to burst into the room. Just as he was about to release his fury, something Azim said caused him to relax. Speaking to someone else in the room, he distinctly heard Azim mention his rabbi's notebook.

He paused and listened.

"… those two Jewish swine nearly recovered it, but Allah was with us. Mr. Willingham is in possession of it. I have Rajah making arrangements with him to give it to us even as we speak."

All his great strength seemed to flee from Judas upon hearing that Tobin had lost the notebook. His knees turned to water, and he sank to the floor and gasped for air with shallow breaths.

The noise of his falling grabbed the attention of the people in the sitting room. The three men turned in unison and stared at him. Between two of them, Judas's eyes met Azim's. Everyone froze in momentary disbelief until one man reached into his jacket.

Judas snapped back to reality and leapt to his feet. He darted into the bedroom, slamming the door behind him. He ran under the doorway to the roof just as he heard the bedroom door slam open. One of the men burst into the room, holding his gun before him. As the man swung the gun at him, Judas sprang into the air, throwing the roof's door open with his turned-up palms. Sounds of automatic gunfire echoed behind him.

Judas landed on the roof, sprinted to the edge, and leaped across to the other building. As he crossed the alley, he looked down to see the two men out of the car, guns in hand, staring up at him. Before they could fire, Judas landed on the other building and ran to the other end. He jumped to the street and sprinted through a crowd of astonished people who had seen him fall from the sky. He crossed the alley and sprinted to the street where his car waited for him.

When he reached his car, he dove in and took off. After a few quick turns, he was on the road leading to Jerusalem. Tonight, he knew, he had to find Tobin and Aaron; but more importantly, he had to find the rabbi's notebook.

# CHAPTER 18

THOMAS WAS TREATED and released from the hospital. He now sat in his room at the King David Hotel, with Michael and Delia seated at a small table by the window. Michael, he observed, seemed to be getting along rather well with his injuries. However, a thick atmosphere saturated with tension filled the room with silence as the three looked at the floor while running their fingers through their hair.

Thomas stood and stretched. He walked to the vanity and splashed cool water on his face. After he patted himself dry with a towel, he stared at his reflection in the mirror. His skin looked worn, and dark circles puffed under each eye. His mind raced through the events of his time since entering Israel. He thought of the life-threatening moments he had lived through and of the fear and apprehension that accompanied each day. But he also thought of the Effect, of its historical and, if he were honest, its professional significance to him.

His eyes drilled back into him from the mirror. The deeper he looked into his own soul, the firmer his resolution became. He silently vowed to let nothing sway him from his quest. From this very moment, he'd be the master of his circumstances.

"It ends here." He turned to see Michael and Delia lift their eyes to his.

"What ends here?" Michael asked.

"From the day I left home, I've been tossed about by my circumstances like a rag doll. No more." He sat at the table and folded his hands across his chest. "I'm going to find the Samson Effect, and neither Azim, nor Jewish assassins, nor anyone else will get in my way. Your uncle has offered protection, and I intend to take him up on his offer."

Thomas leaned back in his chair with his arms folded over his chest. He looked to Michael and then to Delia, who both caught his eyes before they turned to each other. Slowly, Michael's smile grew, and he clenched his fist. "I'll call Uncle Ben right away. We'll be back in Hebron tomorrow."

"Hold up, there. The first thing we're going to do is locate Pastor Willingham and find out how he's involved with the Samson Effect. I'm sure the key to the search is hidden with him."

A knock at the door stopped the conversation cold. Thomas got up and looked through the peephole before removing the chain lock and opening the door. Hanna stepped across the threshold and melted into his arms.

"Thank goodness you're all right. I've been in torment not knowing how bad your condition was." She cupped Thomas's cheek in her right hand, tenderly massaging it with her thumb.

Thomas wiped her tear away with his thumb and pulled her into his arms. He looked into her eyes and gently guided her lips to his. She offered no resistance. When their lips touched, an emotional spark ignited his passion. Thomas had played this kiss over and over in his mind, and by the way Hanna melted into his arms, he knew she had as well. Without breaking either kiss or embrace, he led her into the room and kicked the door shut with his foot.

He pulled her into his chest, her hands slipping behind his head. She ran her fingers through his hair, pulling him, if it were possible, deeper into her lips. Then they slowly, reluctantly, pulled apart from each other. With her still in his arms, he smiled and looked into her eyes. "It's good to see you too."

She smiled, closed her eyes, and leaned her head upon his chest. They silently swayed together as Thomas softly kissed the top of her head. Her fragrance flowed into him and he felt a contentment long since forgotten. He rolled his eyes to his forgotten friends at the table. Both returned his gaze with an affectionate smile, sitting hand-in-hand, obviously feeling towards each other some fraction of what he was feeling now.

"Did I interrupt anything?" Hanna asked softly.

"Actually, we're just about to make plans to return to Hebron."

"You're what? Thomas, no. You and Michael are lucky to be alive as it is."

Thomas took a step back and gently gripped Hanna's shoulders, holding her at arm's length. "I'm not going to pass up an opportunity to find it."

"I don't understand—"

"You don't have to understand it, just accept it. I'm going to do this."

She looked at Thomas, her eyes pleading for him to reconsider. Finally, she softened and smiled back at him. "I suppose it'll be futile to try to talk you out of this." She turned to Michael and Delia and sighed. "When do we start?"

Thomas spun her towards him. "*We*? There's no *we*! I'm not about to bring you into this."

She arched her eyebrows and smiled with confidence. "You have no choice. I represent Ambassador Ben Hur, who, I might remind you, is underwriting your little search. I'm confident he'll want me along."

Thomas looked at Michael, silently pleading for help. Michael shook his head. "She's right. Knowing my uncle like I do, I'm positive he'll insist she go with us. He trusts her more than he trusts me, remember?"

Thomas blew out a frustrated sigh. "Fine, but I'm going on record to voice my disapproval in the strongest of terms."

Hanna shrugged with a wry smile. "Duly noted."

She and Thomas stared at each other until the tension between them grew uncomfortable. Michael pierced the atmosphere by changing the subject. "I need to speak with Thomas alone. Why don't you girls go downstairs and grab something to drink."

Neither woman looked particularly thrilled about being excluded from a conversation, but neither pushed the issue. Delia stepped next to Hanna. "Fine. We'll just have our own conversation."

Hanna took a step back and looked Delia up and down. The look of disgust on her face was unsettling to Thomas. "I can entertain myself while you two discuss what you need to discuss." She turned to Thomas and morphed back to her beautiful, sweet self. "I need to make a phone call anyway. I'll meet you in the lobby when you're ready." She leaned in and pecked him on the cheek, turned, and walked out of the room.

When Thomas turned to see Delia's frozen, shocked expression, he knew he must be abnormally crimson. Michael was reddening too; but by his expression, Thomas knew it was from anger. Before either man spoke, Delia said, "It's obvious how she feels about me."

"I'm sorry." Thomas said.

"Please, under the circumstances, it's nothing to take to heart." Her smile melted the tension away. "I have a long history to make up for."

Michael stepped up to her and brushed her hair from her eyes. "You are truly amazing. It's no wonder I love you so much." He leaned in and kissed her. After a few moments, she pulled away. "I'll be waiting with my tea."

When she left, Thomas began to stutter through an apology, but Michael held up his hand to stop him. "You've nothing to apologize for, my friend." He sat on the edge of the bed. "She's right. It'll take time for them to accept her, possibly just to tolerate her. I'm fortunate she's as patient as she is."

"You're one lucky man, that's for sure." Thomas dropped into a chair. "So, what is it we need to discuss?"

"I didn't want to ask you in front of Hanna, but when you were rushed into the hospital, you told me you think my uncle may be hiding something. What did you mean?"

Thomas ran his fingers through his hair. "I don't know, Michael. Something just doesn't feel right about his relationship with Arnold Willingham. I mean, this man had more information about the Samson Effect than we have, and yet your uncle waited until now to bring us into the loop. And Willingham's son had a photocopy of the parchment you and Caleb found. Tell me if I'm crazy, but it seems your uncle's been dripping information about the Samson Effect to us as he sees fit."

"I don't know what to think. Why would my uncle, who wants us to find it as much as we do, withhold anything from us?"

"Look, I didn't mean to impugn your uncle's motives—"

"No, no. It's obvious he's aware of more than he wants us to know." Michael stood and nodded to the door. "Let's find the women. I have a gut feeling Hanna may be privy to more than she'll offer to share. I say we keep our concerns to ourselves and not arouse suspicion. From now on, we'll do some dripping of our own. Agreed?"

"Agreed."

As they were about to walk out the door, the phone rang. Thomas answered it. "Hello … You're kidding? We're on our way down."

As soon as he hung up the phone, Michael asked, "Who was it?"

"Hanna. She just talked with your uncle. They have the pastor in custody along with the notebook. They're waiting for us at his office."

Fifteen minutes later, the four of them were sitting in Ambassador Ben Hur's reception area. They had only been there a couple of minutes when the office door opened, and Ambassador Ben Hur appeared in the threshold. Behind him, Thomas saw a man with his hands cuffed behind his back sitting in a chair facing the mammoth mahogany desk. At least three men in suits stood erect.

"Michael, Thomas, you both look remarkably well. Come in. I think your quest is about to take a giant leap forward."

The four walked to the door. Thomas followed Hanna in. He counted eight armed men standing on either side of the bound man. After a few more steps, Thomas confirmed the bound man's identity as the younger Pastor Willingham. The man's eyes were wild, darting around chaotically, terror emanating from his quivering body. He rocked back and forth, uttering repeatedly, "No, please, no."

Thomas turned when he heard Michael's firm resolve that Delia was going to enter. The ambassador had positioned his body between her and the door, resolving just as loudly that she was not entering his office. Two guards entered the reception area, obviously to enforce the ambassador's wishes.

Thomas stepped to the ambassador and in a calm, even tone said, "Remember our agreement? If you want me to continue the search, she's with us every step of the way."

The ambassador stared incredulously at Thomas, who waited with raised eyebrows. He then looked at Michael, whose thick brows were definitely crinkled downward. With a slight move of his hand, he waved off the men in the reception room and grudgingly stepped aside for Delia to enter. Thomas shook his head and marveled at her composure during these public affronts against her.

With the conflict over Delia settled for the moment, the ambassador slipped behind the desk and eased into his chair. On the desk before him lay the manila envelope and blue spiral notebook that Thomas recognized as the items he had temporary custody of before he was arrested. His heart raced. He wanted nothing more than to reach out, grab the envelope, and search it to see what was important enough to cause the death of a man.

"Mr. Willingham," the ambassador said, "My patience is gone. I'm going to ask you one more time. What do you know of the items in this envelope?"

Tears streamed down the pastor's cheek. "I told you, I don't know what it is. The detective gave it to me after he interviewed that man." The pastor nodded at Thomas. "Ask him. He brought it from my father's apartment."

"If that's true, then why are you so upset? Makes me think you're hiding something from me."

"I'm not—"

"And why are you so adamant to return home with the envelope and notebook?"

The silence was heavy as everyone waited for the pastor to explain. He bowed his head and quietly gave in to the ambassador. "The men who killed my father were waiting for me and my family when we returned from the detective's office. When I pulled into the parking lot, I saw someone climbing into the window at the back of the house. I turned the car around and fled. Almost immediately, I heard an explosion. I pray if I just give the men what they're after, they'll leave me and my family alone."

Again, silence filled the office. The pastor's eyes darted from person to person, pleading for someone to believe him. Thomas's heart went out to him. He looked frightened. Coupled with the loss of his father and then the attempt on his family's life, it was no wonder he was a nervous wreck.

The ambassador looked at the pastor and then to the others in the room. Hanna and Michael shrugged and raised their eyebrows. Thomas, however, replayed the pastor's story in his mind while matching it against what he knew to be true. There was a piece missing, but he couldn't put his finger on what it was.

"Well, Pastor Willingham," the ambassador said as he folded his hands upon his desk, "I'm going to allow you to leave, but I must insist on keeping the envelope and its contents with me."

"No! You must allow me to take them. I told you—"

The ambassador stopped him by raising his hand. "I'm sorry, but this is a matter of national security."

Delia whispered something to Michael, who immediately produced a pen and a business card from his pocket. She scribbled something on the back and handed it to Michael, who silently read it and handed it to Thomas.

"Please, sir, take a copy of the contents, but you must let me have the originals. My family will die if you don't."

"I'm sorry, but I cannot do that. I'll arrange to have you and your wife protected for a few days or make arrangements for you to return to the United States if you're so inclined."

"He's lying."

All eyes turned to Thomas. "Who's lying, Thomas?" the stunned ambassador asked.

"Pastor Willingham. Oh, I believe him about his run-in with the assassins and the burning of his house, but the only fear he has is he'll miss a large payday by not being able to sell the envelope to Azim."

# CHAPTER 19

EVERYONE IN THE ambassador's office was stunned at Thomas's indictment of the pastor, especially Pastor Willingham, who, at the mention of Azim's name, sat wide-eyed with his mouth gaping open. He recovered rather quickly, but not before convincing Thomas he was dead-on with his conclusion.

"I don't know any Azim, and I'm certainly not trying to sell anything. My father died over this, for heaven's sake. Everything I've told you is the God-honest truth."

"Thomas, maybe you'd better explain yourself."

"I'd be happy to, Ambassador. Everything the pastor said seems plausible, but something about his story just didn't settle with me. I'd no idea what it was, and I was about to shrug it off when Delia wrote this." He placed the back of the business card on the desk and slid it to the ambassador, who picked it up and read it.

The ambassador looked at Delia for a long moment and then back to Thomas. Hanna stepped forward and extended her hand. "What is it, Ambassador?" He handed her the card, which she read aloud: "I've seen this man meet with my brother on two occasions. I'm sure of it."

Willingham jerked his head around and for the first time saw Delia standing in the back of the room. "You!" This time he didn't attempt to recover from his incriminating expression.

"Before I fell unconscious at the pastor's house, I saw a photocopy of the parchment your nephew found. The only way the pastor could have obtained it is if Azim had given it to him. Michael made no copy, and Azim has the original.

Based on that and on Delia's recollection, it's obvious the pastor was dealing with Azim behind his father's back, presumably to sell what his father had on the Samson Effect." He stepped over to the pastor, who refused to look him in the eyes. "How much was Azim willing to pay for the notebook?"

"She's mistaken. I've never seen her or her brother before."

The ambassador addressed Delia for the first time since meeting her. "Are you positive this is the man?"

"I have no doubts whatsoever."

"I don't know why she's saying this," the pastor pleaded, "because I've never seen her before in my life. Please, you must believe me."

The ambassador leaned back in his chair and brought his fingers to his lips. After a few moments, he called over one of his men. "James, put the word on the street that a pastor has come to us with written information about my nephew's current work. Don't give a name or nationality; just say it was a pastor."

"What are you doing?" the pastor asked, fear flooding his eyes.

"Simple. If you're telling the truth, then when Azim gets this message, you'll have nothing to worry about. But if you're lying, well, I'm sure you understand your predicament."

Without pause, the pastor snapped out his response. "My family will take you up on your offer to leave for America immediately."

Thomas felt the surge of victory rush through him. He felt, for the first time, that he was in control of his quest; and he wasn't about to lose that edge. "Hold up, Ambassador." He stepped in front of the pastor. "Mr. Willingham, before you go anywhere under Israeli protection, you're going to answer a few questions."

The ambassador smiled and nodded to an empty chair in the corner of the room. "Please, make yourself comfortable, Dr. Hamilton."

Thomas positioned the chair so he was sitting directly across from Willingham. "Just three simple questions. First, how did you come across knowledge of the Samson Effect? Your father?"

"No, at least not directly. He just returned from a trip to Rome a few days ago. While he was gone, I found the notebook quite by accident."

"Okay, then how did you manage to meet up with Azim?"

"I found the story of a magical weed turning people into Superman entertaining. I mentioned it to a few people, and we had a good laugh over it. Somehow, word got back to Azim, who sent someone to make an offer to me. He said he'd buy the notebook for fifty thousand dollars. By then Dad was back, so I had to wait for an opportunity to take the notebook."

He turned to the ambassador with watery eyes. "Sir, you've known me for years. You know I loved my father, and I would never have gotten into this had I known it would cause his death. I just thought fifty thousand dollars would help me take better care of my family."

"I knew your father, not you. When you lied to me, you spoiled any personal affection I may have had for you. It's only because of my friendship with your father that I'm going to help you leave Israel."

Delia inserted herself into the conversation. "If my brother ever believes you've betrayed him and takes it personally, there's nowhere you can hide from him. You're as good as dead." The whole time she was talking to Willingham, her eyes were fixed upon Michael.

"I'm sorry, but she's right," the ambassador said. Willingham grew still and very pale. Thomas scooted his chair away from him, fearing the pastor was about to be sick to his stomach.

"What's your last question, Thomas?" the ambassador asked.

Delia's words still echoed in his ears. He felt a gut-wrenching pain, not for Willingham, but for Delia and Michael. He knew every day Azim lived could potentially be the last for his friends. He slowly blinked his eyes to help clear his mind. When he opened them, he saw Willingham was as pale as ever. "Last question: what else do you know about the substance that gives men great strength?"

"Nothing. I found nothing except the notebook, and my father never mentioned it to me."

Thomas stood and picked up the envelope and looked in it. He pulled out the rabbi's old notebook that Arnold Willingham had described to him. He flipped through it and slipped it back into the envelope with Willingham's notebook. He then tucked the envelope under his arm. The ambassador leaned forward with a scowl. "What are you doing?"

"Michael and I have a few hours to read over this tonight. Tomorrow, I want the four of us, along with the protection you promised, on a helicopter heading for Hebron." He looked at Michael and smiled. "We still have a couple of caves to search."

*       *       *       *

Thomas held a slice of New York-style pizza with both hands. "Pizza? We're in the Middle East, and you ordered pizza?"

"But I like pizza," Michael countered in defense of his meal choice.

An empty box sat on the foot of Michael's bed while he, Thomas, and the two women finished off their last piece. A chorus of agreements from Hanna and Delia put the issue to rest. Neither woman had spoken a word to each other throughout the meal. Upon their simultaneous agreement about the pizza, they averted their gaze from each other and sat in silence.

Thomas tossed his unfinished crust into the box and rested his elbows on the table, looking from Hanna to Delia. When he looked at Michael, his friend rolled his eyes and shook his head. Thomas's frustration over the friction between the two women had just reached his boiling point. He smacked his hand against the table's surface, cracking the serene atmosphere.

"That's it; enough is enough!" Everyone's eyes swiftly locked onto him, and the chewing came to an abrupt halt. "Here's the deal. Michael and I have work to do, and it's going to take every bit of physical and mental strength we can muster. The last thing we need is for you two to continue with your catty, schoolgirl behavior toward each other."

Both women's eyes nearly popped from their sockets. They were about to respond when Thomas held out his hand. "I'm not through. Either you two decide right now to be civil to each other, at least in my presence—"

Michael interrupted with a weak voice and tentatively raised a hand. "Mine too."

Thomas whipped his head toward Michael, unable to keep the fire from his eyes for being interrupted. Michael dropped his hand and lowered his head, deferring the floor back to Thomas. Thomas took a breath and continued. "Either you two find a way to get along, or Michael and I go to Hebron alone."

Now the fire spread into both women's eyes. Delia was the first to challenge Thomas. "You wouldn't dare!" She whipped her head toward Michael. "Tell him!"

Thomas let out a sigh of relief when his friend answered. "I'm with him. Either you both go or you both stay. Your choice." Michael shook his head and looked at each girl. "I don't know why you're making us go through this; you're both big girls."

Hanna folded her arms across her chest. "I don't care what you say; I'm going. The ambassador won't have it any other way. And, frankly, I'm appalled at your outburst and insinuations."

"Trust me, the ambassador wants me to go far more than he wants you to go." Thomas nodded toward Delia. "If I promised to leave Delia behind if he would order you to stay, how quickly do you think he'd take me up on my offer?"

For a moment there was a chilly silence in the room. Thomas finally decided to thaw the situation somewhat. In a sincere, soothing voice, he said, "Look, Michael and I truly want you to come; heck, we *need* you to come, but not if you're going to constantly be at each other." He picked up the envelope and motioned for Michael to follow. He opened the door and said, "Michael and I are going to my room to start going through this material. You two discuss what you're going to do and then let us know."

They shut the door behind the fuming women. Thomas opened his door and flipped on the lights. The two men melted into their chairs, taking a minute to envelop themselves in this serene haven. With his eyes closed, Michael asked, "Do you think it was wise to leave them alone in there?"

Thomas sighed. "I really don't know."

✳    ✳    ✳    ✳

Judas pulled into the parking lot of Arnold Willingham's church and home. When he saw the burnt shell of the parsonage next door, he knew something had gone terribly wrong. With late evening approaching, the traffic along the busy roadway had already dwindled to a trickle. He parked next to the church building and stepped out of the car.

He looked around in the darkness, hoping to find Tobin and Aaron, but the place seemed deserted. He ascended the steps at the side of the building to the door with the dedicated doorbell to Arnold's downstairs residence. He pushed the button and waited. A few moments later, he hit the button again and glanced up at the video camera the church had installed so Arnold could see from his apartment who was at the door. No sound stirred within the church building. He descended the steps and was about to get back into his car when a voice from the front of the building called to him.

"Can I help you?"

Judas squinted at the silhouette of a man who cautiously took a few steps toward him from the front of the church. "I'm here to see Arnold Willingham."

"Dear God," an elderly female voice said as another, shorter silhouette appeared next to the man. "He doesn't know."

"Know what?" Judas asked as he stepped toward the couple.

The two did not run, but the woman's hand quickly clutched the man's arm. As he approached, Judas could finally make out the sullen details on the elderly couple's faces.

The old man shook his head and spoke quietly. "Pastor Willingham died today—"

"Was killed," the woman clarified. "Oh, it's so terrible. Were you a friend of the pastor?"

Judas had only met Willingham occasionally when he and Simon had accompanied the rabbi to Jerusalem. However, the affection the rabbi had for him made Judas give no thought in sending Aaron and Tobin to him after the rabbi's death. "Yes I am," Judas answered weakly. "I'm shocked to hear of his death. The burnt house, was it recent also?"

"Today. The firefighters just left." The old man shook his head. "Praise the Lord the pastor's son and family were spared."

"That is fortunate." Judas thought for a moment. "Perhaps I could speak with the pastor's son. Two friends of mine were staying with his father. Maybe he could tell me where I could find them."

The couple froze, their eyes wide and their mouths gaping open. Judas grew uncomfortable at their reaction and silence. "Sir, do you know where I might find the pastor's son?"

"Friend, let me make a call to see if I can find them. Mind waiting here for a few minutes?"

"No, I ... I guess not." He watched the man nudge the woman, snapping her from what appeared to be a trance, and the two disappeared around the front corner of the building. Judas reluctantly stepped back to his car and leaned against the hood.

A few seconds later, the silence was shattered by the start of a car's engine and the squealing tires. Judas bolted from the car and ran to the front of the church in time to see the old couple fly from the church drive onto the street. He watched as their taillights disappeared around the corner of the first intersection.

Whatever was going on, Judas knew it would be best if he left immediately. He jogged to his car, but a familiar voice from the darkness behind the church stopped him cold.

"Rabbi."

He peered into the darkness. "Tobin? Is that you?"

Two figures emerged from the darkness. When they approached the car, Judas let out a sigh. "Tobin, Aaron, what's going on?"

"Get in the car. We have to get out of here, now!"

Aaron slipped into the backseat while Tobin slid behind the wheel and started the car. Without arguing, Judas went around to the passenger side and got in. Before he even closed the door, Tobin took off.

"Tobin, what's going on?"

Tobin held up a hand and picked up a cell phone. He punched in a few numbers and waited.

"This is Tobin. We have the rabbi … Israeli police will soon be after us. I need to ask you to trade cars with us … thank you. We'll meet you out front in a couple of minutes."

Tobin ended the call and dropped the phone into his lap. Without taking his eyes from the road, he began filling Judas in on what was happening. "The police are looking for Aaron and me for killing the pastor. The old couple you were talking to knew that and probably headed for the police when they linked you to us. They've been there since the house burned down. Aaron and I found a hiding place close to the church, hoping to see you if you came tonight."

"But how did you know I'd be here? I wasn't planning to be here for a week or two."

Tobin turned to Judas. "What? Didn't my sister call you and ask you to come?"

"No, no one called me. I came because I heard you'd lost the envelope I gave you."

Tobin fixed his eyes back upon the road. His audible swallow confirmed he was unaware Judas knew he had lost the envelope.

"Please tell me you have the envelope."

The car's engine was the only noise Judas heard.

"Tobin? You didn't lose the envelope, did you?"

Tobin closed his eyes for a moment and nodded.

"Dear God, no! This can't be happening. Do you know what was in that envelope?"

Neither Tobin nor Aaron answered.

"The location of the power of the Lord's Strength and the key to access it!" Judas balled his hand into a fist and, in frustration, brought it down. His hand sliced through the glove compartment as though it were a Styrofoam egg carton.

They heard sirens whine in the distance. Judas felt a surge of anger sweep through him like he had never felt before. All he wanted to do was lash out at Tobin and break his neck with his bare hands. It took every ounce of self-control he could muster to fight off the urge. When his blind rage finally passed, his hands trembled as he realized how close he had come to killing his friend. His bouts of anger were growing increasingly stronger and harder to control. With calm resolution, he asked, "Where is it?"

Aaron spoke up for the first time. "The last time we saw it one of the pastor's American friends had it." He pulled a folded sheet of paper from his pocket and handed it to Judas.

Judas studied the paper. It was the first page of the article written by Dr. Thomas Hamilton. There was a picture of the author in the upper left-hand corner.

"That is the man who took the envelope," Aaron said. "Tobin and I heard him and the pastor talking about what we protect. The doctor called it the Samson Effect."

The conversation stopped when Tobin whipped the car into the drive of a dark house silhouetted in the light from a full moon. Outside, a woman stood waving them forward. The three men got out of the car, and the woman ran to Tobin, draping her arms around his neck and kissing him on the cheek.

Tobin took a step back. "Rabbi, this is my sister. She's going to help us."

Judas nodded his greeting, yet felt anxious because of the lingering sirens still in the background.

Tobin and his sister exchanged keys. "Take the rabbi's car and go. I'm sure they have the description. If God is with us, you may be able to buy us some time."

Tobin's sister nodded and slipped a piece of paper into his hand. "This is the phone number and directions to a friend's home. He's waiting to take you in and hide you for as long as you need protection."

Tobin thanked her and went to the car. When they were in, he rolled down the window as his sister approached. "I gave him the name of the doctor you're looking for, and he says he knows him. He seemed eager to help you find him." She looked past her brother to Judas. "Godspeed, Rabbi."

Judas smiled and nodded his appreciation. Tobin started the car and turned left out of the drive. In the rearview mirror, he watched his sister leave to the right. He handed the folded directions to the rabbi, who navigated the rest of the way.

Fifteen minutes later they pulled into the circular drive of a large, middle-class home situated in the midst of a suburban neighborhood. The front-door light came on, and a thin, middle-aged man met them at the door. "May I ask which of you is the rabbi?"

"That depends," Aaron said cautiously. "Who are you?"

The man smiled. "Yes, of course. Forgive me." He fished his wallet from his pocket and flipped it open. Next to a Jerusalem police photo ID rested a police badge. "I'm Detective Ari Hazan."

# CHAPTER 20

"PLEASE COME IN and sit down." Hazan extended an inviting hand inside and stepped aside to make way for the three men to enter.

Judas shifted his eyes from Tobin to Aaron, both of whom awaited his instructions. The menacing sirens remained in the background, but still worried Judas enough that he warily nodded to his host and led the others in. They all took a seat on the extended sofa.

"May I offer you something to drink?" Before they could answer, Hazan's enthusiasm erupted. "I'm honored to have you in my home." With a juvenile smile and trying to hide his giddiness, he turned to Judas. "Especially you, Rabbi."

The three men looked at each other quizzically. Judas stood and stepped to Hazan. "Who are you, and what do you know about me?"

The expressions of joy morphed into confusion, accentuated by his shrinking smile. Then, as if baptized with understanding, his eyes widened, and his smile stretched to full length. "The rabbi hadn't revealed the Council to you. Of course."

Hazan's nonsensical comments began to stir the seeds of Judas's anger. Hazan apparently sensed Judas's growing aggravation and motioned for him to sit again as he himself slid into the chair facing the couch. "Let me explain." He nervously eyed Aaron and Tobin. "May we speak alone?"

"No," came Judas's adamant reply. "What you need to say, you may say in front of these two."

All joy washed from Hazan's expression, replaced by nervous indecision. "You don't understand—"

"That's right, and you're not helping me to understand. Now tell me what you wish, or my friends and I will handle our affairs on our own."

"No! You mustn't risk it. Please, Rabbi, it's for your own protection."

Judas stood and unceremoniously strode to the door. "Tobin, Aaron, we're leaving."

"Okay, okay." Judas stopped and turned to the detective. Hazan wiped his brow with his sleeve. "The Council won't like this at all."

They seated themselves, and Hazan let out a sigh. "There's a council of ten who guards the Protector and takes care of his needs. We're all in positions of influence in Israel, and we were to be introduced to you by the rabbi next week."

"The rabbi never mentioned a council to me, either orally or in writing."

"He wouldn't have. For centuries, the Council has existed without written record or awareness by anyone except fellow members, an enforcer, and the Protector himself." His eyes shifted to Tobin and Aaron. "That is, until today. The Council is not going to be happy at all."

"How do you know my sister?" Tobin interrupted.

"When the rabbi told the Council two months ago he'd be choosing Judas or Simon to pass on his responsibilities, I took the opportunity to create friendships with families of both."

"So, she doesn't know about the Council?" Judas asked.

"Heavens, no. She only sees me as a trusted friend."

"I suppose you've heard of the rabbi's death, then."

"Yes. It filled the Council with panic since we weren't sure if he'd chosen his successor and passed on the secret." A smile swept across Hazan's face. "And then we heard stories of a man in Hebron who bent a rifle barrel. Our emotions were mixed, with relief he'd apparently made his choice and with apprehension from the public display of power. It was only when we looked into the rumors that we learned of the rabbi's death."

Judas felt overwhelmed by what he had just heard. Until now, he had believed he, Tobin and Aaron were alone with their great responsibility. A wave of relief washed over him. However, he felt he needed to put Hazan to the test in order to confirm the detective's legitimacy. If there was, indeed, a council as Hazan had described, Judas knew it would not want the secret hiding place of the source of the Lord's Strength revealed to them. The rabbi had insisted he and Judas were the only two people on earth who knew the location.

Judas stood and paced thoughtfully through the room. All was silent as each man watched and waited. He finally stopped and turned to Hazan. "I want you to send someone to bring the secret to me in Jerusalem. It's in danger of being discovered."

"What?" Hazan flew to his feet, and years of tough-nosed interrogation experience took over. "What do you mean, it's in danger?"

The depth of the paleness that washed over Hazan's face surprised Judas. "First things first; I want you to have it brought safely to me now."

Hazan violently shook his head. "But we cannot. We don't know where it is."

Judas peered into Hazan's frightened, dilated eyes. After a moment's hesitation, he said, "I'll tell you—"

Hazan covered his ears with his hands and cried out. "No! No! You must never, *never* share that information with anyone except your successor!"

Judas smiled and waited for Hazan to remove his hands. "I now believe what you told me." He watched as the color slowly returned to Hazan's face.

An audible sigh escaped from the detective's mouth. "For a moment, I feared you were telling the truth about the secret's location being in danger of being compromised."

Judas pulled out the cover page of Dr. Thomas Hamilton's article and handed it to Hazan. "Do you know the man in the photo?"

Hazan gave it a cursory glance. "Yes. I spoke with him today, as a matter of fact. Why?"

"Because I was telling the truth about the secret being compromised. This man has directions to the secret, and the means to access it." He watched Hazan stumble into the chair as the color once again drained from his face. "I need your help in getting it back."

For a moment, Hazan seemed paralyzed. Then, suddenly, he snapped into action. He grabbed the phone and dialed. Placing his hand over the mouthpiece, he said, "We must convene the Council first thing tomorrow morning."

✳    ✳    ✳    ✳

Light from the lamp poured over the table in Thomas's room. He and Michael sat spellbound, poring over the contents of the envelope. Not only did the material in the notebook confirm the ancient writings about the Samson Effect, it also revealed Protectors were still searching for and guarding the secret. A chill ran through Thomas's body as he imagined that somewhere, someone at this very moment had intimate knowledge of this "ancient" secret.

Thomas watched Michael examine the metal key that had weighed down the envelope. "What do you think it is?"

Michael shook his head. "I don't know. The notebook calls it a key that leads to the altar room and then to the secret of the Lord's Strength." Michael turned the key around in the palm of his hand and examined it from every angle. "Doesn't look like any key I've ever seen."

"Let me see it."

Michael tossed the key to Thomas, who examined it for the first time. It was cylindrical and the size and weight of a small stone. There were no carvings on it, only ridges and grooves of varying thickness around its circumference. Thomas imagined if he rolled it on an inkpad and then onto a white sheet of paper, he'd find a pattern that would look like a common UPC bar code. One end of the cylinder was flat with tiny scuffmarks embedded in the surface. The other end was hollowed out. To Thomas it looked like a large thimble.

He absentmindedly stuck his forefinger and middle finger into the hollowed end and began tapping the "key" on the tabletop. He pursed his lips and looked up at Michael. "Do you suppose this really does unlock the hiding place to the surviving sample of the Effect?"

"Are you kidding? Solomon reigned about 900 BC or so. What vegetation do you know of that could have survived for three thousand years?" Michael let out a quiet chuckle. "At least I was on the right track. The Samson Effect is a plant, and if the notebook is correct, the seeds have been lost since the Protector during the reign of King Rehoboam died before letting his successor know what he'd done with them. Apparently, no Protector since has been able to solve the riddle of the seeds being hidden in Satan's belly."

Michael rubbed his eyes with his palm. "I hope that if we find the seeds there's enough left to identify the type of plant they came from."

"If we're really lucky, we'll find dormant seeds that can germinate."

Michael's laughter bellowed out and filled the small hotel room. "You actually think three-thousand-year-old seeds can survive and remain fertile?" He smiled. The slight nod of his head teased Thomas, who knew he was about to be the butt of unmerciful banter. "You're the archaeologist. Ever hear of King Tut's wheat?"

Thomas's cheeks grew hot. "Of course I've heard of King Tut's wheat, but apparently your knowledge of botany and seed viability is pretty limited."

Thomas stared at Michael and shook his head at his friend's implication. Every archaeologist knew of the American airman who, during World War II, came across a street vendor in Egypt who sold him thirty-six kernels of grain he claimed was found preserved in a pharaoh's tomb. The young man sent the kernels to his father, a farmer in Montana, who successfully grew the seeds. Eventually, the public went crazy over what was dubbed "King Tut's wheat."

Science, however, disproved the theory that the kernels came from an ancient tomb, and it eventually identified the grain as a little-known grain from Egypt now known as kamut. Grains such as wheat, the scientist had explained, can remain dormant and viable for about thirty years, maybe ninety under ideal circumstances, but certainly not for thousands of years.

Michael continued his relentless jabs at his educated friend. "Have you ever heard of grain remaining viable after being found in an ancient archaeological site?"

"Not exactly," Thomas intoned in a deep, steady monotone. "But for your information, lotus seeds have been found in ancient lake beds in Manchuria, which carbon 14 has dated as between 830 to 1,250 years old. And guess what? When planted, they sprouted, and some even flowered!"

The smile slowly faded from Michael's face as he took on the appearance of a man lost in deep thought. It was not until now, in silence, that Thomas realized he was breathing heavily. He couldn't believe how easily Michael had pushed his buttons. But, he thought, so what if it showed he was a little ruffled. It was worth it to see Michael's expression right now.

To Thomas's satisfaction, Michael cocked his head and nodded, apparently conceding the point to Thomas. "I see. You may be right. All we need to do is find under which river the Samson Effect seeds are buried …"

"I'm just saying—"

"No, no, no," Michael interrupted. "I agree. You're correct. The seeds must be as big and as rock hard as those thousand-year-old lotus seeds."

"I get your point," Thomas fumed. "I didn't say it was probable, just possible."

"Wow. You might be the first archaeologist to ever find ancient, dormant, viable seeds hidden away by another culture."

"Look, Michael, can we just drop this, please. It's getting old."

Michael's eyes grew as wide as saucers as he mimicked the starstruck expression of a groupie who just ran face-to-face into her idol. He slid a piece of paper to Thomas and, without breaking eye contact, asked, "Would you please sign your autograph for me?"

Thomas's bubbling anger quickly cooled as he took control of himself and realized Michael was just trying to get a rise from him. He whipped a pen from his pocket, scribbled illegible squiggles on the paper, and floated it back to Michael. "You'd better hang onto that. It'll be worth something some day."

There was a light rapping at the door. When Thomas got up to open it, he heard the unmistakable crinkling sound of paper being wadded up. He smiled, shook his head, and opened the door. Delia and Hanna stood side by side, neither looking particularly happy.

Thomas held the door wide open and stepped out of the way. "Looks like we've got company."

Michael craned his neck to watch the women walk through the door. "They seem to be okay. No blood, no bruises." Delia's icy gaze silenced Michael and forced him to sink into his chair.

Thomas closed the door and slipped to the perceived safety of the table next to Michael. "So, what did you two decide?"

"We decided you're right," Hanna said coyly. "Frankly, we're offended you treated us like children, but we both know it's important not to create added burdens on you."

Thomas's apprehension melted away. He looked at Michael and smiled. "Great. It's amazing what we can do if we just act like adults."

"I must say, I'm pleasantly speechless," Michael confessed.

Thomas was relieved that the tension between Hanna and Delia was resolved. He actually looked forward to the morning trip the four of them would make together to the caves. He was about to suggest Hanna accompany him to the lobby for a nightcap when he caught sight of her furious expression. Instead, he froze, not quite knowing what to say.

Apparently, Michael didn't think the anger daggers were aimed at him because he got up and confidently approached Delia. He reached out and gently gripped her arm. "Come on, Delia. Let's get some sleep. 5:00 a.m. comes awfully early."

Delia shrugged her forearm from Michael's grasp. "Hanna and I have booked the last room left in the hotel. We decided it would be better to spend it with each other than with you two. We'll see you boys at breakfast at six."

Together, they turned and marched to the door. They stepped into the hall; but before closing the door, Hanna looked at Thomas with a mischievous grin. "And if either of you want anything more than a cordial, professional relationship over the next few days, we'd suggest you learn real quickly how *not* to speak to us in the future."

# CHAPTER 21

THOMAS AND MICHAEL stepped into the hotel's dining area a few minutes before 6:00 a.m. Delia and Hanna were already seated at a small table for two along the wall. Their breakfast plates and drinks covered the entire surface of the small table, leaving no room for the men to join. As they approached, both women looked up at them and smiled, and then returned to their conversation. Thomas and Michael smiled back and slipped into the chairs at the small table behind them.

The waiter appeared and took their order. In a few minutes, they began dining on a continental breakfast. The men ate their breakfast silently until it became apparent the women were not yet interested in forgiving them.

Thomas cleared his throat, determined not to let the women's icy behavior dampen his excitement for the day's excursion. He matched the women's muted tone as he buttered his muffin. "How do you want to go about checking out the rabbi's house?"

"I've been thinking about that. The house is right in the middle of a Palestinian-controlled neighborhood. How the Jews have been able to retain control over it for centuries is beyond me. Obviously, Azim doesn't have a clue the sample may be in there, or he'd have found a way inside. To tell the truth, I'm not quite sure how we can manage to search for the altar room without calling attention from both the Jews and the Palestinians."

"You do still think it's worth checking out though, don't you?"

"Absolutely. I figured we'd check out the two caves today while we think of a way to get into the house." Michael lowered his already muted volume. "I think it's wise for us to keep the knowledge of the altar room to ourselves for the time being. Right now, you're the only one I have 100 percent trust in."

"I've been thinking the same thing. In fact, I think we should hold everything we find close to our vests until we know it's safe to share it with anyone." Thomas stole a sly glance over his shoulder. "Be prepared to face your uncle's fury and the women's when they find out we've been hiding something from them."

"What are you two talking about?"

Thomas looked up to see Hanna approaching the table. "Oh, nothing of consequence. You two ready for today?"

Hanna couldn't hold in the smile. "To tell the truth, I've not been this excited for a long time."

"Michael, you done eating?" Thomas asked.

Michael picked up the juice and downed it. He stood, picked up a muffin, and took a bite. "I guess." He looked at his wristwatch. "The colonel should be in the lobby in five or ten minutes. Let's wait for him in there."

They entered the hotel's lobby to find Colonel Yarconi already seated on a couch waiting for them. Standing around him were four soldiers dressed in full combat gear, complete with their assault rifles held against their chests. Thomas felt uneasy seeing military personnel dressed to kill standing idly by in such a public place. He glanced at his friends' faces, but they didn't seem to give it a second's thought. He was beginning to realize just how well he had it back home, at least when he wasn't wanted for murder.

Colonel Yarconi stood and extended a hand to Michael. "I see you're already up and ready to go."

Everyone nodded to each other as the colonel introduced the four-man team that would accompany them to Hebron. "You have until sunset," the colonel continued, "to be back in Jerusalem. These men will watch your backs everywhere you go and reinforcements are just a radio call away. Any questions?"

Having no questions, the group followed the colonel out of the hotel and loaded into a military transport vehicle. A few minutes later, they boarded a large helicopter and were soon heading south.

Thomas studied Michael's crude map. They agreed that after checking out Snake Cave Number Three, they would have the pilot fly around Hebron to see if other parts of the city's landscape had features of a serpent.

Michael leaned forward and tapped the pilot on the shoulders. "I need you to sweep around the south of Hebron so I can get my bearings."

The pilot nodded, and the four of them planned their day in detail in order to take full advantage of their borrowed chopper. Every now and then Thomas asked the soldiers questions; but after endless one-word answers and no interaction on their part, he finally gave up and turned his full attention to his friends.

As they passed by a mountain, Thomas interrupted Michael and pointed out the window. "We're here. There's the mountain we were on when you drew the map."

Michael glanced out the window and then looked at his map. Once he was oriented, he again tapped the pilot on the shoulder and gave him directions to Snake Cave Number Three. The pilot made a slight bank to the right, and Michael returned to his conversation with the women. The four soldiers gathered up their equipment and checked their rifles.

Thomas leaned his head against the window and stared into the desert, wondering if everything they were doing was futile. He wondered if the Samson Effect even existed at all. As he silently debated, something in the receding distance caught his eye and jarred him to a rigid posture. With his hands and face plastered on the window, he felt his breath go shallow.

"Pilot, turn around at once. Head back to the tall mountain."

The pilot kept his course but turned to look at Michael for approval. Michael's conversation with the women halted abruptly as all eyes were riveted on him. Even the soldiers froze in their preparation for landing and looked questioningly at him."

"What is it, my friend?"

"Just turn this thing around, and I'll show you."

Michael nodded to the pilot, who drew his attention back to his controls and initiated a much deeper bank than he had previously. Thomas jumped from his seat and moved to the other side of the chopper, squeezing between two soldiers. Soon all eight sets of eyes were peering out the window.

"Bring us within one hundred yards of the northeast side of that mountain."

The pilot moved them into position while Thomas waited to see if anyone else saw what he saw. He didn't have to wait long.

"Good heavens," Michael said with a touch of awe. "The belly of the devil."

By the gasps from the women, Thomas knew they saw it too. As they hovered next to the mountain, Thomas could clearly see the image of a snake embedded in the cave. The shadows of the overhanging rocks cast a dark, triangular shape of a snake's head against a smooth side of the cave. Right where the eyes should be, Thomas found two small indentations into the mountain. But it was the jaw of the rock serpent that made the sight surreal. A cave opened into the mountain with a stalactite dropping down like a menacing fang. What was apparently another fang had broken off, leaving a thick stump behind.

As the chopper hovered, the sun continued its path across the morning sky. The shadows that gave the snake's head its form slowly receded down the mountain until the surface no longer resembled a serpent. After a few more moments of surreal silence, the group burst out in unison with all kinds of questions. "How could someone see from this vantage point three thousand years ago?" "What are the odds we'd randomly choose the exact moment needed to see the serpent?" "How could the surface not have changed through erosion?"

Thomas silently listened to the chaotic chorus around him, but it was not enough to drown out his own thoughts. He sat back in his seat and marveled at their luck. It was about time he had some luck. He didn't know, nor at the moment did he care, how this discovery could have happened. A deep satisfaction drifted through him because it *had* happened. He heard Michael giving the pilot anxious instructions to land. When they touched down, a maverick thought came out of nowhere, something the elder Pastor Willingham said. If God wanted him to find it, he would. Thomas shuddered at the thought, yet still not bringing himself to believe in a deity. He tried to summon back the feelings of satisfaction; but the maverick thought lingered, cutting into his joy like a two-edged sword.

\*     \*     \*     \*

At 7:00 a.m., the first members of the Council began filing into Detective Ari Hazan's home. Hazan confided to Judas that this would be the first time since he had joined the Council that he would actually get to meet the chairman, who had always been out of town when the Council convened. In fact, since no one talked of Council matters, he did not even know the name of the chairman. Judas couldn't tell if Hazan was more excited to meet him or the chairman.

As the Council members started arriving, Judas remained alone in the kitchen and immersed himself in prayer while the other three men removed furniture from the living room and arranged the chairs into a circle. As more people entered, Judas finished his prayer and moved to a place in the kitchen where he could see the front door. Two well-dressed men in their fifties walked in and made brief greetings to Hazan before being seated.

Hazan's housekeeper brought a tray of refreshments to the men, who took a cup of espresso and then returned to their whispered conversation. Judas noticed that the men ignored Tobin and Aaron, only giving them cursory glances and shaking their heads. Over the next half-hour more men joined the group, until all ten were present. When the tenth man entered, Judas noticed that the expression on Hazan's face changed markedly. It was as if he had seen a ghost.

Once all the men were seated, the chairman of the Council cleared his throat, immediately ending the gentle murmurs in the room. "Before we begin, I must insist that you and you leave this house at once." The chairman pointed to Tobin and Aaron, who looked to Judas for guidance. After a brief pause, Judas nodded, and Hazan escorted them through the room and out a sliding door in the kitchen, where he seated them at a table next to the swimming pool. Judas smiled and nodded to them through the window and then turned his attention back to the chairman.

When Hazan returned to his seat, the chairman continued. "On behalf of the Council, let me tell you how honored we are to finally meet you, Rabbi." Nods and verbal agreement broke out in the room. When silence returned, the chairman said, "Please accept the heartfelt condolences on the death of your rabbi. I assure you it was as painful for us as it was for you."

Judas noted the sincerity in the chairman's eyes. The room was deathly silent until Judas's quiet response thundered through the room. "Thank you. I'm sure it was hard on you."

"Of course, these are not the circumstances in which we wanted our first meeting with you. Apparently, the rabbi made no mention to you of the Council or of our purpose."

Judas shook his head.

"Very well. For thousands of years this Council has existed for one purpose: to provide for the needs of the Protector of the Lord's Strength. I believe you know Detective Hazan; let me introduce each member to you."

The chairman went around the circle introducing each man. Some, Judas had heard of, but most he had not. In the group was a bank president, an import/ export entrepreneur, an army general, two mayors of prominent Israeli cities, a high-level official in Israel's Foreign Ministry, a multibillionaire who had his hands into everything, and a member of Parliament.

"And finally, that leaves me. My name is Benjamin Ben Hur, Israel's ambassador to the United States."

Suddenly Judas felt a wave of inferiority sweep over him. In his presence were some of the most powerful men in Israel. Even his great strength couldn't suppress the trembling that overtook his hands. Had he wanted to say something, he knew he wouldn't be able to. His mouth felt like someone had stuffed wads of cotton into it.

He glanced around the room. The eyes of these powerful men locked upon him only exacerbated the problem. Then his eyes met Detective Hazan's eyes. The familiar face was instantly soothing. Hazan was the only man in the room who he was not intimidated by. In fact, the more he considered Hazan, the more out of place the detective seemed in the presence of these men.

"Forgive me, but may I ask how a police detective became part of this Council? His station in life hardly seems to fit."

Judging by the detective's reaction, it seemed as though Judas had just stripped him naked in the midst of a jeering crowd of strangers. The detective averted his eyes from everyone as deep crimson colored his dark face. Instantly Judas regretted asking the question. He hadn't meant to humiliate Hazan.

The ambassador humanely broke the oppressive silence. "Each member of the Council chooses his own successor in much the same way as the Protector chooses his. Once every member approves the choice, we use what influence we may have to elevate, in your words, his station in life. Detective Hazan's predecessor died of a sudden heart attack before we had a chance to groom him for the position." The warmth of the ambassador's smile as he turned his attention to Hazan seemed to hearten the detective and take the sharp edge from Judas's question. "No need to worry. In short order he will be sitting among us as an equal in every sense of the word." The ambassador then turned back to Judas and in a nonaccusatory manner asked, "Does that alleviate any worries you have, Rabbi?"

Judas's embarrassment blossomed, and he let the issue die with a simple nod of his head.

"Good. Now before we administer the oaths and take up the issue that has brought us together today, we must have a confirmation that you have, indeed, received the sacred knowledge you claim to have."

"Of course," Judas said. "Tell me how you wish me to prove it."

"I believe a demonstration of your strength will suffice." For the first time since the meeting had started, the ambassador's eyes squinted and his voice became gravelly. "You are still under the effect of the Lord's Strength, aren't you?"

Judas gulped and silently nodded. Without taking his eyes from Judas, the ambassador said, "General ..."

The general rose from the chair and marched through the circle in an even cadence until he stood next to Judas. Judas looked up at him, wondering what demonstration the Council had in mind. It quickly became evident as the general reached for his holstered gun and pressed the barrel to Judas's temple. Judas's heart raced, and his eyes flew open. His brain sent messages to his muscles to flee, but the shot came too quickly.

Instinctively, Judas yanked the gun from the general's grip and smashed it in his hand as though it were a plastic toy. Shouts of "Rabbi" filled the house as Tobin and Aaron burst through the back door to their rabbi's aid.

"I said out!"

Tobin and Aaron stopped at the ambassador's shout. Their helpless eyes were glued to the rabbi as they waited for him to fall.

But he didn't.

The general bent down and picked up the pieces of his gun. The curious expression of every council member instantly changed to that of deep, almost godlike, reverence. Murmurs of "Rabbi" again filled the room.

Hazan, the newest member of the Council, ran up to Judas and pressed his fingers to Judas's temple. His expression betrayed his complete bewilderment. "But how? This is not possible. By Solomon's Temple, he's only flesh and blood!"

The ambassador's laughter filled the room. "How, you ask. It is of the Lord. The stories of Samson and the Judges, of King David's amazing feats, none are myths. You see the seriousness of our duty, don't you Ari?"

Hazan nodded feebly. "I've seen what gunshot wounds do to the human body, especially from point-blank range. The skin isn't even broken." He whipped his head toward Judas. "Do you feel any pain?"

Having not yet recovered from the shock of being shot in the head, Judas slowly shook his head while reaching his fingertips to his temple.

The ambassador's tone came soothingly and full of reassurance. "Ari, Ari, please my friend, if not for faith then accept what your own eyes have seen." The ambassador looked at the faces of the men in the circle. "It's a rare thing for our faith to be strengthened like this. The time will come when our work and sacrifice will be rewarded abundantly. The Messiah will come, and when he does, he'll restore Israel to its full glory. By this gift, the Army of God will once again be invincible."

The ambassador walked over to Judas and dropped to his knees. Following the custom of their spiritual father, Abraham, he slid his hand under Judas's thigh and administered his oath. "I swear on all I have and upon my very life to provide for you your every need, freeing you to answer the Lord's call. My riches, my possessions, my life are yours until the Lord breaks this bond by death."

Every member of the Council lined up behind the ambassador and administered the same oath, word for word, with adoration and sincerity. The last to pledge himself was Hazan. His voice trembled as he spoke his words. Rather than adoration and sincerity, Judas perceived fear in Hazan's voice.

When they finished and were seated, the ambassador moved to the issue at hand. "Now, about the secret which the rabbi protects being compromised; put your fears to ease. My nephew and his friends have the rabbi's notebook. I assure you it will be returned safely to him."

"But you know as well as we all do there can be no knowledge of the secret outside the Council," the general said.

"I know, and the time will come when those who know must be silenced."

"Even your nephew?" asked the bank president.

"If he does not accept the gift of succeeding me on the Council, yes." Judas perceived no doubt, no remorse in the ambassador's words. "However, we've never been so close in finding the source of the Lord's Strength. Give them time. The Lord may be answering our prayers through them."

Each Council member considered the request and agreed. The ambassador adjourned the meeting with a warning that caused each member to leave with a distressed spirit. "Azim Ebadi's sister has bewitched my nephew and searches for the secret with him. If they do find it, she'll be his Delilah and betray him to her brother. We all know what he'll do with the gift." Fear enveloped each member, and none attempted to mask it. "We must commit all resources to silence her when and if the secret is found … even if it means my nephew's death."

# CHAPTER 22

Two SOLDIERS CLIMBED to the mouth of the cave while the other two remained at the foot of the mountain. Already, the sun's heavy rays bore down on Thomas, heating the sweat his shirt had soaked up. He looked over his shoulder toward Michael and the women. Delia scaled the surface with the agility of a mountain goat. Hanna climbed much more tentatively, though Thomas was still impressed with her progress. It was the first time he remembered beating Michael in a physical challenge, yet victory over a man with cracked ribs was hardly something to celebrate.

Thomas could see the agony masked behind the determination etched on Michael's face. Each grunt from Michael echoed from the mountainside, and yet they seemed to give him the nudge he needed to make it up, inch by inch. Thomas looked up at the soldiers who waited to pull him to the level surface at the cave's mouth. He reached out a trembling hand to the soldier's vice grip, which pulled him the rest of the way.

He pulled the canteen from his belt and drained half its contents, dismissing Delia's earlier warning to conserve. A cool flush revitalized the strength the climb had zapped. He looked down at the approaching climbers, ready to lend his hand, but was relieved when the two soldiers made it clear they could handle it without his help.

He walked to the cave's entrance and peered inside. The opening led back about fifteen feet before sharply turning to the right. The passageway was just big enough for them to crawl into, one by one. He gripped the remaining stalactite fang, trying to envision the serpent's image he had seen from the helicopter. No matter how hard he tried, however, he could not re-create the vision from this vantage point. If not for the uncanny timing of their flight, he knew there was no way they would have been able to find the spot.

He turned to the rustling sound behind him and saw Delia's deep bronze arm extend and grip the soldier's hand as he hoisted her the remaining way up. She grabbed her canteen and tipped it back, gulping a little more water than her own advice should have allowed. Thomas smiled and dropped to a sitting position next to her. "I'm impressed. You're not even winded."

"Looks can be deceiving," she answered between breaths. "If you weren't in my way, though, I'd be up here already."

Thomas smiled. "Sure you would." He crawled to the cave and started inside. "Want to see where we're going?"

Delia followed close behind until they reach the first turn. Thomas took out his flashlight and aimed the beam into the black void. He cringed when he saw a steep pitch downward that extended beyond the light's reach. "Great," he mumbled as images of his painful slide in the other cave flooded to mind.

"You two, wait for us."

Thomas looked back at the cave's opening and saw one of the soldiers kneeling in and shining his light at them. "This is as far as we're going without you. Just wanted to get an idea of what lay ahead."

"What do you see?" Hanna's unmistakable figure silhouetted in the cave's entrance.

Thomas tapped Delia and pointed toward the exit. "Nothing really. Just a chute going down into the cave."

They emerged from the cave and saw Michael lying on his back with his hand shielding the sun from his eyes. He made no attempt to mask his exhaustion. As Thomas approached, he saw Michael's canteen lying empty next to his sweat-drenched body.

"You going to make it?"

Michael pulled his head to Thomas and held up a finger as he tried to catch his breath. "Yeah … just give me … a minute."

For the next few minutes they rested, and each ate a granola bar they had packed. One of the soldiers poured part of his water into Michael's canteen. When everyone seemed rested enough to continue, a soldier knelt next to the cave's entrance.

"If you're ready, let's get going."

As he entered the cave, Thomas stopped him. "I think it's best if I lead. I know what we're looking for, and I need a full view of what's before me."

"Sir, I think it's best I lead."

"You can be right behind me. We're more likely to run into trouble from behind anyway."

The soldier looked at his partner, who nodded. He stepped out of the way to let Thomas take the lead. Within a few minutes, the train of explorers was halfway down the steep chute. The walls and floor were rugged, winding and narrowing along the way. Thomas was sure the passageway was naturally formed, but the discarded water bottles and plastic wrappers let him know others had been down this way recently. His stomach tightened as he thought of the prospects that someone else may have found what they were looking for.

They continued down until the tunnel's grade began to level out. This must be the belly, Thomas thought. He shined his flashlight in front of him. It looked as if this part of the snake's belly was alive. The tunnel walls undulated and shivered in the darkness.

Thomas froze, not sure he wanted to go farther. "What is it?" the soldier behind asked.

Thomas squeezed next to the wall, giving the soldier a view ahead of him. "I don't know. Looks like the tunnel is alive."

"Alive?" Hanna asked.

The soldier reached to his hip and pulled up something. "Everyone, put your face to the ground and cover your heads. Don't look up until I give the word."

"Why? What's out there?" Thomas asked when he saw the soldier pull out his pistol.

"Bats. By the looks of it, thousands. A few gunshots should scare them out of here."

Thomas dropped to the ground and buried his face under his arms. He didn't like the thought of thousands of bats making a mad exodus out of the cave and flying chaotically over him. He closed his eyes and cursed himself for insisting to be in the lead.

For a few seconds, the silence eerily hung with anticipation.

The stuttering cracks of bullets pierced the silence, and the cave echoed with unnumbered screeches. Thomas not only heard the cries, he also felt them reverberate from head to toe. He wasn't sure, but he thought he also heard a woman's scream buried in the frightening screeches.

Then bats began to swarm. Thomas felt the rush above him and the wind from their flapping wings beating down upon him. Every so often one of the bats touched the top of his head or bounced from his legs. Every muscle in his body tensed as the roar of screeches rumbled above him. It went on and on until Thomas wondered if their exodus would ever end.

After what seemed an eternity, the screeches faded in intensity. Thomas began to feel hope that the ordeal would soon be over. He realized he had been holding his breath and let the stale air spill from his lungs. He gasped, sucking in rich oxygen.

Peaceful contentment washed over him. It was almost over. As he raised his head, a hand gripped his shoulders and forced him back to the ground. "Get down!" As soon as his face hit dirt, Thomas heard another round of gunfire.

The surge of bats increased but this time died away after a few seconds. Soon every sound receded until absolute silence returned. Thomas remained prone until he heard the all clear from the soldier. Only then did he lift his head.

He looked over his shoulder to see everyone slowly raising their heads. Thomas sucked in a breath and crawled forward. The stench left from the bats nearly overpowered him as he moved farther through the chute. A chamber quickly opened to a room about fifteen or twenty feet high and wide enough for the group to walk around freely in.

He reached to the wall to steady himself, and his hand pressed on something cold and slick. He pulled it back to find it covered with guano. He shined the light into the room and saw a slick layer of bat dung covering the floor. Maggots were squirming in it, their white bodies highlighted against the inky, dark mush. Cockroaches scurried across it surface. With the group silently urging him forward, he wiped his palms on his shirt and stood in the entrance. Stepping aside, he made room for each person to enter and listened to the "Yucks" and "Oohs" as they did. Someone's stomach retched. Thomas could have sworn it was from one of the soldiers.

He stepped carefully, feeling the guano ooze over the laces of his hiking boots. "Careful, the footing is slick." He continued to trudge through the murk while shining his light along the walls. He completed the room's circumference, finding no other exit. This was the end of the line.

"Well, what do you want to do now?" Michael asked, completing his own survey of the room.

"I don't know." Thomas massaged his closed eyes, trying to ward off his disappointment. "It's too much of a coincidence not to be the location we're looking for."

Hanna shined a light around the room. "Did you find anything that gives a clue as to where the Samson Effect may be hidden?"

"No," Thomas answered. "No markings, no sealed passages, nothing."

"Well, there's only one more place to look."

"Where?"

Hanna pointed her light at the guano.

"What? There?" Thomas looked to the floor and then to Hanna. "You think it's buried in bat dung?"

"Not exactly, but we may find something on the floor under it." She didn't wait for a response but started at the back corner of the room and used her boot to slide the guano away, revealing a smooth, stained surface.

"And what exactly are you looking for?" Michael asked.

"I don't *exactly* know. I was hoping you would tell me."

Thomas slid his toe through the guano and wrinkled his nose. "I guess it's not going to hurt to check." Everyone spread out at the back of the cave, side by side. Even the two soldiers agreed to help. "All right, we're looking for anything out of the ordinary."

"Out of the ordinary? What exactly does that mean?" Delia asked.

"It means anything that shouldn't naturally be here; a carving, a mark. I don't know. Just yell if you think you've found something."

Thomas heard Delia's muffled response, and knew she meant him to hear it. "That clears it up."

He didn't comment. Instead, he began sliding the guano away with his foot. Quietly, the others followed his lead. They were at it for fifteen minutes when Delia's shrill cry stopped the others in their tracks. "I've found something! Quick, look!"

Thomas sloshed over to her, followed by the others. Delia's knees sank into the guano as she frantically cleared an area two feet by two feet with her hands. A thin line formed a near perfect square, enhanced by the guano. Ignoring the sticky mess, Thomas dropped to his knees and ran his fingers along the line. "It's a cover. I'm sure of it."

He ran his fingertips along the surface of the rock slate. In the upper left corner, his fingers felt the indentation of surface carvings. He reached for his canteen and poured water on the corner. The water and his fingertips removed the guano enough for an etched image to become visible.

Delia gasped. "The mark."

Michael thrust his hand down and ran it over the etching. His fingers froze. He looked up at Thomas, and the two of them broke out in simultaneous laughter.

Michael motioned a soldier over. "You have anything to pry this up with?"

The soldiers began using every tool they had to try to pry up the stone, but nothing worked. Finally, they tried another tactic with Michael's approval. One soldier placed a chisel on the corner opposite the mark and picked up a stone. The cavern echoed from continuous poundings until, finally, the chisel broke through.

The soldier removed the chisel and Michael shoved his fingers into the hole. "It's hollow."

The hole made it easy for the soldiers to pry off the stone cover. Thomas shined his light into the cavity and saw a layer of tiny, white, coarse rocks about four inches down. Delia picked up one of the stones and examined it. "Salt. It's salt."

Michael examined one of the stones also. "I believe you're right."

Thomas started digging, throwing handful after handful of salt out of the hole. After removing about ten inches, his fingers struck a solid object. With renewed fervor, he dug around the object and uncovered a clay jar. He pulled it up and examined it. The jar was plain with no markings, and the top was still sealed. As he turned it over he could tell something was in it. It felt like sand or pebbles falling free within it.

Thomas held the jar delicately in his hand, gently brushing off the fine white dust with his thumbs. "We need to get this to a lab."

With deliberate swiftness, Michael grabbed the jar and thrust it against the stone lid. It shattered, spilling out yellow-white crystals. As the crystals spread away, a single dark sphere about the size of a golf ball rested on top.

Thomas's heart sank. "I can't believe you just did that!"

Michael picked up the sphere. "Come on, you wanted to know what was in there as much as we did."

Michael's utter disrespect for the ancient vessel caused indignation to bubble up inside of Thomas. However, the expressions on everyone's face made him bite his tongue. He picked up the yellow crystals and let them slip through his fingers. His indignation fled when he realized what he was holding. "Of course," he whispered.

"What?" Hanna asked.

He picked up more crystals and let them fall through his fingers again. "It's honey. Salt and honey, two of the most reliable forms of preservation in the ancient world."

"You mean this ball is a seed ... *the* seed?" Hanna asked. "But it's three thousand years old."

Thomas held out his hand and Michael handed him the seed. "Nothing lasts forever, but the size and thickness of the seed, coupled with the honey and the salt to keep moisture and bacteria away—"

Hanna gasped. "You mean it may germinate after three millennia?"

Michael popped the bottom of Thomas's hand and snatched the seed from midair. With an infectious smile, he said, "There's only one way to find out."

# CHAPTER 23

AMBASSADOR BEN HUR'S limo screeched to a stop next to the entrance of the King David Hotel. Without waiting for his driver, the ambassador threw open his door and stormed from the car. Colonel Yarconi and the four-man team that had escorted Michael's group to Hebron stood at attention. As the ambassador reached the front door, Colonel Yarconi fell in beside him, followed by the four soldiers.

"No one's answering their phones," the ambassador said through clenched teeth. The hotel's general manager waited silently by the front desk and then joined the group when they entered.

"My men and I have knocked on all of their doors. No answers there either."

They squeezed into an elevator and the general manager pressed the button for the third floor. The elevator jerked and started its ascent. "Which one of your men witnessed the discovery?"

Two men lifted their hands. "We did, sir," one of them said.

"And what happened after the discovery?"

"Sir, we boarded the chopper and flew back to Jerusalem. When we landed, we drove them back to the hotel."

The ambassador removed his glasses and stared icily at the soldier. "Then what?"

The soldier gulped, but kept his composure. "Then we headed back to base per orders."

The elevator slowed and stopped. The doors opened and the ambassador led the group to Thomas's room and pounded on the door. Without waiting, he nodded to the manager who unlocked the door. The ambassador stepped in, looked around, and checked the bathroom. The room was empty. The empty closet caused the ambassador's stomach to churn. He yanked out the dresser drawers and found them empty as well.

He pushed his way through the crowd that had filled in behind him. He grabbed the manager firmly by the upper arm and dragged him into the hall and to Michael's door. The manager fumbled with the keys before finally opening the door. The ambassador pushed him out of the way and marched into the room.

"Michael!"

He opened the closet and pulled out the dresser drawers, finding everything empty.

"Ambassador, here."

The ambassador turned to Colonel Yarconi, who pointed to an envelope on the nightstand addressed to him. He picked it up and ripped it open.

*Uncle Ben,*

*We did it! Yahweh was with us! Now that we have it, we believe we are in the greatest danger. I know you won't understand, but Thomas and I have vowed to keep this discovery to ourselves until we can authenticate it. We're safe and the women are with us, though they don't know what our plans are either. Rest assured, as soon as we determine it's safe, we'll share the discovery with you. I don't ask you to understand, just to please trust me. Michael.*

The ambassador's eyes bored a hole through the letter. He could feel his cheeks catch fire, and by the expressions on everyone's faces he knew they all could see it. He clinched the note in his fist and threw it to the floor. "Colonel, I want your men to do what it takes to find my nephew. You know what's at stake." The colonel nodded and pulled his men out of the room with him.

The ambassador shot an angry look at the manager. "That will be all." When the manager ducked out, he picked up the phone and called the hotel operator.

"This is Ambassador Benjamin Ben Hur. Please call the Jerusalem police and locate Detective Ari Hazan."

In less than two minutes, Detective Hazan came on the line. "Hazan, my nephew and his American friend have found the secret, and now they're gone. Find them!"

\*        \*        \*        \*

"I don't understand why we're here," Delia protested. "Why are you hiding this discovery?"

"I don't understand either," Hanna added. "I especially don't understand why you're hiding it from the ambassador. Above all, I really don't understand why you're hiding it from us. Just tell me, what did you do with the seed?"

Thomas tried to sound empathetic. He hated keeping the women in the dark, but in truth, no one had been searching as long as or with as much heart as he and Michael. Both knew they would create hard feelings in the people they cared about and possibly alienate them for good, but until they could resolve all lingering doubts about everyone's motives, they had agreed to pursue the rest of their plan themselves. That now meant they would need to try to get the seed to germinate; and if it did, test it to see if the legends of its power were true.

Michael had dropped the three of them off at a friend's house. His friend's family was out of the country for three months, making it a perfect place for them to remain under the radar. Michael had gone on to drop off the seed to a botanist friend. He had told her they found a seed in an ancient burial site; and if she could help it germinate while keeping quiet about it, they would give her all the research documentation she needed to write a paper on it for one of her journals. She was more than eager, knowing that if she were the first to grow a seed from antiquity, it would catapult her career.

Thomas lifted his eyes. The two women looked betrayed as they awaited an answer to their questions. He was frustrated with himself, knowing anything he said would only deepen the gulf forming between them. "I just hope you'll trust us. Our lives are in danger; and until Michael and I can guarantee your safety and the safety of the seed, we're not involving anyone deeper into this." He slouched, realizing how pathetic his reason truly was.

Hanna blinked in apparent disbelief. "Thomas, we're already deeply involved with this. If you're afraid Delia or I will tell anyone, we promise we won't. I swear I won't even tell my boss." She looked with pleading eyes to Delia, who supported her with a vigorous nod.

"Hanna, Delia, please, I know this is hard; but I promise you two will be the first to know everything, and you'll witness the secret that's hidden within the seed. But for the moment, our minds are made up." He inwardly cringed, knowing the words came out harsher than he intended.

To his surprise, the women didn't argue or pout. They seemed, at least temporarily, resigned to the decision.

"Well," Hanna said, "you don't expect us to stay hidden here with you until the seed germinates, do you?"

"No, of course not. We trust you to keep our location quiet."

"And if we don't," Delia interjected, "the seed is still hidden, and we'll be found to be untrustworthy, correct?"

"I didn't say that, but it ..." Thomas paused, knowing he couldn't finish the statement. The women looked away, defeat in their eyes.

"Promise if you tell one of us, you'll tell us both," Delia said. The women held each other's gaze for a few moments. Thomas couldn't tell whether it was a look of camaraderie or of jealousy. When they finally broke their gaze and looked at him, he simply nodded.

✳    ✳    ✳    ✳

Rajah stepped out of the passenger backseat of Azim's Mercedes. The driver opened the other backseat door, and Azim stepped out into the desert sand and stifling heat. Still, as always, Azim wore his Armani suit, silk tie, and polished leather dress shoes. Rajah, in his khakis, polo, and loafers, was already sweating after leaving the cool, refreshing, air-conditioning less than a minute earlier. Azim, however, never sweated. At least, not noticeably. When he did, it was not due to the sun but to his fuming temper. At the moment, though, he was happy and, thus, dry.

They approached an abandoned, dilapidated hangar left over from an attempt to build Hebron's first commercial airport in the desert. The only other site left was the single cracked runway half overgrown with weeds. When they were within a few feet of the large hangar door, it slid open and Sofian emerged with a smile and upbeat demeanor in spite of his soaked hair and shirt. He greeted Azim and Rajah and then led them into the hangar.

As soon as the men entered, it was as if they had stepped into a sweltering oven. Not only was it hot, but the air was also heavy and carried a putrid stench.

Azim's joy didn't falter. He strutted in and went straight to the single chair that sat in the center of the hangar. Behind, the door slid shut and the windowless hangar grew as dark as a moonless, starless, desert night. The darkness quickly scattered when Sofian turned on the semi-ring of electric lanterns strung around the chair. As they approached, the men felt the added heat radiating from the lamps. The tied and gagged man in the chair summoned the strength to lift his head and pry open his swollen eyes just long enough to see his visitors before exhaustion pulled his head back down.

Azim's dress shoes clicked on the concrete and echoed thunderously through the cavernous hangar until he came within three feet of the chair. When he stopped, silence washed over the scene to such an extent that Azim could hear the man breathe. His breath had a shudder in it as if he was so terrified he couldn't keep the terror from finding a way to boldly advertise itself.

Azim smiled.

"My family ... please—"

Sofian's backhand struck the man's cheek with vicious force. "Don't you ever speak in Mr. Ebadi's presence without consent, you filthy swine!"

Fresh blood flowed from a gash in the man's cheek over crusted, dried blood. The man lifted his head only high enough for his eyes to meet Azim's eyes. Azim could not make out the whites of the man's eyes through the narrow slits and the bluish-black puffy lids. Heeding Sofian's warning, the man merely nodded.

This is a good day, Azim thought to himself. This is the day he would take a giant step toward the ancient prize he'd been striving to possess. He looked down at the man and smiled. It was one of those occasions where he felt benevolent.

"Sofian, I believe this man has the utmost respect for me." He looked at the man again and smiled. "Isn't that correct?"

The man nodded immediately but still held his tongue.

"I thought so. I'm sure he doesn't want to be here any longer than we do." Azim beckoned with his hand. "A chair and something cool to drink."

A man emerged from the shadows with a padded folding chair followed by another man with a tall glass of ice in one hand and a clear pitcher of water in the other. The man with the chair unfolded it and set it before Azim. Azim adjusted it and placed it facing the man so close that his shoes brushed against the man's knees when he pulled one leg over the other.

The man with the water stepped forward and poured a thin stream of water from the pitcher into the glass. The sounds of ice clanking against the glass and the low rumble of falling water echoed in the hangar. Azim watched the man in the chair. His swollen eyes were riveted to the glass. Azim watched him, with great effort, force his dry tongue through cracked, bleeding lips. Azim could actually hear the man's dry swallow over the trickle of water.

A cheerful "thank you" from Azim stopped the water flow. He reached out and took the glass. The man's eyes remained locked onto the water, and his tongue had managed to crack the entire length of his now parted lips. With epicurean satisfaction, Azim sipped the water and then leaned back in his chair.

"Very good water." Azim called into the shadows. "I'm done. Please take the glass away."

The man who had brought the water reemerged from the shadows. The bound man quickly became alert. Azim saw anxiety pour from his prisoner's expression as the man came to take away the water. Azim reached forward with the glass but before handing it off, he tipped it, allowing the water to trickle onto the dusty concrete floor. The man in the chair groaned and strained against his bonds, trying to capture a few precious drops of the ice-cold water onto his tongue. Azim could see the veins in the man's neck as his mouth stretched for the water that trickled only inches away. A train of ice fell over the rim and shattered on the floor. As the last of the water dripped to the floor, the man's dry tongue extended so close to the trickle Azim was sure he must have felt the coolness that radiated from the water against his tongue.

Finally, the last drops of water fell. The bound man quit straining and slumped into the chair. Azim waited until the man quietly started to cry.

Azim spoke with a calm, even voice. "I don't want you to die, nor do I want your beautiful wife or lovely children to come to harm. I just want what you promised me." The man sobbed steadily but quietly. "Give me what you promised and I'll overlook your attempt to flee from me to the United States."

The man struggled to answer because of his dry, swollen tongue and his inability to stop sobbing. "I told the others already, I no longer have the notebook. The police took it."

"If that's true, it doesn't bode well for you." Azim leaned forward and placed his hands on his knees, making sure the man could see his holstered gun beneath his jacket. "If you've truly lost the notebook, then you've failed me, and I don't take it well when people fail me, Mr. Willingham."

The pastor's sobs grew louder and echoed in the hangar. With great effort, he groaned out his words. "I don't have it."

Azim sighed and stood. "I'm sorry our relationship has to end on a sour note."

"My family, please, let them go."

"You've no need to worry about them, or anything for that matter." Azim reached into his jacket and pulled out his gun. In one swift motion, he lifted it to Willingham's forehead and pulled the trigger. Willingham's body jerked and then slumped.

Azim holstered his gun, and the men in the hangar moved with the swiftness and grace of a ballet production, each silently and expertly cleaning the mess. Two men ended the dance by lifting Willingham, one by the shoulders and the other by the legs, and melting into the shadows.

The clicks of Azim's footsteps echoed in the hangar as he, Sofian, and Rajah approached the exit. The doors parted a few feet and the sun's rays cut the blackness like an intense laser beam.

"I'm sorry, Azim," Sofian said. "We did everything we could to pull the information from him."

Azim smiled and squeezed Sofian's shoulders. "I know you did, my friend." When he turned to leave with Rajah, Azim heard the unmistakable sigh of relief escape from Sofian.

The car's driver stood rigid with Azim's door open. Azim walked to the car and slid in while Rajah helped himself in on the other side. The car made a U-turn and headed back to the city.

"I don't understand how you can still be happy," Rajah said. "What did I miss?"

Azim's smile grew. "An old friend at the King David Hotel spotted my sister last night and was kind enough to call me. My friend agreed to keep an eye on her and, in doing so, described a manila envelope she and her companions seemed extremely interested in."

Rajah's jaw fell. "You found Delia? Give me the word, and I'll have her to you this very evening."

"Patience, my friend. At the moment, I'm more interested in the envelope, or should I say the notebook my friend saw them pull from it. Besides, I received a call from my friend a little while ago that informed me they all checked out in a hurry."

"How can you not be frustrated? You seem to always be one step behind."

"Because my friend, I was able to find out where they went." Azim patted his breast pocket. "I have the address of the house they're staying in right here. Now, it's just a matter of waiting for them to lead me to the Samson Effect."

# CHAPTER 24

FOR THREE MONTHS, Thomas and Michael waited with the women for the botanist to do her thing. Thomas vividly remembered the euphoria that swept through the house when she had called less than two weeks after receiving the seed to report the appearance of tiny sprouts. The daily updates Michael, in his excitement, had insisted on receiving grew monotonous for everyone and quickly turned into weekly updates. Even the botanist seemed surprised at the sprout's rapid growth. Her own excitement was evident as she reported one week that she had not been able to identify the plant. It was a new, undiscovered species.

A few weeks ago, however, they had received a call from her that rivaled the excitement of her initial call. The plant had produced five seeds that were quickly maturing. Last night she had asked to meet so Thomas and Michael could pick up the plant and four of the five seeds in exchange for the promised research on its discovery. Since tomorrow was the Sabbath and the facility would only have a skeletal crew of nonorthodox Jews, they agreed to meet then at 6:00 a.m.

Thomas lay in bed and looked at the clock. Midnight. Although he had consumed no caffeine, his body felt like it was jacked up on ten pots of coffee. He and Michael had invested over a year of their lives searching for the Samson Effect. They both suffered injuries and lived under the threat of death, and they both lost people close to them. As far as he knew, he was still a wanted man in his own country.

But in less than six hours he would be holding in his hands the thing responsible for all of it.

His bedroom door cracked open, followed by a soft rap. It wasn't Hanna; she never knocked. A deep voice called from behind the door. "Thomas, you awake?"

Thomas rolled over and turned on the lamp sitting on the nightstand. "Yeah, come on in."

Michael slipped in and sat at the foot of the bed. "I'm having a tough time sleeping myself. I can't believe it. It actually exists." He gripped Thomas's leg and squeezed it in excitement. "Do you know what this means?"

"Hey, I'm as excited as you, but you do know there's a possibility this is still just a legend. We may find out this plant is nothing more than a heck of a burger topping." He tried to look serious, but Michael saw through him.

"You can't wait to see what it's like to be Samson, can you?"

"I'm serious." He couldn't maintain his facade any longer. A betraying smile stretched across his face. "No, I guess I can't." After a brief fantasy played through his mind, his deeper analytical thinking surfaced. "We're going to have to test this thoroughly and build safety nets into our experiments, especially on how it affects mental health. If it's more than a legend, then there may be a correlation between it and mental illnesses I've researched."

Michael's spirit did not dampen one iota. "Sure. Absolutely. We'll be very cautious." He squeezed and shook Thomas's legs again. "I can't wait to walk up to it tomorrow, pluck off a leaf, and see how quickly the strength starts flooding into me."

Thomas bolted from the bed and towered over Michael. "That's exactly what I mean about safety! You've no idea what—"

Michael fell onto his back, holding his stomach while laughing. "I'm kidding, Thomas. Take it easy. Of course we'll be careful."

Thomas felt his cheeks flush. He sat down on the bed next to Michael and shook his head with a smile. Of course Michael would take safety seriously. Michael sat up and patted him on the back. "We better get some sleep. Tomorrow morning is already here."

"Yeah, I guess you're right. Is Delia still putting the pressure on you to tell her more about the plant?"

"Are you kidding? It's become a nightly chorus by now. 'Don't you trust me? Don't you love me? How can you shut me out?' I tell you, she was wonderful for a while, but now I believe she's taking it personally."

"What do you tell her?"

"The truth. I do love her; and when I'm positive we're all safe, I'll tell her." He looked at Thomas and shook his head. "Don't worry, I didn't tell her anything."

"Oh, it's not that. Lately, Hanna's been needling me for more information too. To tell the truth, I think Delia's put her up to it. Hanna doesn't like to appear weak in any way; and every time I tell her no, I can see the humiliation in her eyes. Makes me feel like a louse."

"Are they still drinking on the verandah?"

Thomas rolled his eyes. "Yeah. They're strengthening each other up to slowly chip away our resolve. I think I liked it better when they hated each other."

"Well, why not come clean now? Once we get the plant, there will be nothing to hide anymore."

Thomas thought for moment. "Why not? We've been here three months and all has been quiet. We have to leave in a few days when your friends return anyway. Let's go find them."

They entered the upstairs media room and walked through to the balcony. The women sat at a small round table sipping wine from their nearly empty glasses. Michael picked up two clean wine glasses from the shelf next to the sliding door before entering the veranda. The women hushed their conversation, acknowledging their entrance with smiles and tipped glasses.

Thomas pulled up a chair and sat while reaching for the wine bottle in the ice bucket. "Mind if we join you?" He pulled out the bottle and shook it. It was empty. "Looks like you two had a pretty good time tonight."

The women looked at each other and started giggling. Michael sighed and looked at his watch. "It's late anyway." He pulled up the fourth chair and wedged himself up to the crowded table. "We wanted to talk with you anyway."

Delia drained the last of her wine and smiled. "About what?"

"Well, you two have been patient beyond expectation, and Thomas and I figured it was safe enough to bring you fully into what's happening with the Samson Effect."

Delia's mouth flew open, and she looked at Hanna with a look of genuine surprise on her face, which Hanna parroted. "Really?"

"Really," Thomas answered, taking Hanna's hand. "Thank you for putting up with us."

After telling them about the plant's new seeds and their planned trip to the lab in a few hours, Delia leaped to her feet and swooned, steadied by Michael's arm. "This calls for a toast. I'll be right back with a bottle of wine."

"Let's hold off until tomorrow night, okay?" Michael said with a touch of concern in his voice.

"Nonsense! This is too big." She took a step and staggered.

"At least let me get the wine, then. You come sit down."

"No!" Everyone looked at her when she exclaimed. She smoothed her blouse with her palms and took deliberate steps to the sliding door. "I'll be fine." She didn't wait for a response but kept walking with dogged determination.

The three eased uncomfortably into their chairs, knowing it would be futile to try to stop her from her mission. "Guess you can see which one of us had the better part of the bottle," Hanna said sheepishly.

Thomas and Michael answered Hanna's endless questions about the Samson Effect with zeal. After ten minutes, Michael looked at his watch and stood. "I'd better make sure she's all right."

No sooner had the words left his lips, than he saw Delia enter the media room carrying a bottle of champagne. She stepped onto the veranda and held the bottle between her legs. When she popped the cork, champagne bubbled out. She brought the bottle to her lips, trying to capture as much as she could.

"I thought this called for a real toast."

Hanna giggled and extended her glass, receiving as much champagne on her arm as in her glass. The men smiled and extended their glasses as well. With their glasses full, Michael helped Delia to her seat and offered a toast. "To the sweet reward of costly perseverance." They raised their glasses and sipped their champagne. Five minutes later, Thomas helped Michael carry Delia to bed.

\*　　　\*　　　\*　　　\*

At ten till six in the morning, the four met the botanist at a side entrance to the lab. Michael and Thomas had made a half-hearted attempt to talk the women into waiting for them at the house; but after they heard about the seeds, the men knew it was futile. Michael introduced everyone to Rachel, who warmly returned their greetings before leading them to her office.

Once in her office, sipping the fresh coffee she had offered, they seated themselves around her desk. All eyes locked onto the potted plant sitting on the corner of her desk. Thomas looked at the delicate flowers that bloomed at the end of thin bamboo-like stalks. Any other day, he would have confidently sworn it was an orchid.

Rachel glowed over the interest they showed in her plant. "Isn't it beautiful?" They silently nodded, lost for words.

"Is this the ..." Michael was too overwhelmed to finish his question.

A puzzled look covered Rachel's face for a moment before being replaced by a comprehending smile. "Oh no, this is my prized orchid." She gently touched her fingertips to the flowers. "It's one of the rarest in the world. I only bring it here for special guests."

Thomas's shoulders, along with the others', instantly sagged. Rachel looked hurt but quickly recovered. "I suppose you're anxious to see the product of the seed you've entrusted to me. I want you to know it's garnered a lot of interest among the staff. It wasn't easy to dodge their questions. It was only when I took the lab director into my confidence that he blessed my secretive work."

"You told someone about it? But you promised. I specifically asked you—"

"I know, I know, but something like this is hard to keep hidden. It doesn't exactly blend in with anything else." She paused. Everyone's attention was riveted to her. "It was your promise of full disclosure and collaboration that actually swayed the director to give me the freedom I've needed to nourish it with the secrecy you've insisted on."

Michael was clearly struggling over her decision to involve someone else, in spite of her promises not to. Thomas knew Michael was wondering the same thing he was wondering: how many others knew about the plant?

Rachel ended the awkward silence by standing and gesturing to the door. "If you'll follow me, I'll show you what I mean about it not being able to blend in." She stepped to the door, followed by the group. Thomas felt like he was about to enter a new, unexplored tomb. In a few seconds, they found themselves standing in a greenhouse full of trees and plants in full bloom. The heavy, wet air was a noticeable contrast to the cool night air in which they had arrived.

Rachel stepped through the maze of plants and stopped next to the plant they had all come to see. She didn't need to point it out. With only a few steps into the room, everyone saw the plant they knew had come from the thick seed. Rachel was right; it truly was like nothing they had ever seen.

"We've dubbed it, 'The Burning Bush.'" Rachel stepped aside to let the four eager people examine it more closely. It was a small shrub planted in a five-gallon container. The trunk broke out in all directions about an inch above the soil. The branches looked like a handful of millipedes scattering in every direction. Tall, thin, green leaves shot horizontally up along the branches. They were as narrow as fern leaves but grew between six and ten inches long. None was at an angle; they all grew straight up.

As Thomas reached out to touch the leaves, the slight breeze from his hands caused the leaves to dance. The leaves themselves were dark green with a burgundy tint to them.

"Watch this," Rachel said. She reminded Thomas of a child who had found a strange bug along the creek and was eagerly coaxing people to witness her good fortune. She picked up a clipboard that hung on the wall and began waving it back and forth a few inches from the plant.

The leaves caught the breeze and began dancing. With the light reflecting off the leave's red and green sheen, Thomas instantly understood just how aptly they had named it. The leaves looked like flickering flames burning the bush. As the breeze died away, so did the botanical flames.

Everyone was speechless.

"Well?" Rachel finally asked. "What do you think? Didn't I tell you it was unlike anything you've ever seen?"

"Yes you did," Michael answered in awe. He stared at the plant so intently he looked like he was in a trance. He reached for the pot and hefted it into his arms. "Thank you," he said, without breaking his gaze from the plant.

Rachel breathed a sigh of relief. "When you share your findings on the plant with me, that will be thanks enough."

Thomas cringed. He knew it was coming eventually, and when it did, sparks would fly. He took a step back and waited for the fireworks to start.

Michael broke his gaze from the plant and looked at Rachel. His hesitation was just enough to let Thomas know this was going to be harder for him than he thought. "Rachel, I … we need to—"

"You'd better not be telling me what it sounds like you're telling me. We had an agreement. You promised."

"And I *will* follow through on that promise. This plant is more important to Israel's national security than you could imagine."

"Spare me your cloak-and-dagger story. We had an agreement, and I mean to hold you to it."

As if summoned by the power of her mind, a security guard entered the greenhouse. He stopped about ten feet away and stood silently, as if waiting for Rachel's order to attack. Thomas saw the pistol holstered at his side and began to feel the fingers of circumstance wrestle control from him once again. Banking on the premise that they were all on the same side, more or less, he decided to defuse the confrontation and negotiate a deal everyone could live with.

"Rachel, Michael's right. He should have been more open with you, but he was trying to protect you. A number of people have died over this plant already." He paused to study her reaction, but her determination did not waver. "You can go with us and when we're sure it's safe, you can have everything you need to begin your research today."

Thomas's spirits rose when she seemed to contemplate his offer. No one made a sound. They looked at her and waited. "I don't know," she said hesitantly. "I'd better get the director on the phone." She reached into her pocket and pulled out a cell phone. Before Thomas could think of a convincing way to stop her, the security guard started walking toward them. Rachel's fingers paused on the cell's buttons. "Please take that plant and hold it while we sort this out."

The guard kept walking, passing by Michael and the plant. A look of anger crossed Rachel's face. "I said … wait a minute. Who are you? Where's Matt?" Her anger melted into confusion, and then her eyes grew wide as the guard reached for his gun and leveled it at her head. She stumbled backwards, pleading through barely coherent words. "No … please …"

The gunshot echoed in the greenhouse, causing the four of them to gasp. Thomas watched Rachel slump to the floor and then followed the security guard with his eyes toward Michael. Out of instinct, he folded Hanna into his arms and turned his body so he was between her and the guard.

Three more men entered the greenhouse where the guard had entered. One had a rifle trained on the group. When Thomas saw the other two, he felt his knees weaken. It was as if he was caught in a nightmare, unable to flee from the monster.

"Azim!"

"Hello, Dr. Hamilton. I must commend you and Michael on a job well done. I knew my faith in your abilities wasn't misplaced. Rajah, please get the plant."

Michael offered no resistance. He handed the plant to Rajah and slumped like a man thoroughly beaten. Only when his narrow eyes lifted to Delia did Thomas see a semblance of strength in him. Venom saturated his words. "You really had me fooled."

Delia vigorously shook her head. "Michael, I—"

Michael turned his back, stopping her in midsentence. He tried to remain stoic, but his quivering lips betrayed him. Delia looked shocked rather than angry. She closed her eyes in resignation, but she couldn't keep a lone tear from falling when he turned his back on her.

"Enough!" Azim cried out. He nodded to the security guard. "Give us five minutes, and then take care of them." He gestured to Rachel's body. "Take care of her too."

The guard nodded and walked over to a wheelbarrow leaning against the wall behind him. He wheeled it next to Rachel's body and then looked at his watch.

"Time to come home, sister. You and I have a lot to talk about." He turned and led her toward the exit, whispering something into her ear. Rajah and the other armed man fell in behind.

Thomas felt Hanna pull away from his embrace and take a step toward Azim. He attempted to pull her back, afraid Azim needed little encouragement to put a bullet into her on the spot. She shook off his hand and kept walking.

"What about me, Azim?"

The moment turned surreal for Thomas. Hanna smiled and had the worshipful look of a prom queen enamored with her quarterback boyfriend. Azim stopped and looked back at her. Hanna took it as her invitation to run to him. The love she had in her eyes for him stabbed at Thomas again and again. He let her slip from his fingers like quicksilver, feeling totally naked and exposed. As if she wanted to cast one more stone at his heart, she turned and gave him a wicked smile.

She reached her hand to Azim, who wrinkled his nose at it and scoffed. "Get away from me, Jewish swine."

The smile faded from Hanna's face. "What? Azim, I love you." She reached for his hand again but he used it to backhand her cheek. The force of the blow made her stagger backward a couple of steps before it sent her sprawling on her backside.

Thomas jogged to her and knelt down. Anger bubbled inside, but he didn't know quite where to aim it. He reached to gently wipe the blood from her swollen lips but she pulled her head away in defiance. The word choked from his throat. "You?"

Contempt oozed from Azim. "You think I'd have anything to do with an Israeli sow? The thought makes me sick." He turned on his heels and led the rest unceremoniously to the door. "Five minutes," he said to the lingering guard before exiting.

Hanna cried out and sobbed, unable, or unwilling, to hide the tears. Michael looked at Thomas, his eyes widening in comprehension, then streaked with terror. "Delia," he whispered. He turned to go after her in spite of the armed guard blocking his path.

Thomas grabbed his arm. "No, Michael. Not yet." He felt Michael tug against his arm but ease up as he sized up the guard. Resistance oozed from him, leaving him limp. He turned to Hanna and looked down at her. He summoned the vilest substance he could and spit it on her face. Hanna didn't look at him. She still sought after Azim, holding an arm outstretched toward the door.

Her betrayal ate at Thomas. It took all of his will to replace the humiliation and hurt with anger. He pulled Michael aside, leaving Hanna to wallow in her own broken spirit.

Thomas checked his watch. "We've got less than five minutes to clear our heads and find a way out of this or Delia is as good as dead."

Michael nodded.

Thomas hoped his friend's head was clearing. It would take every ounce of mental prowess they had to get out of there alive. He subtly surveyed the room for anything that would give them a fighting chance. The wheelbarrow and Rachel's body were next to the guard, about seven feet in front of them. Rachel's cell phone had cracked into two pieces when it fell and lay a few feet away. Thomas was growing uneasy, fighting the thought that everything was futile.

Then he noticed the shelf under the table next to Rachel. A pair of manual hedge trimmers with twelve-inch blades rested on the shelf. The crude outline of a plan formed in his head as he quickly surveyed the rest of the room. He glanced at his watch. Two minutes left. He prayed the guard would hold off, taking the five-minute countdown ordered by Azim literally.

He walked next to Michael and nodded toward the space behind him. "See that table?" Michael looked at a table full of plants about six feet behind them and nodded. "I'm going to go over and check Rachel's body. When you see me place my fingers on her neck to check for a pulse, I want you to run as fast as you can for that table, flip it over, and hide behind it."

"Why? What are you going to do?"

Thomas checked his watch. "No time to explain. Just trust me."

Michael looked into his eyes for a moment and then nodded. Thomas turned and headed for Rachel's body. His plan would result in their salvation or their massacre. Success hinged on perfect timing.

The guard thrust his gun at Thomas and babbled something in Arabic. Thomas looked at him as he knelt next to Rachel. The guard glanced at his watch and smiled, keeping his gun trained on him.

Thomas took a deep breath, hoping Michael was watching. He held out his fingers and applied them to Rachel's neck. The silence seemed to last an eternity but he finally heard Michael's footsteps pounding the floor followed by a loud crash. Trusting the guard had averted his attention to the commotion, he reached for the hedge trimmers and in one swift motion swung around as he stood to his feet. When he stopped, all twelve inches of both blades stuck into the guard's abdomen. He and the guard stood face-to-face, eye-to-eye. Without blinking, Thomas pulled the handles apart with all his strength and felt the blades separate inside the guard.

The guard's mouth fell open, and Thomas watched the life fade from his eyes. He heard the pistol hit the floor and released the trimmers. The guard crumpled to the floor, and Thomas picked up the pistol.

The greenhouse was silent. He turned to see Michael's head slowly appear from behind the table. Then he turned to Hanna, whose cries were replaced by an occasional sniffle. She stood and walked to him.

He wanted to take her into his arms and hold her, yet at the same time he wanted to use his own backhand to give her lips a twin cut to match the one Azim gave her. When she held her arms open, his own arms opened as if they had a mind of their own. Her body pressed against his.

"Everything's going to be okay."

When she squeezed her arms around him, his body nearly melted. She held him for a moment and then pulled away from him just enough to look into his eyes. She smiled as a tear fell from each eye. She gently ran her hands down each of his arms.

"I'm so sorry. Please forgive me."

The pace of her hands quickened. It registered in Thomas's mind what she was doing, but not in time to stop her. She gripped his hand and pulled the pistol's muzzle into her stomach. Her fingers found his trigger finger and it was over. She fell forward into his arms.

His reaction surprised him. He felt pain and hatred, but they were overshadowed by pity. He knelt and laid her body peacefully onto the floor. Michael ran over and stared. Thomas stood, tucked the pistol into his waistband, and walked to the door. "Let's find Delia."

# CHAPTER 25

AMBASSADOR BEN HUR dragged himself into his bedroom at 11:30 p.m., unusually early for a Friday evening in Washington, DC. He passed by his wife and slipped into their adjoining bathroom. He leaned forward and sighed at his reflection. His crow's feet were deepening and his hairline plowed deeper into his gray hair.

He shook his head, remembering how it wasn't too many years ago his diplomatic duties carried him deep into the night. But not anymore.

He started brushing his teeth, when he heard his private line ring in the bedroom. He glanced at his watch; less than twenty minutes until his aging body demanded its rest for the evening. He didn't hear a second ring and assumed his wife had answered the phone. He fought to keep this inconsiderate late-night intrusion from fanning his anger.

When his wife came into the bathroom with the cordless handset, his anger began to simmer. "Who is it, my dear?"

She covered the mouthpiece with her hand. "It's Michael. He needs—"

Upon hearing his nephew's name, adrenaline coursed through his veins, waking every cell in his body as he yanked the phone from her. "Michael, you have some nerve disappearing for three months. Where in heaven's name are you? What have you done with the seed?"

"Uncle Ben, I need your help. I … Thomas and I lost the seed. Azim's got it."

"What?" The ambassador slammed his palm against the wall, startling his wife, who looked at him with sickening worry. He spun away from her and marched into his closet. "How could this have happened? How could you have been so foolish? You should've come to me when you found the seed."

The ambassador began changing into his navy-blue pinstriped suit while fumbling to keep the phone to his ear. "We were going to call you today but Azim knew we were on our way to pick up the plant and followed us. We were betrayed."

The ambassador stopped buttoning his shirt and leaned against the closet door. "Plant? You found a way to grow the seed?" The harsh tone in his voice softened. With those few words, Michael had vindicated his dedication to the Council's purpose. His satisfaction was short-lived when he remembered Azim. "Betrayed? I told you that Jezebel would turn on you when she had the opportunity. Your hormones have cost us—"

"It wasn't Delia. Hanna told Azim."

"Hanna? Don't be ridiculous. She wouldn't have—"

"Listen to me! I'm not going to argue about how or why Azim was able to find out about the plant, I just need you to send someone to help us get it back."

"No. Stay where you are. I'll find a way to recover the plant."

"Azim has Delia."

The ambassador's lips quivered in silence.

"Look, Thomas and I are on our way to Hebron. Help us if you will. Regardless, we're going."

"Don't be a fool, Michael. The peace in Hebron is fragile. If you and your American cowboy friend go in there with guns blazing, you'll make it nearly impossible to get the plant back. Please, wait where you are. I'll send someone to take care of things."

"Do you know the kind of damage Azim could do if he and his men consume the plant? We're going."

The line disconnected. The ambassador knew profoundly what would happen if Azim found a way to prepare and consume the plant. He finished dressing and met his driver downstairs. On the way to the Ronald Reagan International Airport, he called his pilot to have him prepare to leave as soon as possible. He then called Colonel Yarconi and ordered him to Hebron to detain Michael and Thomas without creating an international incident. His last call before boarding his flight was to arrange an emergency meeting of the Council upon his arrival in Tel Aviv.

He had done everything he could from this side of the Atlantic. He prayed the Lord would interfere with whatever plans Azim had until the Council could meet. And he prayed, fervently, that his nephew would not make matters worse.

\*       \*       \*       \*

The sun's rays over Hebron's desert felt heavy upon Thomas's head and neck. He and Michael had made it undetected to the craggy hills a few hundred yards behind Michael's compound. The landscape they surveyed seemed serene except for six soldiers the Israeli army had dispatched to protect his home. Michael leaned against the rock and grimaced.

"You okay, Michael?"

"I'll be fine." He ran his fingertips across his ribs and smiled. "That sprint to the table in the greenhouse didn't help much."

Thomas looked around the rocks. "Why don't you stay here and tell me how to get into the compound. I'll bring back what we'll need."

Michael shook his head. "If they catch you without me, they'll detain you. We don't have the time for them to learn you're no threat."

"It's your home. Why don't we just walk up to the front door? They're protecting it for you."

"Uncle Ben made it clear he didn't want you or me to proceed. I've no doubts he's issued orders to detain us if we're found. I can't let that happen. The longer we wait, the less of a chance we have of finding Delia in time."

Thomas looked back at the compound and counted the soldiers again. "If you're right about your uncle, we'll need to do this quickly. This is one of the first places they'll look for us." He shook his head. "I don't know how we're going to make it across open desert without being spotted. And even if we do make it, we have no idea how many soldiers may be in the courtyard or the house."

"Hey, where's that competitive spirit of yours?"

"I've never had an open desert between me and assault rifles, and an invalid in tow."

"True," Michael said, "You've only had to deal with the bombing of your office, escaping U.S. authorities, being locked in a dungeon, caught in the crossfire of a shootout, escaping seconds before your execution—"

"Okay, okay, I get your point—"

"This will be a piece of cake, even with an invalid in tow."

Thomas rolled his eyes. "So, how are we going to get in?"

"I've been watching the soldiers walk their patrol. If we wait until the two soldiers on either side of the compound walk from the rear toward the front, *and* if the soldier on the roof lingers long enough before walking towards the back, we should have enough time to make it to the right corner of the wall. We scale it and drop behind the shed in the corner of the courtyard."

Thomas stared unblinkingly at him. "Yeah, piece of cake. And if the stars and moon line up, we'll be able to walk out the front door, to boot."

"I'm serious; this can work."

"Okay, let's say we make it to the corner undetected. How do we get over the ten-foot wall?"

"That's the part I'm dreading. You'll have to stand on my shoulders and once you're on top of the wall, pull me up."

"Are you crazy? You can't hold my weight in your condition."

"Look, my ribs have been healing for three month. They're fine. Besides, I have a better chance of lifting you than trying to pull you up the wall."

"I can't believe we are even thinking of doing this. There's no way it can work."

"It has to work, for Delia's sake."

The determination on Michael's face set Thomas's resolve. He sighed and shook his head. "Tell me why you think it's absolutely necessary for us to risk this."

"Because I have the weapons and equipment we'll need if we're going to try to penetrate Azim's compound. Think of this as a dry run."

Thomas threw up his arms. "Okay, let's do it."

They waited a few minutes until everything finally fell into place. The two soldiers patrolling the sides of the compound reached the rear at the same time and turned to walk toward the front. The soldier on the roof lingered for a moment before turning from the rear and heading to the front. Thomas felt a hollow feeling of anticipation grow in his stomach. Michael pushed him forward. "Go."

He sprinted into the open desert, and a sense of vulnerability washed over him. Now, only one thing focused in his mind: making it to the wall. When he had covered half the distance, a troubling thought raced through his mind and threatened to paralyze him where he stood. How were they going to get out of the compound once they got in?

*   *   *   *

Delia sat on the edge of her bed locked in her room. The guard outside her door refused to answer her command to release her. She paced the floor and thoroughly searched the room for anything that would help her escape. She knew better than anyone what was going to happen when Azim grew tired of letting her worry about her predicament. Blood was not enough to stay his vengeful fury.

She walked to the window and pulled the curtains aside for the tenth time. And, for the tenth time, she spotted the armed guard faithfully patrolling his station below. The fear and respect toward her the guards had once shown were gone. It infuriated her that they treated her as a common enemy and not as the sister of Azim.

The thought of Michael entered her mind again. Each time it did, she conjured the strength to expel it. Now was not the time to grieve. If she did, she knew she'd have nothing left in her to find even the remotest chance of escaping.

She drew on every tactical experience she had, knowing no plan was perfect, not even one of her brother's. Somewhere there was a flaw. If she could find it, no matter how small it was, she knew it could be fatal.

She prayed to Allah she hadn't missed it.

The door opened, driving her thoughts away. Her escort stepped in and gripped her arm. "Come!"

She shrugged her arm free and conjured up the cold, steady expression she knew sent fear into others. "Hello, Sofian." Her penetrating stare didn't have the effect she was seeking. Sofian's eyes squinted as a smile curled from the edge of his lips. His reaction turned her blood cold and sent a shiver up her spine. Something about him was very different.

Sofian led her from the bedroom, through the maze of hallways, and to her brother's plush study. When she stepped into her brother's office and saw him sitting behind his desk, her blood froze. Azim stared at her, anger flaming from his eyes. He held out his hand and gestured to a chair across the desk.

She obeyed his silent command and waited for him to speak first. He rose from his chair with a smile and walked around the desk. Her flesh began to crawl as she awaited his twisted habit of greeting her. It was his ultimate show of dominance over her, one she had never been able to stand against. Even now, she felt herself turning into the frightened little girl only he could bring out in her. He approached and leaned into her. Fear paralyzed her every move except for the shallow breaths that stabbed her lungs.

His lips hovered so close to hers that she felt his warm breath upon her. She tried to summon the inner strength to pull away from him, but it never came. She resigned herself to the abhorrent display of affection and waited with closed eyes.

Moments dragged on and then the warm breath disappeared. She tensed, awaiting the touch of his lips while fighting the urge to retch. But even with her eyes closed, she sensed his presence receding from her. She opened her eyes and caught a blur of motion in her vision followed by an intense flash of white light. Her neck twisted violently to one side, and a warm numbness seeped into her face. She lifted her head to her brother, who was massaging his right fist in his left hand. She lifted her fingers to her lips and felt the warm, sticky ooze. The numbness went away, replaced by a stinging, throbbing pain. She felt a pebble roll upon her tongue and spit it to the floor. Gliding her tongue along her teeth, she discovered a hole created by a missing upper front tooth.

For the first time in her life, she wasn't afraid of her brother. Hatred fueled her fury. She hated what he had turned her into. She began to laugh, seeing the blood spray from her mouth through her peripheral vision.

"You find this a matter to laugh about, sister?" He spewed the words through clenched teeth.

Her laughter regressed to a bloody smile. "I do, brother. Oh, I do very much."

He cocked his head and squinted with curiosity. "And what, by Allah, do you find so funny?"

"The fact that you're a little man who thinks he's big." Azim's face reddened and his fist clenched. "And before the night's out, I will kill you."

For a brief moment, Delia saw in her brother's eyes the fear she had often witnessed in her targets' eyes the moment they knew they were about to die. Never, until this moment, had she seen it in her brother. As quickly as it came upon him, however, it left him.

"You'd be wise to hold your tongue, Delia. It's only by my grace you're alive for the moment. I may be a small man, but not too small to hold your insignificant life in my hand."

Brother and sister stared into each other's eyes, neither blinking nor looking away. "Why," Azim said, finally breaking the silence, "did you betray me? Why did you turn your back on Allah for a Jew?"

Delia appraised Azim's sincerity as genuine. Somewhere in her hatred for him, a glimmer of familial love flickered. "I didn't betray Allah. My dedication to him made me try to stop you. Not me, brother. You betrayed Allah by the evil you've done in his name, by what you've turned your own sister into."

She had no tears for Azim. Only pity. "Set your things in order, Azim, for today I finish his will."

Delia knew she had just cut off any hope of reconciliation between her and her brother. Fate had been set. Tonight, only one of them would be alive. She entrusted the outcome to Allah's hands.

Azim's voice roused her from her thoughts. "Before you die, I want you to witness Allah bestowing his glory upon me. Your last thought before death will be confirmation that I've been his faithful servant." He shook his head. "You could have been by my side when it happens."

Azim lifted his phone and called for Sofian and Rajah. They entered the office followed by two armed men. "Make everything ready at the hangar. Tonight, we begin laying the building blocks for Allah's new kingdom. The three of us will unite the world to his cause. The final jihad is about to sweep upon the infidels, purifying the earth for Islam."

Delia saw the maddening hubris deep within her brother's eyes, far beyond his usual arrogance. Something was happening in his mind. Her anxiety was more potent over this than when she contemplated her own death. "What do you mean, Azim?"

His lips curled into a smug smile. "Yes, I want you to hear, to know the plan Allah has put into my heart. You'll understand I am truly his prophet and humble servant."

"Please, Azim, no," Rajah insisted. Delia heard panic in his voice. "We mustn't tell her. If too many people know, all could be lost."

"Silence!" Azim's command echoed in the office. "Nothing can go wrong. The future has been ordained. Now sit!"

Rajah turned to Sofian with wide, pleading eyes. "Please, help make him understand!"

Sofian shook his head and a few chuckles escaped his lips, but he didn't respond to Rajah's pleas. Delia watched the strange scene unfold before her, nearly convinced she must be in the midst of a nightmare. Rajah always spoke with calm wisdom, but now he looked and acted like a frightened child.

Azim's glare locked onto Rajah. He stepped up to Rajah and extended a hand, wrapping his fingers around the frightened man's throat. His lips curled into a snarl as he lifted Rajah effortlessly into the air. "I said sit."

# CHAPTER 26

SMALL WISPS OF dust rose behind Thomas and Michael as they sprinted from the safety of the craggy rocks, across the open desert, and finally to the back corner of the compound wall. Thomas threw himself against the wall and sucked in oxygen as he watched Michael take the last few painful steps to him. So far, he heard no gunshots or shouts from the guards, but he knew it was only a matter of seconds before at least one guard walked his post to the rear of the wall. If he showed up before they made it over the ten-foot wall, Thomas knew it was over for them.

Michael stumbled to Thomas's feet, clutching his ribs in his arms. His grimace silently cried out in pain. Thomas stooped to help him to his feet. "Michael, I don't think you can handle my weight. Umar did major damage to your ribs; three months isn't enough time for you to do this."

Michael's hair matted to his forehead, and his face was covered with a moist sheen. "I'll be fine." He took out his leather wallet and bit down on it. He then turned to the wall and knelt down, bracing his palms against the flat surface.

"You don't have the strength to do this."

Michael looked over his shoulder and shot a commanding look at Thomas. He gave one curt nod and furrowed his brows, emphasizing that Thomas needed to act now. Thomas knew the soldiers were somewhere just around the corner. He nodded and rested one foot on Michael's shoulder.

Michael took three deep breaths and nodded. When Thomas felt him rise, he thrust himself up, scratching at the wall's smooth surface for any opportunity to remove weight from his friend.

Somehow, Michael kept rising. Thomas's fingertips finally found the top of the wall and his adrenaline did the rest. He lay on his stomach and straddled the top of the wall. He looked down at Michael, who was pulling himself to his feet. He reached down a hand and gripped Michael's wrist. His adrenaline was gone, and it took every drop of strength in him to pull Michael to the top.

Thomas swung his legs inside the wall and was about to ease himself down and drop inside when Michael's leg knocked him off balance. He tumbled down behind the shed and heard a loud snap when he hit the ground, followed by a stabbing pain in his side. He rolled to his back and gripped his lower left side. He knew immediately he had cracked a least one rib on the cinderblock that had broken his fall.

Michael dropped beside him, and they both gritted their teeth and held their sides to keep the pain from betraying their presence. Michael scooted to the edge of the shed and poked his head around the corner. A few moments later, he scooted back to Thomas.

"I didn't see anyone in the courtyard or in the house through the windows. If Yahweh is with us, we'll only have to worry about the guard on the roof."

Thomas dropped his arms and leaned against the shed. He closed his eyes and felt Michael gently lifting his shirt. When Michael's fingers explored his wound, the stabbing pain flooded back.

"Broken."

"No kidding, Sawbones." Thomas shook his irritation from his head. "Let's focus on getting into the house; we'll worry about this when we're inside."

Even in the pain, they made the trip from the shed to the house with relative ease. Michael slipped his key into the lock of his utility door, and they silently stepped inside. After a careful search, Michael declared the house vacant. They spent the next few minutes tending to their wounds. The ever-present footsteps above reminded them they weren't alone.

"Let's get what we came for," Thomas said when Michael finished applying the bandage to his ribs. Michael nodded, and Thomas slipped off the countertop. With every step, his appreciation for what Michael had endured grew stronger.

They walked into the garage and through a door at the other side. Thomas stopped cold. As he looked around the room, he saw everything from handguns and assault rifles to crossbows and knives either on the wall or behind glass-covered cabinet doors. "What in the world is a linguist doing with an arsenal like this?"

Michael milled about as if it were the most natural thing in the world for him to be around such an arsenal. "I'm a Jew living in Hebron, remember? And not just any Jew, but the nephew of the ambassador to the U.S." He swung a rifle with a telescope onto his shoulder and handed one to Thomas.

"What's this for?"

"This is how we get out of here and, in your words, 'walk out the front door, to boot.'"

"Wait a minute. The soldiers may be in our way, but they're not the bad guys. I'm not going to put a bullet into an innocent man."

"Relax." Michael walked to a desk drawer and unlocked it. He picked up a box with a blue label and read it. When he seemed satisfied he had the right box, he opened it and pulled out a tray of odd-looking needles. He divided them into two piles of four.

"These are harmless tranquilizing darts. The rifles are made especially for them. Once they find their mark, the man drops instantly, albeit safely." He began loading one group into his rifle. "Ever shoot a rifle?"

Thomas shook his head.

Michael stopped loading for a second, clearly unhappy at Thomas's lack of experience. He shrugged it off and continued loading his rifle. "Don't worry, the guns are made for even a novice to use. All you have to do is line the crosshair on your target and pull the trigger. There's no noise and no kick. Just takes a steady hand."

Thomas still didn't like the thought of shooting a man, even if it was with just a tranquilizer dart. Michael loaded his rifle and handed it back to him.

Michael picked up a duffel bag and packed it with two pistols, two silencers, a GPS tracking chip and a handheld GPS monitor, a lock-pick set and two Tasers. He then walked over to the desk and pulled a three-ring binder from the drawer. "This is perhaps the most important item."

"What is it?"

"It has, among other locations, a detailed map of Azim's compound. This will give us the best chance at navigating through it undetected."

Thomas was duly impressed. Michael's high-tech, 007 gadgets made him feel they just might have a chance in spite of their injuries.

He followed Michael to the attic door and eased up the ladder behind him. Only the knowledge that Michael's injuries were worse than his kept him from entertaining the thought that he wouldn't be able to continue. They moved to the only window in the attic. Thomas glanced outside. The view overlooked the flat part of the roof where the soldier patrolled. Michael set down the duffel bag and pulled the rifle from his shoulder.

"I'll take out the guy on the roof. When I do, crouch and slip out to the west side and wait for the guard to move to the middle of the wall. When he does, put a dart in his neck. If you aim for a clothed part of his body, you'll run the risk of hitting something that will deflect the dart—"

"And that would be bad."

"Very. Just take a breath and wait for your shot. When you take it, make sure he's out of view of the other soldiers. Then crawl to the front and meet me."

Thomas nodded and watched Michael ease into position at the window. He cracked it open and stuck the barrel through the opening. The guard had just finished surveying the rear of the compound and headed toward the front. Thomas held his breath when the soldier glanced in their direction, but Michael remained steady. The soldier finally glanced away and continued his walk to the front.

When the soldier reached the center of the roof, Thomas saw him grab his neck and fall unconscious to the ground. He had hardly heard the shot at all.

Michael nodded, and Thomas eased through the open window and crouched to the west side of the roof. Michael exited the window behind him and crouched around the dormer to the east side.

When Thomas drew near to the edge of the roof, he dropped to his belly and bit his tongue to endure the fire that burned in his side. He saw the soldier facing toward the front of the compound and waited for him to turn and head back to the rear. When he passed by, Thomas put the crosshair on the center of his neck.

He pulled the trigger and the soldier fell silently to the ground. A euphoric feeling washed over him that made him temporarily forget his pain. He turned to find Michael already halfway to him. He gave Michael the thumbs-up sign and met him toward the front of the roof.

"Piece of cake," Thomas whispered.

"Good. Three down and three to go." They peered over the edge of the roof. One soldier sat on a rock in the shade of a tree eating his lunch. The other two walked together. Thomas could barely hear their muted conversation.

"This is going to be easier than I thought," Michael said. "Let's go for the two with the guns first. On three, you take the one on the left and I'll take the one on the right, then we'll both go for the one eating lunch."

Thomas nodded. "Poor guy." They dropped to their stomachs and took aim.

"Ready?"

Thomas nodded.

"One … two … three …

Michael's target fell immediately, but Thomas's had bent down just as he'd pulled the trigger. The soldier eating lunch grabbed his gun and leaped to his feet. He screamed out a warning and pointed to the roof but fell to the ground when Michael found his mark.

The remaining soldier spun with lightning-quick reflexes and sent a shower of bullets in their direction. "Shoot!" Michael commanded.

Thomas felt paralyzed. Bullets whizzed by. He knew Michael was out of shots, and he had only two left. "He's going for the radio. Shoot!"

Thomas sucked in a breath and looked over the edge of the roof. The soldier was jogging toward the truck while pointing his rifle behind him and firing blindly. Thomas looked through the telescope and followed his moving target. When the soldier was a few feet from the truck, he fired.

The soldier didn't fall.

Thomas's hands began to shake, knowing he only had one shot left. He looked through the scope. The soldier flew all around his field of vision.

He knew he had only seconds left before the compound would be swarming with soldiers. He took a deep breath and started to pull the trigger.

Before he knew what happened, the rifle flew from his hands. Michael dropped down beside him and immediately pulled the trigger. The soldier stiffened and fell to the ground with the radio mic in his hand.

They waited in silence for an unaccounted soldier, but no one else appeared. Michael stood, surveyed all four sides of the compound, and then tossed the rifle to his feet.

"Piece of cake."

They returned through the attic and retrieved the duffel bag. Within minutes, they walked through the front door. They limped down the steps and looked at the damage they had done. They then dragged themselves to the garage and slipped into Michael's sedan. They both popped a few pain pills before Michael started the car and headed for Azim's compound.

A few minutes later, they pulled into an alley and parked next to a trash container. Michael pulled out the map of Azim's compound and began explaining the layout to Thomas. It seemed vaguely familiar to Thomas, especially when Michael pointed out the cell Azim had cast them into when he first arrived in Hebron.

"I'm not even going to ask how you got this map."

Michael gave him a knowing smile and then explained his plan and the route they would take into the compound. Thomas cringed at the thought of more sneaking around while his side was still on fire. However, the thought of finding Delia kept him focused on Michael's words as he followed the route along the map.

A tapping sound on Michael's window caused them both to freeze. They slowly looked up to see the car surrounded by men aiming their rifles at them. Thomas thought of the high-tech spy gadgets in the back seat. He shook his head and let out a sigh.

Michael forced out the word through clenched teeth. "Azim!"

∗      ∗      ∗      ∗

Delia sat across from her brother, horrified that he had already processed and consumed the plant. She thought of the three Jewish men who were cast into the fiery furnace and of the young rabbi who had bent the steel barrel of a rifle. The thought of her brother possessing power that made him nearly indestructible made her sick to her stomach.

"I'm sure you've figured out by now Allah has given me the strength of Samson. I can't explain what it's like knowing that no power on earth can stop you."

He paused for her to comment, but she remained silent. He shrugged and continued. "So you see, sister, one of us *will* die tonight, but it can't be me." He waved a dismissive hand at Rajah. "I gave him the same gift, yet he cowers. He was much braver before he became indestructible. Look at him."

Delia turned to see Rajah. He sat, wringing his hands and mumbling about doom while rocking in his chair.

"Sofian, on the other hand, is strong. He knows the future Allah has laid before us."

She looked into Sofian's eyes. They were hollow, almost as if his own soul had been taken from him and replaced with a demonic spirit. Somehow, she knew he would never again cower to her. Unadulterated fear pulsed through her body. She felt as if she were caught in the inner chambers of hell.

Sofian smirked and held a pistol to Rajah's head. Delia knew he wanted nothing more at this moment then to put a bullet in Rajah's head.

"Put down the gun," Azim said in a pacifying voice. "Rajah will come around. He's just adjusting to the gift."

Sofian stared coldly at Azim and pressed the pistol's muzzle onto Rajah's temple.

"I said put down the gun."

The authority in Azim's voice caused Sofian to reluctantly obey, though his eyes told everyone he didn't like it.

When the tension dissipated, Azim continued. "Tonight, we meet with the leaders of our faith. We will demonstrate Allah's gift and lay out our plan to recruit soldiers for the greatest, most glorious jihad ever. When the day is declared, my indestructible soldiers will come out of obscurity all over the world and accomplish what rulers throughout the ages have desired: global domination. All the earth will be Islam."

All vestiges of her brother were gone. Delia looked at him, knowing that arguing or reasoning with him would be futile. She shook her head. "You're mad, Azim. This can never work. The world won't sit by and let you take over. All you'll end up doing is causing a lot of bloodshed; but, in the end, you will die."

"That's right, Azim," Rajah said. "Listen to her. Our enemies are all around. Can't you see that?" He glared at Sofian. "Even he'll look to usurp your power. It's in his eyes."

Sofian gave a half smile and rolled his eyes. Azim got to his feet and held out his hand to silence everyone. "Enough. Rajah, Sofian, let's go."

Someone knocked on the door, and Sofian opened it. The man on the other side insisted on speaking to Azim. Sofian stepped out of the way, and the man walked briskly to Azim. He leaned in and whispered something into his ear. Azim's head snapped up in surprise. "Are you sure it was them?"

The man nodded.

Azim mulled over the information, and a smile crept across his face. He leaned in and whispered something into the man's ear. The man nodded and left the room. Azim turned to the guards. "Take Delia to the cell and keep her there until I return."

Each man grabbed one of Delia's arms and led her out of the office and down the hall. She turned to see her brother lead his group the other way down the hall. She shook free of the men. "I know the way."

The men looked at each other and held tightly to their weapons, but they allowed her to remain free of their grip. When they reach the doorway that opened to the stone staircase that led down to the cell, they nudged her with the tip of their rifles and ordered her through the door. She complied while her mind began creating a plan for her escape.

The narrow staircase was only wide enough for one person at a time to descend. She slowed her pace in order to give herself a few more precious seconds to solidify her plan. Halfway down, however, she began thinking about Michael again. She knew her grief had to wait; otherwise, she would risk making a fatal mistake. This time she found it difficult to remove the images of him turning his back on her and the hurt on his face when he believed she had betrayed him. Her heart ached knowing he died before they had a chance to hold each other one last time.

The man behind her nudged her forward, snapping her from her thoughts. Once they reached the bottom, she slowed and let the men move to her sides. One of them dug into his pockets and pulled out a key ring.

The moment they stepped around the corner, she spun and drove a palm into the nose of one of the men. The feel of the impact told her he was dead before he hit the floor. Her inertia sped her spin, and she almost simultaneously kicked the other man's head against the wall. Within seconds, both men lay dead at her feet.

She picked up the keys to the cell and dragged one of the men to the door. She unlocked the thick heavy door, forced it open, and started to drag in the first body. When she looked into the cell, her legs grew rubbery; and she stumbled against the doorframe for support.

Thomas and Michael sat against the wall looking equally stunned. She quickly recovered, and every ounce of hopelessness in her instantly vanished. "You're alive! But how?"

Michael pulled himself to his feet. "We came to rescue you."

# CHAPTER 27

"I HATE TO break this up, but shouldn't we be going?"

Michael and Delia ignored Thomas's plea and held their embrace, unable to kiss because of Delia's split lip. Thomas left the cell and pulled the two dead men inside. Once finished, he gripped his side and slid to a sitting position against the wall.

"Thomas, what happened to you?"

"He broke a rib or two. Couldn't stand me getting all the sympathy."

Delia looked with concern from one man to the other. Thomas reached into his pocket, pulled out three more pain pills and swallowed them dry. "Can we finish catching up after we get out of here? Delia, you *can* get us out of here, can't you?"

"Maybe. My brother's men are crawling all over the place. Fortunately, many left with him a few minutes ago. We'll never have a better opportunity to try."

They grabbed the rifles dropped by the dead men. "Uh, Thomas, maybe Delia and I should take these."

Thomas grudgingly gave up his rifle to Delia but made no argument.

They followed her up the stairs. She cracked the door and waited until the hallway was clear before sprinting out. They heard footsteps coming toward them from around the corner and ducked into a supply closet. They remained silent until they saw the shadow under the door pass by.

When he felt it was safe to whisper, Michael asked, "Where are we going?"

"Before she died, mother had a room at the end of the hall. If we make it there, we have a chance."

"I memorized the map of this compound," Michael said. "There's no room at the end of the hall."

One look from Delia silenced Michael. "As I was saying, if we make it there, we should be fine. The tough part will be slipping through the window and sprinting across the open courtyard without being spotted. If we make it to the back gate, we just slip through it and lose ourselves in the bazaar a block away."

"This may be a stupid question," Thomas said, "but doesn't your brother have guards to protect the rear of the compound?"

"He has two, but the one on duty right now is lying in the cell we just left."

"Let's hope he hadn't planned on being gone long enough to find someone to watch his post for him."

They followed Delia's plan without incident and in five minutes found themselves lost in a sea of merchants and shoppers. They made their way to the spot where Michael had left his car. "Praise be to Allah, it's still here," Delia said.

Michael gave his keys to Delia and jumped into the backseat. He stretched out, forcing Thomas to the front seat. Delia started the car and eased it down the alley and onto the road.

She drove around the busy streets and caught them up on her brother's insane plan. When she finished, Thomas felt ill.

"Where's the plant and the seeds?" Michael demanded.

"I don't know. I haven't seen them since we left the lab. If I know my brother at all, I'm sure he'll have them close to him until he arranges to have them planted."

"You said something about him going to a hangar."

"Probably the abandoned hangar outside Hebron. He uses it every so often. It's big and private."

"Well, let's go," Thomas said. "We have to stop him."

"You don't understand. This hangar is in the middle of a flat area of desert. He'll be able to see us coming from a mile away. There's no way to sneak in. It's why he often meets there."

"We can't just let him carry this out. If he does have the seeds on him, we have to find a way to get them back before he grows them in some hidden-away location. This may be our only chance."

"I know that! But you didn't see him. He has the gift. It'd be suicide to approach him, and you two look half-dead already." Thomas noticed the knuckles gripping the steering wheel were white. She slowed her breathing. "Do you understand if he sees us alive again, his patience will be gone? He'll kill us on the spot."

"I believe Michael and I are very clear about his intentions for us."

"I want to stop him as much as you do. I'm out of options. I'm open for suggestions."

She was right, Thomas thought. It would be suicide to confront Azim tonight, or perhaps ever. Besides, after his performance on Michael's roof, he felt the least qualified to create a plan. "I wish I did have a suggestion for you. What do you think, Michael?"

He glanced in the backseat. Michael had his ear to the cell phone. He identified himself and launched into an abbreviated account of what had just happened to them and of Azim's plan. He never said another word except "Thank you" before ending the call.

"Who was that?" Delia asked.

"That was our ticket to see your brother tonight."

＊　　　＊　　　＊　　　＊

The Council convened in a conference room at a Tel Aviv bank located a few miles from the airport. All ten members were present. The ambassador finished his call with Michael and reviewed with the Foreign Ministry official the plan he and Michael had just created. When they completed their conversation, they joined the others around the table.

A hush fell over the room as everyone waited for the ambassador to speak. "Let me begin by apologizing for my nephew's foolish and reckless behavior. Fortunately, he's come out of hiding. He's been able to successfully grow the seed."

Excited murmurs filled the room.

"Unfortunately, he lost the plant and the five seeds it had produced to Azim Ebadi."

The excited murmur turned to anger and fear. The ambassador stood and slammed his fist onto the tabletop. The sharp crack silenced everyone. "Let me finish!"

He had everyone's undivided attention. "Azim and two of his top men have ingested the plant." The ambassador swallowed. "They're as strong as Samson." By the time he had told them of Azim's master plan, everyone at the table looked like broken men.

"We must get the seeds," the general said.

"We have a plan to accomplish just that. Jonathon has an agent in the foreign ministry who has infiltrated the Palestinian leadership in Lebanon. He's been invited to attend Azim's 'coming out' party tonight. I've arranged for him to pick up Michael—"

"Hasn't your nephew done enough?"

Everyone stared in silent anticipation, no one yet hinting as to whether they agreed with the general or not.

"No one feels as badly as I do about what he's done, but lest you forget, no one has seen the seeds in over three thousand years, and they'd still be lost if it weren't for Michael."

The general glared at the ambassador but finally submitted with a nod. The ambassador took a deep breath and continued. "As I was saying, I've arranged for Jonathon's man to pick up Michael and take him to the hangar. That should get him close enough to find a way inside."

"This is your brilliant plan? It's a suicide mission," the general scoffed.

"I didn't say it was brilliant, it's just the only plan we could put together under the circumstances."

"There's no way he can do that without help. Listen to me. I've planned and participated in hundreds of covert operations in my career."

"I'd welcome any suggestions from you, General."

"Yarconi and his men are good. Call him. Give him the objectives and let him draw up the plan."

The ambassador nodded. "Thank you, General. I'll call him when we adjourn." Speaking to the entire Council, he said, "I'll contact each of you when we hear something. I'll be here for the evening, so anyone who wishes to stay, may. I'll also call the rabbi and have him join me here immediately. I don't want him in Hebron tonight. Any questions?"

The general parted his lips but looked around the table and eased back into the chair.

"Something on your mind, General?"

The general stared at him for a moment and then shook his head.

"If there's nothing else, we're adjourned."

The Council members rose from their chairs and the buzz of conversation filled the room. The ambassador had picked up the phone to call Colonel Yarconi when the general stepped up to him. He lowered the phone. "I take it you did have something to say."

"It's about Michael. I felt it best we talk in private."

The ambassador squeezed his lips and nodded. "I appreciate that. What is it?"

"When you contact Yarconi, make sure your nephew is not involved. He'll only be a liability."

"There's no way Michael's going to stand by and not do anything, even if I order him to."

"Find a way to keep him away from the hangar, even if you have to have him arrested."

✳     ✳     ✳     ✳

"Tobin, Aaron, I want you to leave at once and meet Ambassador Ben Hur at this address in Tel Aviv." He handed Aaron a sheet of paper. "Tell him I said it's my sworn duty to protect our secret, and I'm going to do what I have to do to carry out that duty. Stress to him that the Lord will take care of everything. Things are not as hopeless as they appear."

The two men looked at Judas, their eyes begging him to let them stay behind and face whatever challenges he was facing. However, they obeyed without question.

When they left, Judas thought of the altar room. Part of him was glad the key was gone. It might have proved to be too much of a temptation to take another dose of the mixture. He would face Azim as a mortal man and kill him this very night. He dropped to his knees in prayer, asking for the Lord's favor and praying that his rabbi was accurate when he delivered the oral knowledge of The Secret to him. He stayed in prayer until twilight and then rose, retrieved the dagger from his bedroom, and strapped it to the inside of his thigh.

Before he left, he changed into his rabbinic robe and tunic. He felt the dagger against his leg with each step. He continued his walk through the streets of Hebron until he arrived at Azim's compound. Without fear, he stepped up to the guard at the front door. He ignored the rifle barrels only inches from his chest.

"Tell Azim Ebadi the Protector of the Lord's Strength wishes to speak with him now."

# CHAPTER 28

FOR THE FIRST time in his life, Michael cursed his uncle. He looked at his watch again. The man from the Foreign Ministry was supposed to have met him across the street from the Tomb of the Patriarchs thirty minutes ago. Thomas knew Michael better than anyone. He could see Michael's pain and disappointment buried beneath his anger.

Michael leaned over the front seat and took the keys from the ignition. "I can't wait any longer. I'm going to the hangar. You two get out."

Delia grabbed his arm. "What are you talking about?"

"I said, get out. I'm not about to drag you two into the arms of death with me."

"Then don't go," Thomas said.

"Have you come up with a brilliant plan? You know as well as I do Azim must be stopped tonight."

Thomas struggled to find words of wisdom that would deter Michael, but he hit a dead end. In frustration, he blurted, "You can't ..."

Michael leaned back in the seat and rolled his eyes with a chuckle. "Even you know I'm right."

"I'm going with you."

Thomas whipped his head toward Delia. "You can't be serious." He looked from one to the other. "What are you going to do? Just walk up to him and beat him into submission?"

Neither answered.

"At least get a weapon. Azim's men cleaned out everything you brought."

"Not everything." Michael stepped out of the car and opened the trunk. He was back a minute later with two pistols and a box of ammunition. He loaded the pistols and handed one to Delia along with an extra clip and a handful of bullets.

"You two are serious, aren't you? In case you've forgotten, we're dealing with an enemy of biblical proportions. *Biblical*, Michael! Jawbone of an ass and fiery furnace proportions."

Again, neither answered. Thomas threw himself back into his seat and shook his head. Then, the fire flared in his side again.

"This is as far as you go, my friend. I never intended to entangle you so deeply in this. I'll call for someone to pick you up when we leave."

Thomas didn't move. Where was he going to go? How long could he outrun the authorities; long enough to be swept away by Azim's army of Samsons? He knew Michael was right; they didn't have the luxury of waiting for the cavalry. They had to do something tonight if they had a prayer of stopping Azim. He laid his head against the headrest. "Give me a gun." The words caught in his throat. He never would have thought he'd ever have to shoot another human.

"Thomas, please—"

"You said it yourself. It's now or never. Besides, I don't exactly have any place to go." He reached his arm into the backseat. "Well?"

"I'm afraid I only have two guns. If you go, you'll be unarmed."

Thomas knew it wasn't logical, but a wave of relief swept over him. "Well, I guess I'll have to trust you two for protection, won't I?"

"You know the guns probably won't stop Azim."

"I'm going."

*            *            *            *

Two of Azim's men pulled the battered rabbi from their car and dragged him to the hangar door. Judas held his left hand in his right hand, trying to keep his three broken fingers from touching anything. The pain in his fingers far surpassed the pain from the lacerations on his face and the burns on his arms. He wished they had killed him, but he knew Azim was eager to see the famed rabbi from whom the Lord had departed.

The door slid open, and his escorts threw him into the hangar. He stumbled and fell at Azim's feet. "So, this is the mighty rabbi." Azim rolled Judas onto his back with his foot. "How long before I need another dose in order to keep *my* strength?"

Judas didn't answer. Azim reached down and picked him up by his tunic, holding Judas in midair. "Answer me." When he refused to speak, Azim threw him to another man fifteen feet away. "Sofian, see what you can do to get him to talk."

Sofian wore the grin of a boy who was about to pluck the wings from a fly before squashing it in his hands. As he bent down to pick Judas up, Judas choked out the answer through bloody, swollen lips. "Two weeks."

Judas heard Azim's shoes click on the concrete as Azim approached. He tried to lift himself when the clicks stopped next to him, but his rubbery arms buckled under his effort.

"Thank you, Rabbi. The more you cooperate, the less painful your death will be." He picked Judas up again and carried him to the back row of folding chairs his men had set up in the hangar. There were at least one hundred chairs but fewer than ten people huddled together in the first row. He felt his strength drain away, and he had to stretch out on the two chairs next to him. He closed his eyes and listened to Azim release his anger behind him.

"This is it? Ten people?"

"Azim," Rajah said, "the religious leaders don't know you yet—"

"Yet! But they will, and when they do, they'll regret their arrogance toward me. These ten people shall be rewarded for their faith when I lead Allah's army to victory."

Judas heard Azim's footsteps fade away toward the makeshift stage up front. "Bring him."

Sofian grabbed Judas's right foot, yanked him to the floor, and dragged him down the aisle as if he were dragging a dog by the collar. Once they reached the stage, Sofian lifted him above the platform and tossed him at Azim's feet. When Judas opened his eyes, he was looking out over the chairs at people who were clearly bewildered by Sofian's show of strength.

Azim's voice thundered through speakers across the empty hangar. "My dear friends, thank you for answering my invitation on such short notice. As I said in my invitation, today is the day Allah has chosen to begin fulfilling his promises through his prophet Mohammed. Today is the day you and I can answer his call and be rewarded by our great faith in him."

Judas tried to pull himself up, but his strength was gone. He listened to Azim tell the sparse crowd about Allah's gift to him, and Azim promised a demonstrations that would prove he was Allah's new prophet. Despair washed over Judas as Azim revealed details about the gift with uncanny accuracy. He was the first protector since the days of Moses to lose the Lord's Strength to Yahweh's enemies.

He was so weak. As hard as he tried, he was powerless to do anything to stop Azim. Then, Sofian made his task nearly impossible by grabbing him like a ragdoll and dragging him back to a folding chair behind the meager crowd. Conflicting emotions washed over Judas as he melted into the comfort of the chair while despair enveloped him as he realized he would have to watch Azim shining victoriously on stage.

Then the demonstrations began.

Azim stepped up to a sedan parked on the stage and ran his fingers delicately across the fenders. "When the jihad begins, I will have thousands of soldiers all over the earth. Some will be operating the bullet train between Paris and London; some will be on Wall Street. Everywhere there's power and fortune, my soldiers will be there, awaiting my command to strike. When they do …" His forearm shattered the driver's window, and he ripped the door from the car with one hand and tossed it to Rajah, who caught it like a Frisbee. "… my soldiers will be as strong as we are."

Prayers and praise to Allah rang out from the meager audience. To accentuate his strength, Azim bent down and gripped the front of the car. With but a little show of exertion, he lifted the front end and held the car as steadily as a pair of jacks. He looked over his guests and stoically accepted their praise and reverence. He put an exclamation on his exhibition by dropping the car. It crashed down upon the stage and rocked on its shocks to a halt.

"Imagine what thousands like me will be able to do in the name of Allah."

A sickening feeling bubbled from the pit of Judas's gut. He silently mouthed a prayer to Yahweh, pleading for the gift to return to him as the Lord had granted to Samson, one last time, to kill his enemies. He waited but felt nothing except pain from his injuries. His hand drifted to his thigh. Through his robe, he felt the hilt of the dagger strapped to him.

Judas finally accepted that the strength was not going to return upon him. He prayed for just enough strength to stagger on his feet far enough to thrust the dagger into Azim's belly. He also prayed that what his rabbi had told him about the secret was correct. If so, Azim would die tonight.

He had to find a way to Azim before Azim realized the Lord's protection wasn't complete, before Azim drew his own blood in one of his demonstrations.

Judas somehow found the strength to rise from the chair. His broken fingers were on his dominant hand, so he would have to attack with his weak hand. He squared his shoulders and started walking painfully down the aisle.

\*          \*          \*          \*

Thomas counted seven cars parked in front of the hangar, far less than the fifty to seventy-five they had estimated. The meeting's low turnout most likely accounted for the scaled-back security. Only one man guarded the back door leading into the hangar. Darkness protected them as they crawled the mile across the desert and stopped just outside the illumination of the hangar's light.

Delia checked her gun and snapped the clip into place. "If we can kill the guard, we should have clear access to the door. Once we go through, we'll quickly lose the element of surprise. We must find Azim, Rajah, and Sofian immediately. Shoot for their eyes."

"I'll take the guard's rifle," Thomas said. "I may not be the marksman you are, but if I empty all my bullets in the face, I'm sure at least one will hit the eyes."

"You and Michael know if we fail we'll be dead before the evening is over."

The men nodded soberly. Michael and Delia stretched on their stomachs and took aim at the lone guard. Thomas watched and hoped Azim hadn't shared the Effect with the guards.

Delia and Michael looked at each other and nodded. Then, Delia leaned in for possibly the last kiss she and Michael would share. When they broke, they both took aim and fired.

Bullets silently whizzed from the pistols, one after the other, until the guard's spasmodic body finally fell to the ground. Thomas swallowed two more pain pills and sprinted behind Michael as fast as his cracked ribs allowed.

By the time they reached the back door, Thomas was in torment. He took the guard's rifle from Michael and leaned against the hangar, trying to catch his breath.

Delia reached for the door handle. "Unlocked," she whispered.

Thomas squeezed his trigger and sucked in three deeps breaths to steady his nerves. Adrenaline began masking his pain, but his hand started trembling as he realized he was seconds away from possibly shooting another man. He steeled himself for Delia's worst-case scenario: they open the door to find nothing between them and their targets to take cover behind. They'd be sitting ducks.

He was lost in his thoughts when Delia flung the door open and followed Michael into the hangar. He took another quick breath and followed behind to find Michael holding a finger to his lips. They were standing behind a large platform. Thomas saw the back of the heads of three men and heard Azim's unmistakable voice bellowing from loudspeakers.

The adrenaline was wearing off, and Thomas's pain began claiming its dominance. Delia made a silent gesture with her hands, and he followed her to the left side of the platform while Michael eased to the right side. As he and Delia turned the corner, they had a clear view of the empty chairs on their side of the hangar and of the aisle that separated the two sections. A robed, battered man was walking toward the platform.

Azim broke the cadence of his speech and turned his attention to the man. "Ah, Rabbi, you came to testify to these faithful few."

The rabbi didn't answer. He continued dragging himself forward. When he reached the steps, he dropped to his knees and tried to crawl up them; but he couldn't make it past the first step. He slumped forward and sprawled across the steps.

"Sofian, be kind enough to help the good rabbi up here."

Sofian went to Judas and grabbed him by the collar of his robe. He snapped the rabbi up, carried him with one hand, and dropped him upon the stage.

"You should be a little gentler with our guest," Azim said in mock concern. "Judas, is it? Come here."

Judas struggled to his feet but remained in place and looked defiantly toward the center of the stage. "You come to me. I have a secret message for you from the Lord God."

Azim stepped into Thomas's view. He smiled playfully to the crowd and stopped about six feet from Judas. "What? Allah has given you a message for me?" He played to the audience with dramatic flair. He extended one arm while holding the microphone with the other. He directed his comments to the audience. "Tell me, what is this message God has for me?"

The rabbi remained silent and immovable.

Azim paced along the edge of the stage. "It seems the good rabbi has forgotten his message. Sofian, help him remember."

Sofian came back into Thomas's view and swaggered to the rabbi. His smile was mischievous, and his eyes drank in the opportunity to "help" the rabbi remember. Judas stared at him through swollen blue slits, immovable from either bravery or a lack of energy to protect himself.

Thomas gripped his rifle and inched forward, compelled to intervene on behalf of the defenseless rabbi. Delia reached out a hand to stop him and sternly shook her head. He looked at the rabbi and forced himself to ease back and watch.

Sofian wrapped a hand around the rabbi's neck and lifted him into the air. Judas's legs kicked, frantically seeking solid ground. The words hissed from Sofian's lips. "You had a message?"

Judas's mouth gaped open, but no sounds came out. His narrow slits widened to reveal large, round eyes desperately seeking reprieve while his fingernails clawed at Sofian's arm with no effect.

Thomas rocked on his knees, fighting to break free from Delia's invisible restraint. Just as the rabbi's eyes began to shut, Sofian dropped him to the stage. The rabbi wheezed and clutched his throat.

Azim's voice masked Judas's gasps. "Behold, the famed rabbi of Hebron!"

By the murmurs from the audience, it was apparent they knew of whom Azim was referring. "Able to bend steel and walk unscathed through a shower of bullets. Now look at him. Allah has given his gift to me."

Judas coughed and defiantly struggled to his feet, wavering on weakened legs. It seemed a simple puff from Sofian's lips would be enough to send him toppling to the ground. Sofian reached out and placed his hands upon the rabbi shoulders. "The message ..."

Judas bent down, placed his hands upon his thigh, and stammered through gulps of air. "The message ... from God ... is ..."

He lifted his robe and grabbed the dagger. In one swift motion, he stood and thrust it into Sofian's belly. His legs buckled, but he sliced the dagger down a few inches before collapsing to the ground. Sofian looked down at the dagger protruding from his stomach and then to the rabbi. "This is your message?" He yanked out the dagger and laughed. "Now, I have a message for you."

Sofian took a step toward Judas and stopped. Confusion swept over his face. He reached to his belly and coughed, lifting a bloodied hand. He slowly turned to Azim, raising his hand and staring at Azim with accusing eyes before falling to his knees and then to the floor.

Azim dropped the microphone and ran to him. He rolled Sofian over and stared into his lifeless eyes. His words echoed from a bewildered fog. "But how?"

Another man ran to Sofian and knelt next to him. "I warned you; Allah is punishing us for our insolence!"

Thomas heard a commotion coming from the audience and saw a handful of people running down the aisle toward the hangar door. Delia slapped Thomas on the shoulders. "Now!"

She rose and fired her gun. Thomas heard Michael's gunfire echo from the other side of the hangar. He stood and saw four men running down the aisle with their rifles poised to shoot. His rifle seemed to gain fifty pounds as he lifted it to take aim. His spray of bullets dropped two guards instantly.

Thomas watched Rajah collapse to the floor and a puddle of blood pool under his head. Azim jerked back and slapped a hand over his bloody shoulder and then jumped from the stage and ran to the hangar door. He flew between the two remaining guards, who had dropped to their knees to take aim at Michael and Delia.

Delia gripped Thomas's rifle and yanked him down as a burst of gunfire erupted from the soldiers. She stripped the rifle from him. "Michael, don't let Azim get a way!"

She stood, fired, and then dropped next to Thomas. There was an eerie silence while Thomas waited for the gunfire to continue; but twenty seconds passed, and it was still quiet. He looked to Delia for direction and found her clutching her chest. He knelt and pulled her hand away from her chest.

"I'll be fine." She yanked her hand away. "You and Michael must stop Azim."

"Let me take a look."

"Go!"

He stared into her eyes and slowly nodded. He grabbed her pistol, propped the rifle in her lap, and put his hand on her shoulder.

Delia closed her eyes. "Please, hurry."

Thomas braced himself to face the guards. After three deep breaths, he leaped to his feet and fired. He stopped when he saw the remaining guards were already dead.

"Michael!"

Thomas sprinted behind the stage to the other side. He found Michael sitting against the wall tying his shirt around one thigh.

"How bad are you hurt?"

Michael gritted his teeth as he tied the knot. "I'll live."

Thomas wasn't a medic, but he knew enough to know Michael had lost a lot of blood. He then saw the wound on Michael's other leg. He ripped off his shirt and used it to tie off the second wound.

"Delia?"

"Still alive."

Michael grabbed Thomas's hand, stopping him from finishing the tourniquet. "Tell me the truth."

Thomas resumed tying off the wound. "I am. She's hit, but she'll live."

Delia's voice echoed in the hangar. "Please, go!"

Thomas smiled. "See?"

Michael nodded and grabbed the shirt. "You must stop Azim. He might not be immortal, but he's still as strong as an ox. Be careful."

"I will." Thomas sprinted through the hangar, sickened at the sight of mangled corpses and blood bathing the floor. He looked through the door and saw taillights receding in the distance. Thomas clutched his side and ran as fast as he could run through the door and into open desert.

Everyone was gone. There were no cars, no soldiers, nothing. He stopped to catch his breath, cursing himself for waiting so long to go after Azim. It would be impossible, he knew, to find the seeds again. Something worse than Armageddon would be brewing while the world waited for the final jihad.

He was about to go back and help Michael and Delia when the sound of an engine racing toward him came from behind the hangar. He gripped his pistol, waiting to face whatever monster the desert had given birth to.

An army truck barreled around the corner and skidded to a stop about six feet from him. The headlights momentarily blinded him, and he heard shouts and people surrounding him.

Thomas dropped his pistol and raised his hands. He was aware of the men surrounding him, but the light kept him from seeing anything. It wasn't until the silhouette of a tall man stepped between him and the lights that Thomas finally saw who had come in the truck. He relaxed his arms.

"Colonel Yarconi, call for a medic. Michael and Delia have been shot. They're in the hangar."

"Anyone else in there?"

"I don't think so, but I'd be careful."

The colonel issued a command, and his men began filing into the hangar. A few seconds later one of the soldiers exited. "All clear, but the ambassador's nephew and a rabbi are in bad shape."

The colonel nodded, and the soldier disappeared back into the hangar. Yarconi jogged to the truck and called the medics. He stopped next to Thomas before joining his men. "Send the medics in when they arrive."

Thomas nodded and watched Yarconi disappear into the hangar. A few seconds later, he walked to the truck and climbed into the driver's seat. Before he had a chance to talk himself out of it, he put the truck in gear and sped across the desert in the direction he saw Azim fleeing.

# CHAPTER 29

THROUGH THE REARVIEW mirror, Thomas watched Colonel Yarconi sprint from the hangar toward him and heard cracks of machine-gun bullets thudding into the back of the truck. Yarconi's image faded, and he turned his attention to finding the fleeing car, hoping it was Azim's. As he scanned the horizon, despair crept upon him. He could not see taillights anywhere.

Thomas was about to give up and drive to Azim's compound when he caught a flicker of light in his peripheral vision. The light stopped moving and went out. He killed his headlights and scanned the moonlit silhouettes of hills and rocky crevices for a place to hide his truck.

He found a narrow path about a quarter of a mile from the car Azim had taken and wedged the truck into it. Thomas checked his ammo clip and found two bullets and one in the chamber. He stepped into the back of the truck and looked for another weapon but found nothing small enough to carry with him. He eased out of the truck and followed the dusty, moonlit path toward the car.

The moon shined down upon him like God's spotlight, giving him a sense of utter vulnerability. He hugged the path next to the hills until the car came into view. Thomas held his gun, pointed down, next to his thigh and slowed his pace. It didn't make sense. Why would Azim stop in the middle of nowhere?

Above, he heard pebbles bouncing down the side of the hill. He turned toward the noise but saw nothing. An uneasy feeling grew in the pit of his stomach. He ducked into a blackened crevice, trying to expel the overwhelming sense he was a walking target under surveillance. Again, small pebbles showered over him as he hid in the blanket of shadows.

Farther away, the loose gravel continued to fall. Thomas summoned the courage to step out from the safety of the darkness and saw Azim's unmistakable silhouette walking along the length of the summit about one hundred feet above.

Thomas tucked the pistol into his waistband and started up the rocky surface. A dull pain itched in his side, but he had no pills left to keep the pain at bay.

Surely, he thought, Azim would be able to fly across the summit with ease while he struggled with every step, straining to pull his body up inch by inch. For a moment, he considered climbing back down and walking the perimeter to keep up with Azim; but he dismissed the thought, fearing Azim would disappear over the summit and lose himself in the desert.

So, he kept climbing.

Exhaustion and pain teased him, tempting him to return to the hangar. Fear prodded him to give up. Emotions whispered to him like a red devil on his shoulders: *You can't kill again; if Michael and Delia couldn't stop Azim, what in the world makes you think you can; if he catches you, he'll make you suffer; go back and let the colonel stop Azim.*

Thomas felt his resolve weaken with each thought. His fingertips began to burn, and his arms grew shaky. He forced himself to rebut each excuse to give up. Ironically, it was fear that ultimately dragged him to the backbone-like summit. Not fear of what Azim would do to him if he caught him, but of what Azim would do if Thomas *didn't* catch him.

When he finally pulled himself to the summit, he bent over and caught his breath. The summit snaked into the desert and the full moon bathed the landscape in bright light. In the distance, Thomas watched Azim's silhouette glide across the range at a speed he knew he would never be able to catch.

He realized he would have to give up the element of surprise. He drew in his breath. "Azim!"

The silhouette took two more strides before stopping. Thomas began to shiver. He felt like he had just jabbed a stick into a hornet's nest with no place to run.

Azim remained stationary, as if contemplating the merits of outrunning Thomas or of returning to make sure Thomas could never tell anyone he was here.

It didn't take long for Azim to decide. The silhouette glided across the range at a speed not humanly possible. Thomas instinctively laid his hand upon his pistol, watching the silhouette grow larger at an alarming rate. He finally had to remove his hand in order to fight the urge to use the gun prematurely. He knew *when* he chose to fire his three bullets would mean the difference between his death and Azim's.

Azim seemed to sense danger. He stopped far enough away that Thomas didn't trust his ability to hit his mark. There was no doubt it was Azim, however. The moonlight shined upon him, revealing his silvery, trim beard, his bushy brows, every feature of his face.

"Dr. Hamilton," Azim called out. "What's done is done. Allah has ordained it. Leave now and I will spare your life until the day of the great jihad."

"I see the blood on your shirt. I thought the Samson Effect was supposed to make you immune to bullet wounds."

Azim glanced at his shoulder. "Apparently, I've overestimated its protective abilities. I assure you, though, I haven't overestimated my strength."

Thomas knew he had to find a way to draw Azim closer. If Azim fled, so would his best opportunity to stop him. He began walking toward Azim. "Why are you out here? Why not go to your compound, where you'd be safe?"

"I must ask you to stop right there, Dr. Hamilton, or you'll force me to take away the grace I've offered you."

Thomas kept walking. "Grace?"

"Your reprieve; the few extra months of life I offer."

Thomas didn't stop.

"As you wish."

Azim's calm, soft words sent a deathly chill through Thomas. His muscles tensed. Azim's smile and casual steps toward him caused every sense in Thomas to heighten. He smelled the rocky hills; his peripheral vision was nearly a sharp as his direct vision, locking onto a lone bird gliding through the night sky. His hands grew clammy as he gripped the pistol. Then, in a blur, Azim charged at an ungodly speed. Thomas drew the gun in slow motion compared to Azim's speed. Azim was nearly on him when he fired the first shot.

Azim dodged to the side. Thomas felt the blood drain from him when he realized he had missed his mark. Panic forced him to fire repeatedly until he heard the hollow clicks from the hammer of the gun. Azim stopped inches in front of him and snatched the pistol from his grasp. With one hand, he squeezed it into his fist and dropped the mangled piece of metal to the earth.

"Perhaps you're fortunate, Dr. Hamilton. You'll not have to face the wrath of my army when I purge mankind of evil."

"You? I thought it was Allah and his army."

"Good-bye, Dr. Hamilton."

Azim thrust out his hand and wrapped his fingers around Thomas's throat. Thomas felt himself being lifted and his legs instinctively kicked wildly in the air. His mouth gaped open and he sucked for air, but nothing entered or left his lungs. He grabbed Azim's arm and pulled, but it was like pulling against a steel bar cemented into the earth.

Thomas began to feel light-headed. Azim wasn't going to crush his throat in a quick, merciful death. He was going to let the life slowly drain from him. When he realized his death was imminent, Thomas gave up the struggle; and a calm peace enveloped him. He looked into Azim's wide eyes. Insanity and a perverse joy dripped from them. Arnold Willingham was correct; the Samson Effect did induce mental illnesses.

*The eyes* … He heard Delia's words echo in his head. *Go for the eyes.*

He summoned his last store of energy and lifted his arm. He forced his fingertips apart and thrust his hand forward.

Thomas fell to the earth and gripped his throat, wheezing and gasping for air. Azim covered his eyes with both hands and pierced the night with a terrible shriek. Thomas pulled himself to a sitting position and watched Azim stumble, blood covering his hands.

"My eyes! I'll kill you! I swear by Allah I'll kill you!"

Azim bared his teeth and began swinging his arms in front of him. Thomas scooted away, knowing a blow from Azim's arms would be like getting hit with a pipe wrench. Azim jerked his head toward Thomas, following the sounds of loose gravel as he scooted back.

Thomas picked up the mangled pistol, narrowly missing one of Azim's swinging arms. He continued sliding back, leading Azim to him. He stopped when the hill lost its slope, and the wall fell straight down to the desert floor.

Azim was still flailing and cursing. Thomas felt the wind from his swings as he drew back and bounced the pistol off the summit and over the edge. Azim jerked his head toward the sound and faced the cliff. Thomas drew in his legs and rocked back. Azim turned his head toward Thomas who rocked forward and kicked with all his might.

Azim did not scream; he fell silently to the desert floor.

Thomas crawled to the edge and peered down. Azim's body lay sprawled below, his neck broken and a black spot growing in the sand under his head. He rested before working his way down to retrieve the seeds from Azim.

\*        \*        \*        \*

Thomas sat in the chair next to Michael's hospital bed, again. Delia slept in the chair next to him, bandaged but in remarkably good condition. Michael, however, wasn't as lucky. The doctors told them he had aggravated his broken ribs, and the bullets in his right thigh had cracked his femur. Now he wouldn't be able to ignore the doctor's orders for bed rest even if he wanted to.

"Sorry, we never did get to play a game of tennis. Looks like you're going to have to wait a little longer before you claim your first victory over me."

"Don't be sorry. I've already beaten you in the biggest competition we've had."

"When?" Michael leaned forward but sank back into his pillows when the pain hit.

"Both of us faced the most powerful man since Samson, and I'm the one still standing."

"Only because you didn't get shot."

"Say whatever you want. I faced and defeated Azim, and I'm the one still standing."

The knock at the door stirred Delia from sleep. When the man poked his head through the door, Thomas froze in disbelief.

"Looks like you've seen a ghost," Delia said with a grin.

"I have."

Dr. Clifton Winfred stepped into the room followed by another man Thomas didn't know. "Clifton, you're dead ... the bomb, I heard reports you died when Abbey Hall was bombed."

"A little broken up, perhaps, but very much alive."

An overpowering joy bubbled up in Thomas. He drew his boss into a bear hug. "That's the best news I've heard in months."

Clifton drew back awkwardly after a few seconds, red in the face. "Well, good to see you. I've been working with the Israeli government in Tel Aviv to beg them to reschedule the dig, and I heard you were here. Thought I'd stop by and personally inform you that your sabbatical is over."

"I think I'd better find a lawyer before I try to go back home."

The gentleman with Clifton stepped forward and extended his hand to Thomas. "That's why I'm here. I'm with the American consulate's office." He gestured to Delia. "Your friend has provided ample evidence proving you had nothing to do with the bombing. You're free to go home whenever you wish."

It was finally over. All Thomas could think of was getting back to the campus coffeehouse, kicking off his shoes, and drowning himself in the richest, smoothest, Sumatran coffee he could buy.

The man from the consulate's office handed Thomas an envelope and took his leave. Clifton stepped to Michael's bed and shook his head. "Delia tells me you and Thomas found the Samson Effect. Quite an amazing story, as she tells it."

"All true."

"And the existing seeds were found burned to a crisp?"

Thomas knew that no one in the room would forgive him if they found out he had destroyed the seeds after he had killed Azim. He saw the pain in Delia's eyes. For her sake, he didn't dwell on the fabricated details. "Yes. The only weapon I could find in the truck to defend myself with was a flamethrower. Azim left me no choice."

He thought of how close he had come to taking all the seeds from Azim. He had even held them in his hands, rolling his fingertips over their smooth surface. But after he had witnessed how destructive they could be and how they had driven Azim deeper into insanity, he knew what he had to do. He had watched Azim's body burn until he was sure the seeds had been destroyed.

Clifton's words pulled him from his thoughts. "But what were you two doing in the middle of nowhere?"

Delia seemed to have collected herself and answered. "My brother had set up a place in the hills to grow the seeds. He knew they'd never be safe with him in the city."

Clifton shook his head and patted Thomas on the back. "You had quite an adventure." He looked down into his hands as he moved his fingers around the brim of his hat. "I'm sorry I doubted you. Suppose you'll be glad to return to your mundane life of teaching."

"I don't know," Thomas said as he rubbed his two-day-old whiskers. "I'm thinking about extending my sabbatical."

"Extending it? You've been away for three months."

"I'm thinking of going to Khirbet Seilun for a month or two."

"Near the ancient site for the city of Shiloh?" Clifton shook his head and rolled his eyes. "You can't be serious."

Thomas reached for his hat and put it on.

"What's in Shiloh?" Delia asked.

"Thomas," Michael said, "You better not go without me."

"What's in Shiloh?" Delia again asked, a little more sternly. "Isn't that where Israel stored the Ark of the Covenant?"

"That's not what he's after," Clifton said as he rolled his eyes. "He's going to try to find a telephone that links to God himself."

Delia looked completely dumbfounded. Thomas laughed and stepped to the door. "Clifton, I'll see you soon." He turned to the hospital bed. "Michael, get well."

"Don't you dare go without me!"

Thomas stepped out of the room. He heard Michael cry out his name and then yell for the nurse. He knew he'd see Michael soon, but it felt good to watch him sweat.

Thomas left the hospital and took a bus across Israel to the Dead Sea. The pamphlet he was reading had pictures of swimmers floating effortlessly in the extremely salty water. Because of its high salt content, he read, nothing except bacteria could live in the sea, hence its name.

It was the perfect place to kill all possibilities of anyone abusing the Samson Effect again.

The bus brought him to Lot's Wife, the boat charter he had made reservations with for a day trip at sea. He gathered his bags and stepped off the bus, scanning the sea of people until he saw him. Thomas whistled and waved his hand.

Judas slowly hobbled his way on crutches, and the two met next to the ticket window. "You don't look too bad," Thomas said.

"The doctor said I'll live." Judas looked at the yellow manila envelope tucked under Thomas's arm. "So, what did you need to see me about?"

Thomas handed Judas the envelope. "It's the notebook."

Judas took the envelope and weighed it in his hand. "What about the key?"

"Sorry, but that's everything."

Judas looked over the sea and sighed. "Well, I should be thankful you were kind enough to give the notebook back."

"It's clear to me it belongs with you." The two shared an awkward silence before Thomas turned to the ticket window.

"Dr. Hamilton."

Thomas turned.

"Next time you're in Hebron, maybe you could stop by for a cup of tea. I don't have many friends with whom I can talk about my role as Protector."

Thomas nodded and smiled. "I'd like that." Judas started to hobble away. "Rabbi, something's been bothering me that I hope you could help me with. How were Azim and his men killed so easily?"

Judas paused and looked at the sand. "I probably shouldn't tell you this, but the plant alone isn't enough to perfect the mixture. Without being mixed with another ingredient, the man who takes it is just as mortal as you and me. The other ingredient also helps control its maddening side effects."

"I suppose you wouldn't be willing to share with me what the ingredient is."

Judas looked up from the sand and smiled. "I do have some responsibilities, Dr. Hamilton."

The two men shook hands and Thomas boarded his boat. Thirty minutes later, he was leaning against the rail watching the waves roll as the boat sliced through the water. He wondered what Arnold Willingham, if he were alive, would have said if he could hold the seeds in his hands.

"Well, Arnold, I found it. You almost had me pegged wrong when you said I'd do the right thing." He dug through his bag and pulled out the single seed he had taken from Azim. He rolled it between his fingers one last time, relishing its feel. He then dug out the cylindrical key and held it in his other hand. Afraid to give it much more thought, he wedged the seed in the hollow portion of the cylinder.

Birds glided through the air next to the boat, and two swooped to the water when Thomas let the key fall into the sea. The key disappeared in the frothy white waves, and the birds returned to their flight.

Exhaustion finally extended its dominance over him and he went into the cabin and found a corner seat between an old woman and a young man. He slipped into the seat and pulled out a slim pocket Bible to read about the object he was seeking at Khirbet Seilun: the "telephone to God," as Clifton referred to it. He read a passage from the book of Exodus; but before he finished, his eyes drew closed. A blanket of contentment enveloped him. At least this search would be far more pleasant.

*          *          *          *

The young man seated next to Thomas waited until he heard a snore come from the doctor. He carefully eased over and glanced at the passage that still lay open in the doctor's lap. It only took a few moments for him to realize they were both on the same page. He smiled, knowing his boss would be happy that he had found the doctor and that, apparently, the rumors of his search were true. He reached into his robe and gently rested his hand upon the revolver.

THE END

978-0-595-45172-2
0-595-45172-1

Printed in the United States
125165LV00001B/363/A

9 780595 451722